Peter Cameron has won two O. Henry Awards for his short stories, and his first collection, *One Way or Another*, was widely acclaimed on both sides of the Atlantic. He lives in New York City. *Leap Year* was first serialized in the American magazine *7 Days*.

'An awesomely talented young writer'
*Publishers Weekly*

'Sharp, urban satire . . . a bonbon for the thirtysomething set'
*Kirkus Reviews*

'Mr Cameron is a sharp observer'
*New York Times Book Review*

# LEAP
# YEAR

PETER CAMERON

An Abacus Book

First published in Great Britain by Hamish Hamilton Ltd 1990
Published in Abacus by Sphere Books Ltd 1991

ISBN 0 349 10280 5

Printed and bound in Great Britain by
Cox & Wyman Ltd, Reading

Sphere Books Ltd
A Division of
Macdonald & Co (Publishers) Ltd
165 Great Dover Street
London SE1 4YA
A member of Maxwell Macmillan Publishing Corporation

*for*
*Sal* AND *Don*

# ACKNOWLEDGMENTS

*Leap Year* was originally published in *7 Days*. The author wishes to express his gratitude to Adam Moss, Diane Cardwell, and especially to Pat Towers, for their generous contribution of ideas, criticism, and encouragement. He also wishes to thank the MacDowell Colony, where a portion of this book was written.

# LEAP
# YEAR

# PART
# I

The calendar is based on noting ordinary and easily observable natural events, the cycle of the sun through the seasons with equinox and solstice, and the recurrent phases of the moon. The earth completes its orbit about the sun in 365 days 5 hr. 48 min. 46 sec.—the length of the solar year. The moon passes through its phases in about 29 ½ days; therefore, 12 lunar months (called a lunar year) amount to more than 354 days 8 hr. 48 min. The discrepancy between the years is inescapable, and one of the major problems for man since his early days has been to reconcile and harmonize solar and lunar reckonings.

*The Columbia Encyclopedia, Third Edition*

# CHAPTER

## I

David was the first person to arrive at Lillian's spring cocktail party. Technically spring had started on Monday, but Lillian and her friends were celebrating its commencement four days late.

Lillian was in the bathroom opening seltzer bottles over the bathtub. She was wearing a raincoat. She had dropped the case of bottles and preferred to have them explode in the bathroom rather than on her guests. David sat on the toilet and watched.

"So who's coming to this party?" he asked.

"The usual," said Lillian. "I haven't made any new friends in the past six months. I haven't made any new friends in the past ten years, come to think of it."

"The nineties are going to be the decade of friendship," said David. "Everyone's just going to have a lot of really good friends. The whole notion of lovers and partners and spouses will fade."

"That leaves me two years to fall in love," said Lillian.

"Is Loren coming?"

"Of course," said Lillian. Loren was David's ex-wife. They had been divorced for about a year. Lillian was friends with them both, which was sometimes awkward.

"What about Gregory?" David asked. Gregory Mancini was Loren's boyfriend. He worked for ABC-TV and was over six feet tall. Height was a sore spot with David, who was only five foot six. Loren was about five eleven and very beautiful.

"I guess so," said Lillian. "Unless he got called away on business."

"As a rule I hate people who get called away on business," said David, who was never called away on business. He worked for an in-flight magazine called *Altitude*. He had until recently edited garden books for a small publishing company, but a big publishing company bought the house and fired everyone.

"Is Heath coming?" Lillian asked. Heath was David's boyfriend. No one had known David was bisexual until he had recently announced he had a boyfriend named Heath. It was all very mysterious. Apparently Heath had been David's temporary secretary over Christmas while Lydia Aronso, his real secretary, went home to Costa Rica. Heath was a photographer when he wasn't temping or tending bar, which he did at night.

"Heath is at Lar Lubovitch," said David.

"What's that?" asked Lillian.

"It's some dance thing at City Center," said David.

"He could come over after," said Lillian. "Did you invite him?"

"Of course," said David. "But Heath doesn't like my friends."

"How does he know? He's never met us."

"He just has this feeling," said David.

"So do I," said Lillian. She opened the last bottle of seltzer and held it at arm's length while it fizzed. "I have this feeling I don't like our friends either. Let's just stay in the bathroom all night."

David got up off the toilet and kissed Lillian. Her face was moist with seltzer spray. She reminded him of a passenger on the *Maid of the Mist,* the boat that sailed around Niagara Falls. He had been to Niagara Falls on his honeymoon with Loren. Just for one night, on their way to Canada. That seemed a long time ago now.

ı ı ı ı ı ı

Loren arrived, alone, about ten-thirty.

"Where have you been?" Lillian asked.

"At the airport. Gregory had to go to L.A., and I took the cab out with him."

"How romantic," Lillian said. "Listen, I've got to talk to you."

"Okay," said Loren. "Just let me get a drink."

They rendezvoused in Lillian's bedroom. A glamorous older woman Lillian didn't recognize seemed to be trying on all the coats that were piled on the bed.

"Hi," Lillian said to this person.

"Greetings," the woman said.

"Did you lose your coat?" Lillian asked.

"Oh, no," the woman said. "I'm just trying them on. It's part of my therapy. I'm a shopaholic. It's good for me to try things on and not buy them. I mean, no matter how much I like these, I can't have them. This one's gorgeous."

"It's mine," Loren said.

"Is it?" the woman asked. "Where did you get it? How much did you pay?"

"Could you excuse us?" Lillian asked.

"Certainly," the woman said. She took off Loren's coat. "If you paid more than three hundred dollars, you were ripped," she said.

"A friend of yours?" Loren asked when the woman had disappeared.

"I think she came with Adrienne," said Lillian. Adrienne was Lillian's sister. Her brother was named Julian, and they all worked together at a PR firm. They all hated each other.

"So what's up?" Loren asked. "You look great. Have you lost weight?"

"No," said Lillian, who had spent much of her adult life trying to lose twenty pounds.

"Are you still going to that exercise class?"

"Occasionally," said Lillian. "I drop in to see how out of shape I am. But you'll never guess where I went today."

"Detroit," Loren guessed.

"Wrong," said Lillian. "A sperm bank."

"A what?"

"A sperm bank. You know, where they sell sperm."

"What do you want with sperm?"

"What do you think? I want to get pregnant."

"From a sperm bank?"

"No, not ideally, but this is not an ideal world."

"You're crazy."

"I just went to get some information."

"How did you even find a sperm bank? Do they really exist?"

"They're listed in the yellow pages."

"Under what?"

"Sperm banks," said Lillian.

"You wouldn't really do it, would you?"

"I don't know. My biological clock is ticking away, and I'm running out of options."

"You're only thirty-five. You can have a baby till you're forty. Plus the whole idea of biological clocks is absurd. It's something men invented to make women hysterical."

"You only say that because you've had a baby. You've fulfilled your reproductive cycle."

"You make it sound like going to the bathroom," Loren said. "Anyway, what happens at a sperm bank? You pay for a wad and they stick it in you?"

"Well, that's the basic idea, but it's not as gross as you make it sound. They 'introduce it to your reproductive system.' "

"Sounds pretty gross to me."

"Well, it just depends how you look at it. I mean, when you think about it, sex is kind of gross. Although, not having had any in about a million years, how could I know?"

"Oh, Lillian," Loren said. "It's just hormones. Don't do anything rash."

"Sometimes I think I'm like I am because I've never done anything rash."

"What's wrong with how you are?"

"Well, I'm not exactly the happiest girl in New York."

"I wonder who that might be."

"Sue Simmons never seems to be depressed."

"Come on," said Loren. "Let's stop being antisocial. Let's see if we can find some men to dance with."

ı ı ı ı ı ı ı

"So where's your boyfriend?" David asked his ex-wife as they descended in the elevator. They had departed from Lillian's party simultaneously.

"Flying to L.A.," said Loren. "Where's your boyfriend?"

6

"At the ballet," said David.

"Are you seeing him later?" Loren asked.

"No," said David.

"So what are you doing?"

"Going home," said David. "Going to bed."

"Alone?" asked Loren.

"No," said David. "With General Noriega."

"Is Noriega cute? I haven't seen pictures of him."

"He's gorgeous," said David.

On the street they stood for a moment. They could hear Lillian's party up above them.

"Well," said Loren. "Do you want to share a cab or something?"

"We don't live near each other," David said.

"Don't be so literal. That doesn't mean we can't share a cab," said Loren. "I don't mind going out of my way."

"You don't?" asked David.

"Not for you," Loren said. She raised her arm and whistled.

ı ı ı ı ı ı ı

"We'd like to make two stops," Loren told the cabdriver. "The first is on the West Side and the second is in SoHo." She gave him the addresses and leaned back against the seat.

"What do you want to talk about?" David asked.

"I don't know," Loren said. "I just wanted to see you. I never see you anymore."

"That's usually what happens when you divorce someone," David said.

"Actually, I was kind of in the mood to sleep with you."

"What do you mean?"

"I don't mean sex, necessarily. I just want to sleep with you. In the same bed."

"I don't think that's a very good idea," said David.

"Don't you ever miss sleeping with me?" Loren asked.

"Sometimes," David said.

"Do you sleep with this guy?"

"Sometimes," David said.

"I can't picture it," said Loren. "I can't picture you in bed with another man."

"Then please don't try," said David.

"I can't help it. You have to admit it's weird. To suddenly turn gay."

"I didn't suddenly turn gay."

"You mean you were always attracted to men?"

"I'm attracted to Heath. It's no big deal."

"Are you in love?" asked Loren.

David looked out the window at the dark park and his reflection in the glass. Behind it, he could see Loren's own beautiful reflection, leaning forward, waiting for his answer.

ı ı ı ı ı ı

When Judith and Leonard Connor, Loren's parents, simultaneously turned sixty, they decided to take a year off. They would spend 1988 away from their usual work, away from their life and friends in Ackerly, Pennsylvania, and apart from each other. After thirty-eight years of marriage, they both desired a rest. Leonard, who had recently developed an interest in Buddhism, decided to pursue enlightenment on the subcontinent of India. Judith, a gynecologist, moved to Manhattan. She sublet an apartment in Washington Heights and worked three days a week at a Planned Parenthood clinic.

On the evening of Lillian's party, she was babysitting for her granddaughter, Kate. Judith had picked Kate up at Loren's apartment on Greene Street, and after an early supper at John's Pizza, they took the A train uptown. Kate liked sleeping over at her grandmother's because Grandma had a waterbed.

As they hurtled up the west side they read an old copy of the *New York Times* they found beside them on the seat. Kate couldn't yet read, but she was adept at deciphering pictures.

"What's going on here?" Judith asked, pointing to a photograph of some GIs relaxing in Honduras.

"They're soldiers," said Kate. "Girls can be soldiers if they want." Kate was learning nonsexist role identification at daycare.

"That's right," said Judith. "Do you want to be a soldier?"

"I'm too small," said Kate.

"But what about when you're bigger?"

"I don't know," said Kate. "They look hot."

"What do you think they're doing?"

"They're guarding something. Probably the president."

"Who's the president?"

"Ronald McDonald," said Kate.

"Ronald Reagan," corrected Judith.

"Oh," said Kate. "That's what I meant."

"These soldiers are in Central America," said Judith. "Do you know where that is?"

"In the center?" asked Kate.

"Well, yes," said Judith. "It's between North America and South America. It's south of here." She motioned her hand back toward Columbus Circle. "It's downtown," she said. "Way, way downtown."

They arrived at Bennett Avenue just in time to watch "Jeopardy." Judith and Kate reclined on the waterbed. Kate was occupied with a book of photographs by Diane Arbus, which belonged to the man from whom Judith was subletting. Kate looked at it every time she came over. Judith, who thought the pictures a little inappropriate for a four-year-old, kept forgetting to hide it.

Kate waited for a commercial before speaking. The only time Grandma got impatient with her was when she talked during "Jeopardy." "Look," she said, pointing to a picture of a topless showgirl, "she's almost bare naked."

Judith looked at the picture. "Well, I guess she is," she said. "Doesn't she have pretty breasts?"

Kate outlined the woman's breasts with her small finger. "Do you have pretty breasts?" she asked Judith.

"All women have pretty breasts," said Judith. "That woman's are big and pretty; other women's are small and pretty."

"I don't have breasts," said Kate. "I have ninnies."

"What are ninnies?" asked Judith.

Kate pulled up her shirt and pointed to her nipples. Judith kissed her bare stomach. "I can hear your pizza in there," she said.

"What's it saying?" asked Kate.

"It's singing," said Judith.

"What?" asked Kate.

"Shsh," said Judith. It was time for Double Jeopardy. She lay with her ear pressed to Kate's stomach. "Who was Emma Bovary," she said to the TV.

ı ı ı ı ı ı ı

Later that night, somewhere south of Judith's and north of Honduras, David and Loren's cab emerged from the park and headed west.

"What do you mean?" David asked.

"Are you in love?" repeated Loren. "That's not a particularly cryptic question."

"But it's hard to answer," said David. "At least for me it is. Are you in love with Gregory?"

"No," said Loren. "But I'm happy with Gregory. It's just the opposite of with you."

"And which do you prefer?" asked David.

Loren smiled. She reached out for David's hand but couldn't find it. She stroked the stuff of his coat. "It depends what I'm in the mood for. Whether I want to be happy or loved."

"I would think being loved would make you happy," said David.

"It's not that simple," said Loren.

The cab stopped in front of David's building. Loren found David's sweaty hand in his pocket. She held it. "Kate's at my mother's," she said. "No one will know."

"Anyone getting out here?" the driver asked. "What about the second stop?"

"We've changed our minds," said David. "There is no second stop."

Ms. Mouse, the cat, greeted them at the door. She had belonged to Loren, but when they got divorced she remained in the apartment with David. Loren picked her up.

"I don't think she remembers me," she said. She looked Ms. Mouse in her small, serious face. "Do you remember me?"

Ms. Mouse yawned. Loren put her down and began walking around the living room, checking things out. The only time she ever saw the old apartment was when she came by to pick up or drop off

Kate. David and Loren had joint custody. "You've got a message," she said, indicating the green Cycloptic blinking eye on David's answering machine. "Can I play it?"

"Okay," said David. He was in the kitchen, peeling an orange.

Loren pushed the play button. A man's voice said, "Hi. It's me. I thought I'd call and see if you were home. It's ten-thirty. I just got out of Lubovitch. I felt like coming over, but I guess not. Maybe we can do something tomorrow. Call me. Bye."

"That was Heath," said David.

"I figured," said Loren. "He sounds sweet. And young."

"He's twenty-six," said David.

"Are you going to call him back?"

"No," said David. "I'll talk to him tomorrow."

"If I weren't here, would you call him?"

"Maybe."

"Do you want me to leave?"

"No," said David. He gave her a piece of orange.

"I promise I won't listen if you call him. I'll stay in the bathroom."

"I'm not going to call him. It's late." David sat down at the kitchen table. Loren got a glass out of the dish drainer and filled it at the tap. "There's seltzer in the refrigerator," said David.

"Water's fine," said Loren.

"How are things at the girl's bank?" David asked. Loren worked for the New York Bank for Women. She called it "the institution whose time has come and gone."

"Oh, please," she said. "It's Friday night. I don't want to talk about work."

They sat there for a moment, then Loren stood up. "Let's go to bed," she said.

ı ı ı ı ı ı ı

After they made love, they lay in bed, holding each other. Some of Loren's long hair was in David's mouth but he didn't want to move his head. Finally he sat up and looked at Loren.

"Well?" he said.

Loren smiled at him. "Let's not talk," she said.

They were just about to fall asleep when the phone rang.

"Who could that be?" David said.

"Maybe it's Heath," said Loren. "You should have called him."

"I'm not going to answer it," said David. "It's probably a wrong number."

They sat up in bed and listened to the answering machine.

"Hi," said Lillian. "It's me. I guess you're not home. I thought you were going home. Where are you? Maybe you're at . . . oh, I don't know. I just wanted to talk to you. Everyone's finally left, and I just wanted to talk to somebody. I wanted to talk to you. I'm sad. I'm sorry, this is stupid. I was just lonely. I hate parties. Remind me never to give another party, okay? I hope you're okay. I'll talk to you later. Good night."

"Poor Lillian," said Loren. "You should call her."

"I'll call her tomorrow," said David.

They lay back down, but something had changed. They lay in the darkness trying, but failing, to sleep.

# CHAPTER
2

For her two-hundred-dollar sperm bank consultation fee, Lillian was sent six donor resumes. Instead of being identified by a name, each report had a number, plus a list of statistics: age, weight and height, hair and eye color, I.Q. There was also a self-evaluated temperament profile, where the donors rated themselves (numerically) on such characteristics as passive/aggressive, stable/unstable, artistic/analytical, humorous/sober, practical/romantic. Lillian spent an evening studying these forms. She worked out a system whereby donors scored points for respectable ages, tolerable heights, and high I.Q.s and lost points for excessive weight and personality defects. Number 72428 emerged at the top of the heap. He was twenty-six, six feet tall, brown hair and green eyes; both his I.Q. and his weight were an attractive 165, he was stable, slightly aggressive, artistic, fun, romantic, and, Lillian knew, too good to be true. Number 72428 was obviously lying.

She set aside the forms and went to bed. And as she lay there, alone, she thought, Is this all wrong? Do I really want to have a baby? And the answer was yes, more than anything, yes, and she fell asleep and had a dream. She was pregnant and floating in warm ocean water; instead of weighing her down, her blossoming stomach buoyed her. The water was clear and shallow, and she floated on a current toward a small deserted island. As the island got closer she could see it wasn't deserted; there was someone on it, waving her in, and the closer she got the more familiar the person looked. The surf deposited her gently on the shore, and David leaned down to help her up.

ı ı ı ı ı ı ı

The next day Lillian met Loren for lunch at Burger Heaven. Their waitress was an older woman whose hair looked as if it had just been done. All the waitresses in Burger Heaven looked like that. There was something tribal about them. Lillian wondered if they all lived together.

"So what happened the other night?" she asked once they had ordered.

"What night?" asked Loren.

"After my party. You and David left together."

"Did we?" asked Loren.

"Yes," said Lillian. "So nothing happened?"

"What are you talking about?" said Loren.

"I just wondered if anything happened between you and David."

"No. What could have happened? We're divorced. Everyone keeps forgetting that."

"I just wondered because I called David after the party and he wasn't home."

"Maybe he was at his boyfriend's," said Loren.

"Maybe," said Lillian. "I just wondered."

The waitress delivered their beverages. "Enjoy," she told them.

ı ı ı ı ı ı ı

In Heath's photographs everything is out of focus, but some things are more out of focus than others.

"These are interesting," the woman viewing his portfolio said, "but they look kind of unfocused."

"That's the way they're supposed to look," said Heath. He had dropped into this gallery on his way to work. He worked as a bartender at a restaurant in Tribeca called Cafe Wisteria. He always referred to it as Cafe Hysteria. Every night on his way in he tried to stop in a different gallery and have his portfolio rejected. It was a good way to start an evening of insanity.

Heath lived in Brooklyn with his ex-boyfriend, Gerard. Gerard was a dancer with Alvin Ailey and an insufferable egomaniac, but Heath couldn't afford to move out because he had invested about $3,000 building a darkroom in the loft. It wasn't really that bad living with a horrible ex-lover: Gerard was on tour a lot.

"What are you trying to do with them?" this evening's gallery owner asked.

"I don't know," said Heath, aware that that was a bad answer. "I want each photograph to be like a little world, with all this stuff happening in it."

"Well, as I said, I find them interesting. Unfortunately, we don't represent photographers, so we can't be of much help to you."

"Don't you represent Holly Pierson?"

"Well, yes, but she's more of a . . . well, I think her work transcends these categorizations."

"Oh," said Heath. "How nice for her."

The woman zipped his portfolio shut. "Well, we thank you for the look. We're always interested in new artists."

"How nice for them," Heath said.

ı ı ı ı ı ı ı

The Cafe Wisteria was continually changing managements. Since Heath had been there, three different people had owned it. The cuisine and decor were in constant flux. At times it all got a little out of synch, and the effect was surreal—Cajun food in an Italian country-kitchen setting. Currently the food and decor were billed as American Bistro, whatever that was.

When Heath arrived about five o'clock, the restaurant was empty. He helped set tables with a waitress named Tammi. She was a performance artist and was always trying to get Heath to come to her performances, but because they were scheduled at inconvenient places and times, like the Staten Island ferry at five o'clock in the morning, he usually passed.

Heath was folding napkins. He was a great napkin folder. His mother had taught him six different ways. Tonight he was making them look like pine cones, only the napkins were too big—they looked more like corn cobs.

"What are you doing after work?" Tammi asked.

"I don't know," said Heath. "I might see David."

"Is he the yuppie?"

"I guess so," said Heath.

"He seems kind of old for you," said Tammi. "I mean, he wears a suit and everything."

"I like men in suits," said Heath.

"Well, listen, do you guys want to come hear this band? My brother's in it. They're supposed to be really great. They're called the Barbara Bushwhackers."

Heath laughed.

"A lot of people think George Bush will never get elected because Barbara Bush looks like his mother. They think she should dye her hair. Personally, I've always voted for president on the basis of the wives. I think most women do. Do men? Maybe everybody does."

"I wanted John Anderson to win in '80. Then we could have had a first lady named Keke."

"The Duke's wife is named Kitty."

"I like Keke better. I'd like to hear Dan Rather say 'Keke.'"

"What about Tipper Gore? There's a name."

"She's the one that wants to censor music lyrics. She doesn't sound too groovy."

"She probably wouldn't like the Barbara Bushwhackers, then," Tammi said.

⌐ l ⌐ l ⌐ l ⌐ l

Around ten o'clock Anita, the hostess, told Heath he had a phone call. He picked up the phone behind the bar and said hello.

"Is this Heath Jackson?"

"Yes," said Heath.

"This is Amanda Paine. We spoke earlier this evening at the gallery. The Gallery Shawangunk."

"Yes," said Heath.

"Oh, good," Amanda said. "You remember."

"Of course," said Heath. "We talked about Holly Pierson."

"Exactly!" The woman laughed. "What a memory! Well, I'm sorry to bother you this late and at work, but I've just had the most interesting talk with my colleague, Anton Shawangunk, about your photographs. And I found the more I described them, the more my interest was piqued. I'm sorry if I was brusque before, but, well, it seems to me that your work is just complicated—I can't think of a better word for it—and I'm so used to looking at work that is so easy, you know, so *evident,* that I think my critical eye has atrophied. I've gone blind, so to speak. But I do so hope it's not a tragedy. What I mean to say is that I hope we haven't missed our chance at Heath Jackson."

"You mean you're interested in representing me?"

"Well, of course I can't promise that. What we'd like to do—both Anton and I—is to have another look at that fascinating portfolio. Would that be possible?"

"I don't see why not," said Heath.

"Super! We were thinking perhaps we would meet for lunch. Would that suit your schedule?"

"I think I have some free lunches," said Heath.

"Well, let's see . . . today's Tuesday. How about Thursday next? At Raoul's. Do you know Raoul's? On Prince Street?"

"Of course," said Heath. He had applied and been rejected for a waitering job there—he couldn't fake a good enough French accent.

"Then we'll see you there, on Thursday April fourteenth, about one o'clock?"

"Fine," said Heath.

"Well, it's been nice talking to you, and I look forward to lunch. See you then." She hung up. So did Heath.

"I need a Tecate with lime," said Tammi. "Who was that? El yuppie?"

"No," said Heath.

"Who was it?"

"That was either the sickest woman in New York or my savior. I'll find out next week."

# CHAPTER
## 3

Loren was lying in bed, listening to "Morning Edition," watching Gregory's head appear and disappear. Every time it appeared, his face was redder and more contorted: He was doing his sit-ups. She was supposed to be counting for him, but she had lost track. She was thinking about David and wondering if he was listening to "Morning Edition." Throughout the day she would often find herself thinking of David, wondering what he was doing. It was funny, she thought, how the heart and the brain worked at different speeds when it came to forgetting someone. Some days she would be curious about David, some days she would desire him, and other days would pass without a thought of him. Those were the best days, when she felt entirely consumed in her new life and truly divorced. Today, apparently, was not going to be one of them.

Gregory collapsed on the floor, out of sight. "How many?" he gasped.

"Fifty," Loren guessed.

"Are you sure?" Gregory asked.

"Yup," said Loren. "On the button. Come here. Let me feel."

Gregory stood up and fell, face down, beside her on the bed.

"Turn over," Loren commanded.

Gregory turned over, and Loren looked down at his flushed, handsome face. His brow was sweating; his skin was hot and moist. She stroked his stomach, pinching for fat. "Not bad," she said.

Gregory opened his mouth and beckoned her, downward, with his tongue. He had been back in town for a week, and she had not told him about spending the night with David. She wanted to. She felt maybe if she told Gregory, tried to explain it to him, she might herself better understand it: this incomprehensible, impossible, seemingly unwitherable need—or was it love?—for David.

ı ı ı ı ı ı

Uptown at David's, Kate was brushing her teeth. She had recently learned about the perils of cavities at daycare and vowed she would never have one. She brushed her teeth with a ferocity that David, who was supervising, found alarming in a four-year-old.

"Easy does it," he suggested. "Nice and easy."

"What?" asked Heath from behind the shower curtain.

"Nothing!" David shouted. "I was talking to Kate." Heath turned the water off.

"Heath, are you bare naked?" Kate asked.

"No," said Heath. "I have my swim suit on."

"What color is it?"

"Flesh," said Heath.

"We have to bring a potato to daycare," said Kate.

"What for?" asked David.

"I don't know," said Kate. "For art."

"I don't think I have any potatoes," said David. "We'll have to stop at the store."

"I want a big one," said Kate. "Can I pick it out?"

"You may," said David. "Enough brushing." He unarmed her. "Now spit."

Kate spat and studied the foamy design in the sink. This spit interpretation was a ritual step in her morning ablutions. "It looks like a fish eating popcorn," she concluded.

Heath emerged from the shower, a towel around his waist. "It looks more like a Jackson Pollock to me," he said.

"Go get dressed," David said to Kate. "Your clothes are on your bed. If you need help, call me. What kind of juice do you want?"

Kate thought for a moment. "Cran-raspberry," she said. She turned on the tap, washed her art down the drain, and departed.

David closed the bathroom door. "Was there enough hot water?" he asked.

"Yes," said Heath.

David watched Heath dry himself. Heath's body was slight and white and, to David, always surprisingly beautiful. The first time he had felt this unexpected attraction to Heath had been last December. The offices of *Altitude* were miserably overheated, and Heath had worn a loose-fitting, short-sleeved bowling shirt that had slid up his arm as he pointed to something—a man dancing with a small Christmas tree—on the roof of the opposite building. David looked at the dancing man, and for a brief perplexing moment he realized he wanted to be looking in the other direction: at Heath's bare upper arm, at the shadow of hair he had glimpsed beneath it, at the whole elegant, upraised limb, but by the time he turned his head Heath had lowered his arm, the sleeve had descended, the hand was hidden in Heath's pants pocket. So David had looked at Heath's face, and Heath had looked at him.

"What time is your lunch?" David asked.

"One," said Heath, who was finally having his lunch with Amanda Paine and Anton Shawangunk of the Gallery Shawangunk. "What do you think I should wear?"

"I don't know," said David. "I don't eat lunch in SoHo. Something black and groovy. Wear your sunglasses."

"I wish I smoked," said Heath.

"Daddy," Kate called from her bedroom.

"What?"

"Are there boy potatoes and girl potatoes?"

|     |     |     |     |     |     |     |
| --- | --- | --- | --- | --- | --- | --- |

Lydia Aronso, David's assistant, was the director of South Americans for Jesse Jackson (SAJEJA), a position that of late seemed to occupy most of her energies during the working day. She assured David that after the primary things would return to normal.

"Hello, baby," she said to David, when he arrived at his office. "If you want coffee, I have to send out. The coffee machine exploded."

"You know I don't drink coffee," said David. "I never drink coffee."

"You could have changed," said Lydia. "There is a capacity inside each of us to change. And that's how we're going to change this country. And the only way this country will change is if Jesse Jackson is elected president . . . "

"Please, Lydia, save it."

"But you're uncommitted. You've said as much. You are an uncommitted Democratic voter. And therefore it is in your power to change this country."

The phone rang. Lydia picked it up. "Hi, *Altitude*," she said. She had to—it was a rule.

David went into his office and opened his briefcase. Inside it was a large Idaho spud. "Shit," he said. He picked up the potato.

Lydia came into his office. "It's the cartographer," she said. "What's with the potato?"

"It's Kate's, for daycare."

"Aren't you carrying this healthy snack thing a little too far?"

"It's for arts and crafts. I forgot to give it to her. Call for a messenger. We'll messenger it over."

⌐ ⌐ ⌐⌐ ⌐ ⌐ ⌐ ⌐

Heath had left his portfolio at home so he took the subway from David's to Brooklyn. Gerard, his roommate, had returned from tour and was lying on the couch watching "Jeopardy," drinking a Diet Cherry Coke, and smoking. Like most dancers, he had a very strong love-hate relationship with his body. He was always either admiring or poisoning himself.

"Hi," said Heath. "When did you get home?"

Gerard just smiled cryptically. He seldom spoke before dusk.

"I'm going out to lunch with a gallery owner," said Heath. He couldn't help boasting. He and Gerard had always been competitive.

"Is it a boy gallery owner?" asked Gerard.

"Yes," said Heath.

"He probably just wants to fuck you."

"I don't think so," said Heath.

"Of course you don't think so," said Gerard. "You're Mr. Naivete 1988. Where were you last night?"

"Out," said Heath, who hadn't yet told Gerard about David. For some reason he was embarrassed about his relationship with David. It was just a little weird to be dating an older, divorced, short in-flight magazine editor. It was certainly a change from Gerard.

"I haven't heard of Club Out before," said Gerard. "Is it for people who are out of it?"

"I'm going to take a shower," said Heath, ignoring Gerard's remark. He had gotten sweaty on the subway.

"What's the Yukon Time Zone," Gerard said to the TV.

Heath went into the bathroom and took his second shower of the morning, shaved the patches under his jaw he had missed earlier, and put aftershave on his face and chest. He thought he smelled too strongly of Aramis so he got back in the shower. Then he dressed as groovily as he knew how.

Gerard had moved from the couch to the floor. He was still smoking, but he had begun stretching. "Jeopardy" had been replaced by "Charlie's Angels." Kate Jackson was holding a gun on a fat man in a walk-in freezer. "Your lunch date called," he said.

"She did?" asked Heath. "Amanda Paine?"

"That's the one," said Gerard.

"What did she say?"

"She said it was an April Fool's joke and that you should give it up and move back to Charlottesville."

For a second Heath believed him. He sat down because he felt faint. He could feel the life drop out of his head, swoosh. For a second he hated Gerard with a pureness that amazed him, and this hatred help bring him back to his senses.

"I'm kidding," said Gerard. "Talk about Mr. Gullible. She just changed the place. You're supposed to meet her at Shawangunk's apartment. Seven twenty-one Fifth Avenue."

"Where's that?" asked Heath.

"It's the Trump Tower, baby," said Gerard. "The big TT."

# CHAPTER
# 4

Since it was such a gorgeous spring day Judith decided to sit in the park for a while. She wasn't due at the clinic until one o'clock. She found a sunny bench and sat reading *The Odd Women* by George Gissing. Presently she looked up to find a man sitting on the opposite bench, gazing at her through binoculars. She gave him what she hoped was a discouraging frown and returned to her book.

But the man persisted. She looked up again. He was slight, middle-aged, and Asian. This time she scowled in a way that could not be misinterpreted, but of course it was. It seemed to attract rather than repel him, for suddenly he was sitting beside her on the bench.

"I am sorry," he said. "I see I have annoyed you. But it was the birds, not you, at which I was looking."

Judith nodded and continued reading.

"And now I have insulted you, I fear," he continued. "I did not wish to imply that you are less attractive than the birds."

Judith gave him a weak smile.

"It is a beautiful day," he said.

She knew better than to respond.

"Would you like to see?" he asked, offering his binoculars.

"No thank you," Judith said. She stood up, with the purpose of looking for another, quieter locale.

"Don't go," the man said. "I will go if I am bothering you. I am so very sorry. This is your bench, and you must stay."

"Oh, no," said Judith. "I'm leaving. I deed the bench to you."

The man smiled. He had extraordinarily white teeth. They were the whitest thing around for miles. Judith stood for a moment, hoping he would smile again.

"It is a beautiful day," she said. You should leave, she thought. But she knew suddenly that she would not: It was the day. It was the sunlight in the air, the trees full of blossoms and birds. It was all so benevolent. No harm can come of this, Judith thought, not today.

"May I have a look?" she asked.

She was rewarded with another smile and the binoculars. She held them to her eyes. She was not sure what she was seeing: It was all out of focus. But she was sure it was beautiful, this mess of sky and leaves and windows glittering in the sun.

ı ı ı ı ı ı ı

The lobby of the Trump Tower was all marble and mirror, and Heath had to concentrate hard not to walk into any walls. He had a phobia concerning mirrored walls ever since he had walked into one at Bendel's and broken his nose.

He maneuvered his way safely across the dim lobby and announced himself at the desk. He was told he was expected and directed to an elevator that rose with NASA-like speed. Amanda Paine was waiting for him in the corridor, smoking a cigarette.

"Ah, so you got my message," she said.

"Yes," said Heath. "Hello." He tried to shake her hand but she had extended it for another purpose—to give her cigarette to the elevator attendant.

"Would you dispose of this for me?" she asked him. He nodded and disappeared behind the closing doors. Amanda turned to Heath. "Anton doesn't allow smoking in his apartment," she explained. She looked different to Heath—taller and more imperial. The dress she was wearing seemed to have been pasted to her body in many little scraps, and her hair was piled high on her head in a manner that suggested the casual but upon closer inspection proved quite intricate. Heath followed her down the corridor.

"I'm sorry we had to change the plan, but at the last minute Anton decided he didn't want to venture downtown. People who live uptown think downtown is so hopelessly far away, I've realized. Do you live downtown?"

"I live in Brooklyn," said Heath.

Amanda laughed, as if this were a joke. "That's right," she said. "I had to dial seven-one-eight. Don't you just hate seven-one-eight? It was much nicer when we were all two-one-two, don't you think? One big happy family."

She opened the door and they entered the apartment. It was smaller than Heath had imagined. Two walls were floor-to-ceiling smoked glass. Heath felt as if he were suddenly wearing sunglasses.

"Anton's showering," said Amanda. "Could I get you a drink?"

"Maybe just some water," said Heath.

"Still or gazeuse?"

"Whatever," Heath said.

Amanda disappeared into a galley-sized kitchen. Heath looked around. He was afraid to get too close to the glass walls for fear of tripping and crashing out. There was no art in the apartment. The floors were pickled wood, and the furniture seemed to be an eclectic mix of Louis XIV and Native American. The walls that weren't glass were hand-painted with very small mauve- and raspberry-colored freckles.

Amanda reappeared carrying a large tray, which she set down on an Indian ceremonial knife-sharpening rock that apparently doubled as a coffee table. On the tray was a bottle of champagne, a bottle of Badoit water, three glasses, and a large silver tureen filled with ice, oysters, and violets. Heath assumed the violets were decorative.

"I should tell you something about Anton before he makes his appearance," Amanda said, pouring the Badoit water into two glasses. She handed one to Heath. The air around it was alive with spritz.

"Thank you," said Heath.

"Anton is many things to many people," Amanda said. "The

gallery is just one of his divertissements. He is actually quite a naif when it comes to art. However, you may be catching him at a bad time. His wife has recently bolted—she's in Europe—and, unfortunately for us, it's mostly her money he's playing with."

If there was something else Amanda meant to tell him about Anton Shawangunk, Heath would never know, for at that moment the man himself entered the room. He was a large, handsome man, younger than Heath had imagined: He couldn't have been much more than fifty. His complexion, neither red nor brown, reminded Heath of polished maple furniture, and his long hair, wet from the shower, was combed back from his face in a dark, slick mane. He was wearing a celery-colored linen suit over an open-collared shirt. He was barefoot.

"Hi," he said. He picked up an oyster and slurped the bivalve from its shell. A bit of seaweed clung to the cleft in his chin.

"Good afternoon, Anton," said Amanda. "This is Heath Jackson, the photographer I told you about. He's come to show us his portfolio."

"I'm all eyes," said Anton.

"Well, then, let's not delay," said Amanda. "Let's look at your art, Mr. Jackson."

Heath unzipped his portfolio and handed it to Amanda. She began to flip through the photographs. "Come look," she said to Anton, who was pacing around the room.

"I will when you're done," said Anton. "Do you want an oyster?" he asked Heath.

"Sure," said Heath. He selected an oyster and ate it a la Anton Shawangunk.

"Have you exhibited before?" asked Amanda.

"In New York?" asked Heath.

"New York or Europe. You've shown abroad?"

"No," said Heath. "Just in New York."

"Where?"

"At the New Prospect." The New Prospect Cafe was a restaurant in his neighborhood that had let him hang some of his photographs in the restrooms.

"I've not heard of the New Prospect," said Amanda.

"It's in Brooklyn," said Heath.

"Who care's if he's shown before?" said Anton. "We want to discover talent, not prostitute it." He was looking out the window, down toward Fifth Avenue and the park. All the trees in the park were surrounded by hazy nimbuses of green or white or pink, and even the hermetically sealed smoked glass could not obscure the fact that spring was rubbing itself against everything in the city, which seemed to be bathed in a post-coital glow.

"I know," said Amanda. "That's why I was asking. I wanted to make sure he wasn't overexposed. You should look at these, Anton. They're really very interesting."

"I don't want to look at them," said Anton. "Not now. I want to go outside. I want to go to Paris. It's April, for Chrissakes. Let's all go to Paris."

"I can't go to Paris," said Amanda. "I have a gallery to run."

Anton turned away from the window. "What about you, Mr. Jackson?" he asked. "Can you come to Paris?"

Heath didn't know what to say, because he didn't know what was going on. "What about my photographs?" he finally managed to ask.

"I'm sure they're wonderful," said Anton. "Amanda, tell me, are they wonderful?"

"I already told you what I think," said Amanda. "I think they're very interesting."

"Well, that settles it," said Anton. "Except for what will we call it? What do you want to call it, Mr. Jackson?"

"What?" asked Heath. "Call what?"

"Your show," said Anton.

Amanda spoke up. "I know what we'll call it," she said. "We'll call it 'Simultaneous Organisms: The Photographs of Heath Jackson.' Do you have a middle name?"

"Edward," said Heath.

"So much the better," said Anton, opening the bottle of champagne.

# CHAPTER
# 5

Loren was looking at an ant that was crawling across her desk. It walked as if it knew where it was going.

Stacey, her assistant, appeared at the door. "Gregory's on one," she said.

"Okay," Loren said. "Look." She pointed to the ant.

"What is it?" asked Stacey.

"It's an ant. How do you think it got up here?"

"It probably came in on your person," Stacey said. "Oh, FYI: Hannelore wants to put a scratch and sniff thing on the money market brochures. I heard her talking to Maureen in the bathroom."

"That's really tacky," Loren said. "What would it smell like?"

"I don't know," said Stacey. "Money, I presume."

Loren picked up the phone. "Hello," she said.

"Finally," said Gregory. "Listen, this has got to be quick. Do you want to have dinner out tonight? I thought it might be nice."

"Sure," said Loren.

"What about Provence? At seven?"

"Okay," said Loren.

"Great. Can you make a reservation? I'm going into a meeting."

"Sure," said Loren. "I'll see you later. Bye." She hung up. The ant was gone, but Stacey was still standing in the doorway. "Could you call Provence and make a reservation for two at seven?" Loren asked her.

Fuck you, thought Stacey. Make your own dinner reservation. "Sure," she said.

। । । । । ।

David and Lillian were walking around the Central Park Reservoir, trying to stay out of the way of the people running around it. This early evening promenade had become a weekly tradition since the arrival of spring.

"You wouldn't believe what I did today," said Lillian.

"What?" asked David.

"We're doing this promotion thing for the Canadian Tourist Board, so we rented this horse and hired a model to dress up as a Canadian Mountie. He was going to ride it around the park at lunchtime and hand out maple leaves. Great, right? So the horse arrives and we immediately get a ticket from the police because you can't have a horse in the street without a permit. Apparently you can ride a horse *in* the park but you can't ride a horse *to* the park. It has to be born there or something. Anyway, we get the friggin' horse to the park and the model shows up, but of course he can't ride. He swore he could but he fell off twice. So that kind of spoiled the Mountie effect. It was pretty pathetic."

"It sounds funny," said David.

"Only in retrospect," said Lillian.

"Most of life is like that."

"Do you think so? I think just the opposite: I think stuff is funny while it's happening and then in retrospect I see how pathetic it is. At least that's how I see my life. How's your life these days?"

"I don't know," said David. "Funny and pathetic, I guess."

"How's Heath?" Lillian asked.

"He's great. This gallery in SoHo is going to show his photographs."

"Really? That is great."

They walked down an incline to check out the people on the tennis courts. Everyone was playing seriously and joylessly, like prisoners who were forced to recreate at gunpoint. David and Lillian continued their stroll. The sun had set behind the castles of Central Park West, and the water had turned dark and choppy. Lillian put her hand through David's arm. Every time someone ran by they could hear Walkman refuse: snatches of tinny music, hovering in the air, then evaporating.

They walked for a while without talking, watching the light drain from the sky, the birds skim low over the water.

"I love the park. It's all so pretty," said Lillian.

"It's a nice night," said David.

"I'm glad spring is here. I really needed a change. I was going crazy. Sometimes I think it's all a trick, though. God makes the weather change, and we feel like we've changed. Doesn't it feel like things have changed?"

David looked up at the sky. It was smudged around the edges with clouds. "Kind of," he said. "I know what you mean."

"But nothing's really changed," said Lillian. "It's just a trick."

"What do you want to change?"

"I want my whole life to change," said Lillian.

"So change it," said David.

Lillian looked at David. He was looking away from her, up at the trees. The very top branches were waving in a high wind. She wondered what he was thinking. She held tighter to his arm. "The changes I want . . . I don't know. I mean, sometimes, you need help, you need someone else."

David looked at her and smiled, but he didn't say anything. As they emerged from the park the streetlights flickered on, and they found themselves in a pool of amber light.

"What are you doing tonight?" Lillian asked. "Would you like to get a drink? Or some dinner?"

"I don't think so," said David, extricating his arm from Lillian's. "I think I'll head home." Actually, he was meeting Heath at the Japan Society to see a movie. He knew if he mentioned it to Lillian he would have to invite her, and he didn't want to. He wanted to be alone with Heath. That's fair, he told himself, but he still felt a little guilty.

"Well, good night then," said Lillian. "It was good to see you. Maybe we can do something this weekend."

"Call me," said David. He leaned over and kissed Lillian's cheek. "Good night," he said. He began walking down Fifth Avenue, along the cobblestone sidewalk, beneath the canopy of trees. When he looked back, Lillian was still standing where he had left her. Although he was too far away to see her face clearly, something in the way she stood alarmed him. She looked as if she were lost—or lost at least in thought—and he stood for a moment and watched the people hurry around her, everyone either going home or going out, everyone walking quickly and purposefully to their singular destinations.

ı ı ı ı ı ı

Gregory ordered a bottle of champagne.

"What's the occasion?" Loren asked.

"Actually, I do have some news," Gregory said. "But first I want to ask you something." He buttered a piece of bread. Loren was looking particularly beautiful tonight, and her beauty unnerved him. I don't want to blow this, he thought.

"What?" Loren repeated. She took a piece of bread but didn't eat it. She tore it into little pieces.

"Do you always want to live in New York?" Gregory asked.

"That's an odd question," Loren said. "What do you mean?"

"Have you ever thought about moving away?"

"Of course," said Loren. "I've thought about it."

"And what did you decide?"

"Nothing. I mean, obviously I'm still here. But I've never had a real reason to think about it very seriously."

"Now you do," Gregory said.

The waiter appeared with their champagne. He opened it deftly and poured two glasses. Gregory picked his up. "Cheers," he said. "To us."

"Wait a minute," said Loren. "What's going on?"

Gregory put his glass down. "I've been offered a new job," he said, smiling. "Producing at Lorimar."

"In L.A.?"

"Yes," Gregory said.

31

Loren sipped her champagne. "Oh, I'm sorry," she said, holding up her glass, "Congratulations. That's great—cheers."

Gregory touched his glass to hers. "Cheers," he said.

"And you're going to take it?" Loren asked.

"I don't know. It depends."

"On what?"

"On you."

"Oh," said Loren.

"I was thinking maybe we should move to California," said Gregory.

"Oh," said Loren. She drank more champagne. A vaguely famous looking woman entered the restaurant. Who is that? Loren thought. Is that Pat Harper?

"What are you thinking?" Gregory asked.

"I don't know," Loren said. "I mean, wow—California. I'd have to leave my job. And what about Kate?"

"You have joint custody. You could work something out, I'm sure."

"I don't know as I'd want to. And what about David?"

"What about him? How does this concern him?"

"Well, taking Kate. He wouldn't like that. It would be horrible. And I don't know, you know . . . I like seeing him. I mean, Los Angeles is pretty far away."

"I think that's good. I think it would be good for you to get away from David. Otherwise you'll never . . . "

"What? Never what?"

"Nothing. It's really none of my business."

"No," said Loren, "tell me."

"Well," said Gregory. "It just seems odd to me. Like it's not really resolved."

"What?"

"You and David. How you feel about each other. At least that's the feeling I get."

"We're friends. I mean, maybe we're more than friends, but is that so strange? We were married."

"But now you're divorced."

"I know we're divorced. It was my idea. I'm glad we're divorced."

"Oh," said Gregory. "It's just hard to tell sometimes. And I just thought, maybe if you moved away, you know, really got far away from him, you could . . . I don't know, figure out better what's going on."

"I know what's going on," said Loren. "Nothing's going on."

"Okay, then," said Gregory, "don't get upset."

"I'm not upset," said Loren, sounding upset, so she said it again. "I'm not upset," she said more calmly.

"Good," said Gregory. He reached across the table and touched her arm. "I'm glad you're honest with me," he said. "I love you."

# CHAPTER

# 6

"I was serious before, you know," Anton Shawangunk said.

"You were serious?" said Amanda Paine. "Good God, let's call a press conference."

"Don't be a bitch," said Anton. "I hate you when you're bitchy."

"I thought you hated me period," said Amanda.

"I never said I hated you. You're such an alarmist. No, baby. I just, you know—my candle for you kind of flickered out."

"You have such a way with words," said Amanda.

"Do you think these oysters are still good?" Anton asked. "Don't they spoil after a while?"

"I'm sure they're fine, darling. Why don't you just slurp them all up? I love watching you slurp oysters."

"Whatever turns you on," Anton said. He picked up an oyster and sniffed at it. "It smells funny," he said. "Here, try it."

"Fuck you," Amanda said.

Anton laughed. "It was a joke, baby," he said.

Amanda picked up the platter of oysters. She took them into the kitchen and dumped them into the garbage. There was a little bit of champagne left in one of the bottles and she drank it. It tasted flat. She went back into the living room.

Anton was lying on the floor, on his back, staring up at the ceiling. He had a bad back and often lay on the floor. When they were having their affair, Amanda had thought it was sweet. She'd often woken up at night to find him asleep on the floor. She'd get out of bed and join him.

"So what's the story with you and that guy?" Anton asked.

Amanda stood gazing out the window. She had the feeling Anton was looking up her dress, but she didn't care. Let the bastard get his sick thrills, she thought.

"What guy?" she said.

"The guy who was here. The photographer. Heath Bar Crunch or whatever."

"His name is Heath Jackson. Heath Edward Jackson."

"So do you have the hots for him?" asked Anton.

"You wish," said Amanda.

"I could care less," said Anton.

"You mean you *couldn't* care less," said Amanda. "At least that's what I presume you mean. God only knows. Actually, I doubt God knows. Anyway, I think he's gay."

"Who, God?"

"No. Heath Edward Jackson."

"So you don't have the hots for him?"

"No. And I wish you'd stop using that expression. I'm an adult. I don't get the hots for people."

"Too bad for you," said Anton. He reached out and clasped her ankle. "So why are we giving him a show?"

"Why do you think?" asked Amanda, shaking her foot from his grasp.

"I told you why I thought. I thought you had the you-know-whats."

"That's not the way I operate."

"That's how you operated with David Vaiden."

"David Vaiden is a great painter."

"So what's Heath Bar Crunch?" asked Anton.

A joke, Amanda said to herself. A sweet talentless goon. "He's a very interesting photographer. You had your chance to see his portfolio, but you were too busy mooning about Paris."

"I'll take your word for it," said Anton.

Amanda smiled.

"What time is it?" asked Anton.

"I don't know. About four," said Amanda.

"I still have time," said Anton. "I'm serious, about going to Paris."

"To chase after Syringe? How *pathétique* of you."

"Her name is Solange," said Anton. "Stop calling her Syringe."

Solange was Anton's wife. When she had found out about Anton and Amanda—she had come back early from a weekend in Mustique and discovered them in bed—she had ditched Anton, and Anton had subsequently ditched Amanda. Amanda was pursuing vendettas against them both.

ı ı ı ı ı ı ı

It was naptime at the New York Bank for Women's daycare center. The babies had been put in their cribs and the older children—Kate included—had unrolled their pallets, laid down upon them, and covered themselves with blankets. Kate liked to cover her head with the blanket so that she could keep her eyes open. It was also good for pretending things. Like you were in a tent, or in a cave. Or frozen in an ice cube.

She traced the blanket's plaid pattern with her finger, and then her finger became a car and the stripes a road. She drove from Daddy's house down to Mom's. She could hear Kate Wallace, who was lying next to her, make seagull sounds. Seagull sounds were made by squooshing your spit between your teeth and your lips.

"No squawking," Miss Coco said. "Eyes closed."

The light coming through the blanket cast a plaid shadow on Kate's body. She could feel her own warm breath trapped around her face. Her finger drove down Greene Street and parked outside of Mom's house. She liked the elevator in Mom's house. It was like a cage. Sometimes when they were in it, she and Mom played circus. Mom was always a chimpanzee. She'd make funny noises and scratch herself.

Miss Coco pulled the blanket off her head. "What are you doing, Kate?"

"Nothing," Kate said.

"Shut your eyes," said Miss Coco. "Go to sleep."

Heath and David and Ms. Mouse were eating Chinese food and watching "Nature." Heath was sitting on the couch, and David lay with his head on Heath's lap. Heath alternately fed cold sesame noodles to himself, David, and the cat. David sucked the noodles into his mouth while Ms. Mouse delicately and deliberately chewed up each thin strand, the way an insect devours a leaf.

"I never knew Ms. Mouse was such an epicure," said Heath.

"Hold it still," said David, meaning the noodle Heath was swinging back and forth above his face.

"I'm hypnotizing you," said Heath.

David opened his mouth under the noodle. "Drop it," he said.

"Wait," Heath said. "I have an idea. Close your eyes. Hold still." He lowered the noodle into David's eye socket.

"This feels disgusting," David said. "What are you doing?"

"Just relax," said Heath. "It's for art." He coiled a second noodle over David's other eye. "Now hold still. I'm going to take a picture." He gently lowered David's head onto the sofa and went to get his camera. He came back and stood over David, adjusting the light meter.

"Hurry," said David. "The MSG is eating through my eyelids."

"There is no MSG," said Heath.

"Yeah, sure—the check is in the mail," said David.

"I won't come in your mouth," said Heath. "Smile." David smiled.

"On second thought, don't smile," said Heath. He took some pictures. David started to get up.

"No, wait," said Heath. "I have another idea. Keep still." He picked up Ms. Mouse, who was watching disinterestedly, and put her down on David's chest, her face poised over David's. He pointed to the noodles over David's eyes. Ms. Mouse sniffed at them and then tentatively began eating. Heath laughed and began taking shots.

"This is great," he said. "It looks like she's eating your eyeball or something. It's disgusting."

"You're sick," said David.

The phone rang. "Hold still," said Heath. "I'll get it." He went into the kitchen and answered the phone. "Hello," he said.

"Hi," Loren said. "David?"

"No," said Heath. "Just a minute."

David stood up, removing the noodles from his eyes. Ms. Mouse licked her tiny lips. David took the phone from Heath. "Hello," he said.

"Hi," said Loren. "Am I interrupting something? Do you have company?"

"No," said David. "That was Heath."

"He's screening your calls?"

"No. I was just indisposed."

"Ah," said Loren. "I can only imagine . . . "

"We were watching TV. And eating Chinese food."

"We used to eat TV and watch Chinese food," Loren said. "Or something like that."

"Did you call me to talk nostalgia?"

"God, no," said Loren. " 'Never look back' is my motto. I was looking forward. I was wondering if I could take you out to dinner some night this week. There's something I want to discuss with you."

"What?" asked David.

"I can't go into it now. How about Friday? Or is that a date night?"

"Friday would be fine," said David.

"Good, then, I'll talk to you Friday. Don't hang up. Kate wants to talk to you."

"Okay," said David. "Good night." He waited a moment for Kate to assume the line. He looked at Heath. He was studiously watching the fish on the TV, trying to appear as if he weren't listening to David's conversation.

"What are they doing?" David asked him.

"Spawning," said Heath.

"I'm sorry," said Loren. "Kate's changed her mind. She doesn't want to talk to you."

"Why not?" asked David.

"She's watching something on TV. Something about fish."

"So are we," said David.

"Well, then, we're just one big happy family."

"Have you talked to Lillian recently?" asked David.

"No," said Loren. "Why?"

"It's just that I saw her the other night, and she seemed kind of sad."

"I think she feels left out," said Loren.

"What do you mean?" asked David.

"Forget it," said Loren. "It's just hormones. I'll give her a call."

"Okay," said David. "Good night."

When he reentered the living room, Heath had put his jacket on.

"Where are you going?" David asked.

"Home," said Heath.

"Why? What's wrong?"

"I don't know," said Heath. "I just don't feel like staying over."

"Why not?"

Heath shrugged. He knew David had a perfect right to talk to his ex-wife on the phone, but it bugged him. He had this feeling lately that maybe he should play it cool with David, so he wouldn't get hurt. He had to figure it out. "It's no big deal. I don't feel like talking about it."

"That's real helpful," said David.

"I'm sorry," said Heath. "I know I'm being a jerk. I'm just in a bad mood. I just want to go home."

"But you were in a good mood just a minute ago," David said. "Was it something I said to Loren?"

"No," said Heath.

"Then I don't get it," said David.

"I know," said Heath. "I mean, neither do I."

# CHAPTER
# 7

Through the crazed horizontal windowpanes of the NoHo Star, Loren was watching people walk to work. It didn't seem to be raining out, yet everyone was carrying umbrellas. They all must have been a little asleep still and had not noticed the rain abate. Her waiter approached with the coffee pot, offering refills, and Loren accepted even though her mug was three-quarters full. She accepted for the luxury of it, for what it implied: She was in no rush, she was a free woman, free to linger over coffee. So she would be late for work. So she would miss the Tuesday Morning Management Meeting. Ever since Gregory had implanted the notion of Los Angeles in her mind, it had blossomed there, a sunny oasis, and she had spent her recent days in rainy, gray New York like a tourist. She would look about her—now at breakfast, later on the subway, or crossing 57th Street—and say to herself, This is New York, this is me in New York, trying to be aware of the city in a way only a visitor can be, really seeing things, and wondering, am I happy here?

ı ı ı ı ı ı

"Wait up!" called Tamra, the receptionist at the Margaret Sanger Medical Cooperative Clinic. "Judith, you have some massages." Tamra always called messages massages. She called everything the sexiest thing she could think of.

Judith accepted the pink slips. She was between patients and had gone out to get some yogurt and Evian. In Pennsylvania she would have died before paying a dollar for a bottle of water imported from Switzerland, but here in New York she didn't resist.

She returned to her office and scanned her messages. Two were from patients canceling appointments, the third was from Henry, the last name looked like Fank—who could that be? Well, there was only one way to find out. She dialed the number, which was answered by a vaguely familiar male voice.

"Hello," said Judith. "This is Doctor Judith Connor. Is Henry—I may have this wrong; I'm sorry—Fank there?"

"Hello, Doctor Connor. This is Henry Fank. Thank you so much for returning my call. It is very kind of you."

"You're welcome," said Judith. Who is this person? she thought. "What can I do for you?" she continued.

"I don't think you remember me," Mr. Fank said. "May I refresh you?"

"Please do," said Judith.

"We met in the park. The Central Park, in Manhattan, last week. We did some chat together—do you remember? And watched for birds."

The man in the park. The incredibly white teeth.

"Of course I remember," Judith said. "Could I ask you how you got my phone number?"

"You had told me the place of your work. This Margaret Sanders Clinic. And I call directory information, and they tell me its number."

"I see," said Judith.

"I call to see . . . to ask you if, well, perhaps you like music? Is that true?"

"Yes," said Judith. "I like music."

"Do you know of Ravi Shankar? He is an Indian musician?"

"I've heard of him," said Judith.

"He plays a concert next week—on the eleventh of May, at Alice Tully Hall, and I wondered if you might be happy to come to hear it with me?"

"Oh," said Judith.

"Am I being rude in asking you?"

"No," said Judith. "It's just that . . . "

"Well, perhaps you must think about it? Maybe you do that, to think about it, and then call me back? Or I could call you?"

It is all well and good to meet a pleasant man in the park, Judith thought, but it is quite another thing to, well, to let things progress. Not when one is a married woman of a certain age; not in New York City in 1988. No, thought Judith, definitely not. "I'm sorry, but I won't be able to join you," she said. "It was very kind of you to ask me, though."

"Oh," said Henry. "I'm so sad. I had hoped . . . "

"I'm sorry," said Judith.

"Perhaps another time? Could you join me another time? You see I have a subscription."

"I'm afraid not," said Judith. "Good-bye." She hung up and discarded the pink piece of paper. She sipped her Evian. She thought of Leonard far away, in India. Ravi Shankar, she thought, how funny . . . what a coincidence. Perhaps it is a sign? And then perhaps I am being an alarmist; what danger is there in a concert? None. This is my year to do things, she reminded herself. To have fun. To meet people and go places. I do not want to return to Ackerly with any regrets. She leaned down and retrieved the pink paper from the garbage. It was stained with coffee yogurt, but the telephone number was quite legible. It marched itself boldly across the page, and Judith found dialing it delightful.

ı ı ı ı ı ı ı

Lillian's law of health clubs was this: Never join. Several times throughout her somewhat sedentary past she had forked over exorbitant sums of money to become that privileged thing—a member— only to discover that once she could have it all, do it all, see it all, *it* all lost its allure. No, never join, Lillian realized. Keep moving, like a shark. Move from free-trial class to free-trial membership, from Nautilus to free weights, from low-impact to top-volume.

Tonight she had talked Loren into a free-trial aerobics class at Tomorrow's Bodies, a New Age fitness salon. The class was very strange. It involved guttural chanting and a lot of sitting perfectly still but visualizing yourself in hysterical motion. This was called telekinetic exercise.

"Well, that's my kind of exercise," said Lillian, après, in the locker room. "Except when we were supposed to touch each other. That was gross."

"That was the stupidest thing I've done in ages," said Loren. "It was a complete waste of time."

"I don't know," said Lillian. "I feel kind of revitalized. Maybe you weren't visualizing enough."

"It was bullshit," said Loren.

"All that telekinetic exercise has made me hungry," said Lillian. "Do you have to go home? Do you want to get something to eat?"

"Sure," said Loren. "Gregory's still in L.A."

They found a Japanese restaurant on Second Avenue and were seated next to an attractive, older couple. "Would you like something to drink?" their waiter asked.

"Do you want to split one of those big bottles of Sapporo?" Loren asked Lillian.

"No thanks," said Lillian. "I'm not drinking anymore."

"Really?" asked Loren. "Why?"

Lillian smiled mysteriously and ordered a seltzer. Loren ordered a Kirin Light. The woman at the table next to them was berating her companion. She was saying, "I'm not trying to tell you 'I told you so.' I'm trying to tell you to listen to me. *Listen to me.* You need help. You need professional, all-American, Grade A help."

"So what's going on?" asked Loren. "Why aren't you drinking?"

"Guess," said Lillian.

Loren looked at her friend. In the warm benevolent light of the restaurant she looked . . . well, not beautiful, but something better: happy. Loren studied her face and tried to decide how that happiness was manifested. It was in Lillian's eyes, which were alive with light; the skin around them was taut with glee. Her whole face seemed poised on the brink of a smile, on the lovely verge of laughter. Loren thought, When was the last time I saw Lillian look like this? She could not remember when.

"Smile," said Loren, smiling herself. Lillian smiled, and Loren leaned across the table and kissed her cheek, and when she leaned back there were tears sparkling in Lillian's eyes, magnifying the light there.

"You're going to have a baby," said Loren. It was a statement, not a question.

"Yes," said Lillian. "At least, I hope so. I don't think I'm pregnant yet. But if everything works, I should be . . . soon."

"So you're going through with the sperm bank thing?"

"Yes," said Lillian.

"When did you decide?" Loren asked.

"A while ago. It was because of David."

"David? Why?"

"I told him I wanted to change my life, and he told me to change it. He made it sound so simple. And it was, once I decided."

Their beverages were delivered.

"Can't you have a little beer?" asked Loren. "Just a little, to celebrate. A little beer can't hurt." She poured some beer into two gold-rimmed glasses, gave one to Lillian, and raised the other. "To you," Loren said, "and to your baby."

For a second Lillian looked doubtful, as if Loren's toast were in some foreign language, then she raised her glass and touched it to Loren's, and they kept the glasses touching there, in the air between them, pressed tightly and hopefully together.

ı  ı  ı  ı  ı  ı

Loren caught an express train and walked home to Greene Street from Union Square. It was a nice night, and Broadway was thronged with people, all elated at the weather, wearing shorts for the first time, eating ice cream cones. Cars drove by, windows open, leaking music into the night. This is New York, Loren reminded herself, this is me in New York. She thought about the City of Angels. She had only been there once, several years ago, for a business conference. She had liked it. She had liked the sun and the cars, the bare, tanned backs of women and the white, confident teeth of men. The palm trees. Here in New York if you looked closely, everyone seemed to be falling apart. I have been falling apart, Loren thought. Maybe I should move to L.A. and put myself back together. She pictured herself driving on the freeway, calm and purposeful. I could learn Spanish, she thought, I could swim in the ocean. I could reinvent myself.

When she got home, Loren discovered Gregory in bed.

"Surprise," he said. "I escaped."

Loren sat down on the bed, leaned over, and kissed him.

"I have to go back tomorrow," said Gregory. "The writer's strike is fucking everything up. You wouldn't believe it out there."

"Why did you come back?"

"To see you," said Gregory. "Come to bed."

"Okay," said Loren. She went in the bathroom. Gregory sat up in bed, waiting. Loren emerged, and he watched her undress. When she got into bed he held her very tightly. He parted her long hair, exposed her nape, and rested his lips there. He moved them, silently.

"What are you saying?" Loren asked. "I can't read lips."

Gregory pulled his mouth slightly away from her neck. When he spoke Loren could hear his words and feel them, too, bouncing against her skin. Each word was interspersed with a kiss: "Will you marry me?"

# CHAPTER

## 8

"David?" Judith called through the door. "Is that you?"

"Yes," said David. It was Friday night, and he had arrived at Loren's for their dinner date.

"Just a second. I have to figure out these locks."

David heard the sound of canisters tumbling and chains swinging. Loren's security system was designed around the premise that more is better. The door opened.

"Come on in," said Judith.

David stood in Loren's front hall, wondering what the proper etiquette was involving ex-in-laws. Was kissing expected, tolerated, or forbidden? He opted for a hug and pressed cheeks. He had always liked Judith.

"It's good to see you," he said. "How are you?"

"I'm fine," said Judith. "I'm having fun here in New York."

"And how's Leonard doing?"

"The last I heard, fine, although he's not the best correspondent."

David followed her down the hall. Loren was standing in the kitchen, talking on the phone. She turned to David. "I'll be ready in a minute. Kate wants to see you. She's in her room."

David went to see his daughter. She was playing with her Little Pony dolls. They were all stacked on top of one another, in trios and pairs, an equine orgy. David leaned down and kissed the top of Kate's head.

"What are they doing?" he asked, indicating the fornicating ponies.

"They're riding each other," said Kate. "See." She helped a pair of them scale the side of her bed.

"Wow," said David. "They can fly!"

"No they can't," said Kate. "They're horses."

Kate knocked the pair of horses off the bed, flinging them to the floor. "They're dead," she announced.

"That's too bad," said David. "Listen, what's new? How's daycare?"

"Okay," said Kate. "I'm going to a birthday party."

"Great," said David. "Whose?"

"Kate's," said Kate.

"There's another Kate?"

"There are two Kates," said Kate. "And three Caitlins."

Kate had been Loren's choice. David had voted for Claire.

"What happened to your potato?" he asked.

"What potato?"

"Remember the potato we bought? That you needed for arts and crafts?"

"Oh," said Kate, resuscitating the dead horses. "That was for doo doo."

"What's doo doo?" asked David, not sure he wanted to know.

"It's when you . . . you make the potato look like someone bad and then you stick things in it."

"That's voodoo," said David.

"No it's not," said Kate. "It's doo doo."

"Who did you make your potato look like?" asked David.

"It's a secret," said Kate.

"Tell me," said David. "You can tell me."

Kate shook her head.

"Is it someone I know?"

No, Kate shook.

"Where's your potato? Can I see it?"

"No," said Kate. "It's gone. I threw it in front of the subway."

Wow, thought David, somebody must be hurting real bad.

Loren appeared at the door. "Ready?" she said. "Kate, be good. Go to bed when Grandma tells you."

ı ı ı ı ı ı

"Could we have a booth?" Loren asked.

"Sure," said the hostess. "This way." David and Loren followed her to the back wall of Spring Street Natural Restaurant.

"Do you want some wine?" Loren asked.

"Sure," said David.

Loren studied the wine list.

"Did you know Kate's learning voodoo at daycare?"

"Really?" said Loren. "How do you know?"

"She told me."

"Well, I'm not surprised. There's a new Haitian woman there. Her name's Coco."

"But don't you think it's weird she's turning kids onto voodoo?"

"Well, I prefer it to Christianity," said Loren. "Remember that awful born-again woman?"

"Yeah," said David.

"I'll look into it. And before I forget, Kate's been invited to a birthday party next Saturday. It's at the planetarium, I think. Charlotte Wallace is going to call you with the details."

"Okay," said David. They ordered their meal. "Do you remember when we used to go to the old Spring Street Restaurant? When we first moved to New York?"

"Of course," said Loren. "That was nice."

At the empty table next to them, a pony-tailed busboy lit a trayful of votive candles. Then he began a pilgrimage around the restaurant, distributing the illuminants, his face bathed in the warm, flickering light.

"Thanks," said David, when their candle was delivered. He held it between his palms as if his hands were cold. "So," he said, looking down at the flame, "what's this all about?"

"A few different things," Loren said, but made no effort to elucidate any of them. "How are you?" she asked instead.

"I'm okay," said David. "Actually I've had kind of a rotten week. But I'm okay." He hadn't heard from Heath all week. He had left messages with Gerard, Heath's roommate, and at the Wisteria, but Heath hadn't called back. David was considering walking down to the restaurant after his meal with Loren: Would that be a good idea? Or should he leave Heath alone?

"That's too bad," said Loren.

David shrugged. "How are you?" he asked.

"I've been a little crazy lately. Something's come up with Gregory that has, well, made me think about things."

"What?" asked David.

"God, this is really hard. I feel awful telling you this."

"What?" asked David. "Tell me."

"Gregory's been offered this job in Los Angeles. I think I'm going to move out there with him."

For a moment neither of them said anything. The music and the talk of the place seemed to well up around them and then abate, as though someone was fiddling with the volume.

"What?" said David. "You're not—I mean, why?"

"I think it would be a good idea. At least to try it. I don't know. If it's awful or something I can move back."

"But why?"

"Wait," said Loren. "Listen." She paused. "I feel like as long as we're both here, you know, in New York, things won't change. And I need things to change. I think we both do. I know that in some ways I'll never find another person like you, you know, someone that . . . I don't know, I'm just comfortable with you, but it doesn't work, you know, it didn't work, and this isn't working out, at least not for me, this being near but not together. I want to get away."

"Oh," said David. He was playing with the candle, swirling the hot wax around the cup. "What about Kate?"

"I'll take her with me. We can work something out—six months and six months or something."

"Forget it," said David. "You're not taking Kate."

Loren was crying. "Don't," she said. "I know it's not . . . oh, fuck."

"Are you going to marry Gregory?" David asked.

Loren shook her head. She leaned back against the booth and tried to compose herself. David looked at her.

"I'm sorry," she said.

David didn't answer. He realized he hadn't been paying close enough attention to his life lately. He suddenly felt strangely disembodied, and now when he tried to inhabit himself, to concentrate on the fact of him sitting there, he felt it all only marginally. Everything flickered at the edges of his vision. He was looking at Loren—she was crying again, her face hidden by her hands, by her napkin, now she was getting up, looking for the ladies room, and he was left alone, still looking at the spot across from him where Loren had been sitting and he could still see her there, and then he finally felt something happening, and with peculiar effort he looked down at his fingers and found them touching the flame. He looked at them curiously, as if they weren't his fingers but a display of some sort: an oddity or a beauty, and he held them there, in the flame—only for a second—but by the time he removed them they didn't look like his fingers anymore, they had changed, and then, suddenly, they hurt.

He lowered them into his water glass. It hissed; a tiny wisp of steam rose. Then he must have fainted, because the next thing he knew his head was on the table, and the glass had spilled. His face was all wet.

ı ı ı ı ı ı ı

"Take us to a hospital," Loren told the cabdriver. "What's closest? Take us to St. Vincent's, at Seventh Avenue and 12th Street. And hurry, please."

"No," David said. "I don't need to go to a hospital. I just want to go home."

"Are you sure?" asked Loren. "Let me see your fingers."

David extracted his fingers from a cup of ice. "They're okay," he said. "Look."

Loren looked at them. "I don't know," she said. "They don't look very good to me. They could get infected or something. I think you should see a doctor."

"I'll go tomorrow," said David. "If I need to. But I don't want to go to a hospital. I'm going home."

"Okay, but then I'm coming with you."

"No," said David. "Could you pull over?" he said to the cab-driver. "Could you stop?"

"We're not going to the hospital," said Loren.

The cabdriver pulled over. "What's going on?" he said. "Where are you going?"

David gave the driver his address.

"Let me come home with you," said Loren.

"No," said David.

"David, really, I think I should. I want to make sure—"

David turned to Loren, his face contorted. "Listen," he said, "if you want to go to California, go to California. Just get the fuck out of my life."

For a moment they just sat there, stunned. Even the cabdriver was silent.

Finally Loren spoke. "Okay," she said. She opened the door and got out. The cab drove away. Loren stood and watched it disappear.

# CHAPTER
# 9

Tammi was rummaging through the goblet of goldfish crackers, searching for the pizza-flavored ones. It was early Friday evening, and the Cafe Wisteria was dead—just a platoon of Japanese businessmen who had wandered up from the Vista and a middle-aged lady nursing a cranberry juice spritzer at the bar. The men were drinking bottles of champagne and acting giggly.

"They're kind of cute," Tammi said to Heath.

"It should be a great tip," said Heath.

"Let's hope so. I need some bucks. I'm thinking about making a movie. I think performance art is dying. You know what I think is next?"

"What?" asked Heath.

"I think bad art films are going to be very hot. After all this Andy Warhol stuff there's gonna be a resurgence of interest in that kind of shit. You don't have a video camera, do you?"

"No," said Heath.

"Too bad," said Tammi. "What's the story with your show? Is it still happening?"

"I think so," said Heath. "I'm waiting to hear from Amanda Paine. We still have to hash out the details."

"That's so wild," said Tammi. "It's un-fucking-believable."

"I know," said Heath. "I just hope it all works out."

"It'll work," said Tammi. "You're golden."

The cranberry spritzer lady signaled Heath. He walked down to the other end of the bar.

"Can I get you another?" he asked.

"Oh," said the woman. "No thanks. I just . . . uh, are you Heath Jackson?"

"Yes," said Heath.

"Hi," said the woman. "I'm Lillian Galton. I'm a friend of David's."

"Oh, right," said Heath. "David's mentioned you. You had the party, right? The spring thing?"

"Yes," said Lillian. "Listen, I'm sorry to come down here and bother you at work and all, but I just thought you'd like to . . . I don't know. You see, David's in the hospital, and I know he's had a hard time getting in touch with you, but I thought you might like to know."

"Jesus," said Heath. "What's wrong?"

"He had an accident with a candle and burned his fingers. And they got infected, and his whole arm blew up. So he's on intravenous antibiotics."

"Is he going to be okay?"

"I think so," said Lillian. "I went to see him today and he seems—well, he seems pretty depressed. And I know, I mean, I know about you and him, although I don't know what's going on, and I know it's not my business, but I just thought you might want to know what happened. I had the feeling he wanted you to know."

"Did he ask you to come down here?"

"No," said Lillian. "But he talked about you."

"Where is he? What hospital?"

"St. Luke's," said Lillian.

"Do you know how long he'll be there?"

"I'm not sure. Just a couple of days, I think." She stood up. "How much do I owe you?"

"Oh," said Heath. "Nothing. Please, it's on me. Are you sure I can't get you another? Or something else?"

"No thanks," said Lillian. "I've got to run."

"It was nice to meet you," said Heath, "and thanks for letting me know about David." He watched Lillian leave. She stood outside for a moment, as if she were looking for a taxi, and then started walking uptown.

The truth was that Heath missed David, although he had been trying to convince himself otherwise. There was something a little frightening about falling in love with someone who didn't completely share your sexual orientation. It wasn't that they had bad or too little sex, it was just that there was always this specter of David's heterosexual past looming. Heath sometimes felt as if he were participating unwillingly in a sort of psychic *ménage à trois*.

"Who was that?" Tammi asked.

"A friend of David's," said Heath. "He's in the hospital."

"Why?" asked Tammi.

"He burned his fingers. I don't know. I haven't seen him in a while. I think you may be right about him."

"What? That he's too old for you?"

"Yeah. I think he's too old and too straight."

"Older straight men are weird," said Tammi. "I used to go out with this guy. He was like forty or something. He used Grecian Formula on his chest hair, because it was turning gray. I liked it gray, you know, it was sexy, but he had this complex about it. Anyway, when we made love he'd sweat, and the dye would run off and stain my tits. It was a mess."

ı ı ı ı ı ı ı

Loren brought David his favorite things: a banana Frozfruit, a can of Diet Dr. Pepper, a copy of *People* with Burt Reynolds and Loni Anderson, finally married, on the cover, and the next week's *New York Times Book Review*.

"Where's Kate?" David asked.

"She's at the planetarium. Remember that birthday party I told you about?"

"Oh, right," said David. "Did you tell her?"

"What?"

"That I'm in the hospital."

"No. I just said you were sick. She sends you a kiss," Loren said. "So you will be all better. Consider it delivered."

"A theoretical kiss," said David.

Loren smiled. "The Frozfruit is melting," she said. "Do you want it?"

"No thanks," said David. "You eat it. I'll have the soda."

They ate and drank very carefully, as if it required all their concentration. David burped. "Excuse me," he said.

They finished their picnic in silence. Loren stood up and looked out the window. "What a pretty view," she said. Then she sat back down.

"I don't know if you want to talk about things or not," she said, "but I just want to say I'm sorry. I feel as if I did a poor job explaining myself the other night."

"I'm sorry, too," said David. "I don't know why I flipped out like that. But it's okay. I mean, you are moving to Los Angeles. You don't have to explain that to me. I think we should stop trying to explain ourselves to each other. It just fucks things up."

"Will you explain one thing to me?" Loren asked.

David shrugged. "What?" he asked.

Loren motioned with her head at his bandaged hand, which sat like a claw in his lap. "Why did you do that?" she asked. "You did it deliberately, didn't you?"

David looked down at his hand. Deliberately, he thought. It seemed a strange word. "No," he said. "It was just an accident."

"Can I ask you something else?" asked Loren.

"Ask me anything," said David.

"Do you hate me?"

David looked at her, then back at his hand. It felt disembodied, like a white-wrapped gift. His feeling tapered off somewhere below his elbow. "Sometimes," he said. "A little."

"I hate you, too," Loren said. "Sometimes, a little."

"Why?" asked David.

Loren nodded again at David's hand. "What you did . . . for whatever reasons . . . I think it was a weak thing to do. I think you've become weak, somehow, that you feel sorry for yourself, that you blame things on me. Things that aren't my fault."

"Oh," said David. And then, after a pause, "I did this, I think, because my heart was breaking. I know that sounds stupid, but it's true. Your moving away and taking Kate—mostly taking Kate—finishes something. The idea of our family. That was still intact, somehow, and now it isn't. And I felt my heart breaking and so I burned my fingers to feel a different pain."

"If that is true, it's sick," said Loren. "You shouldn't hurt yourself for love."

"What should you hurt yourself for?" asked David. "Commerce?"

"No," said Loren. "You shouldn't hurt yourself period."

"You say that because it would never occur to your heart to break. That's why I hate you sometimes . . . I hate your unbreakable heart."

Loren stood up. She looked out the window again, at the pretty view. She felt clear-headed and a little euphoric. I've never understood things so well, she thought; this all finally makes sense to me. It was as if she were standing over a simmering pot and all the liquid had boiled away, revealing the clean-picked, scrutable bones of her marriage.

"If you think that," Loren said, "if you think my heart is unbreakable, you know it less well than I always imagined you did."

She sat back down. For a while they said nothing. They were thinking, We have said terrible, truthful things to each other and if we don't apologize or take them back, there will always be this gulf between us, and they sat on either side of the gulf, feeling it widen between them, and neither of them made a move to speak and when they were as far apart as they could get, they turned to each other and smiled, for they both realized they felt suddenly free, all the knots that had been tying them together so quickly undone, like magic.

Loren stood up. "I've got to pick up Kate," she said.

David nodded.

"Are you okay?" Loren asked. "Is there anything else you want?"

David shook his head. Loren reached down and touched his healthy hand, just for an instant, and then left. A young man was waiting outside the door, holding a sheaf of purple irises. He backed away, smiling at Loren. It was not until she was descending in the elevator that it occurred to her that the young man with the flowers must be Heath.

ı  ı  ı  ı  ı  ı  ı

Loren found a police car double-parked outside of Charlotte Wallace's brownstone on East 70th Street and much pandemonium inside.

Charlotte was standing in the living room surrounded by two policemen, a dozen shrieking girls in party dresses, several mothers, and two clowns disguised as farm animals. "Oh, my God," she said when she saw Loren, "do you have Kate?"

"No," said Loren. "Why?"

"Are you Mrs. Parish?" a cop asked her.

"Yes," said Loren.

"Sit down," said the cop.

"Why?" said Loren.

"Are you sure you don't have Kate?" Charlotte Wallace screamed.

"Wait," said the cop to Charlotte. "Follow me." He led Loren into the kitchen. A maid was pouring half-full cups of obscenely colored punch down the sink.

"Would you excuse us?" the cop asked.

When they were alone, Loren said, "What's going on? Where's Kate?"

"We have reason to believe your daughter's been kidnapped," the cop said. "But please don't panic. We know who did it and we should have her back any minute."

57

# CHAPTER
# 10

"The nurse will get a vase," said David, who had no vessel for the flowers Heath had brought him. David smelled them and then lay them beside him on the bed.

"I'm sorry," said Heath. "I should have known to bring a vase, or a plant, or something. I'm not very good at these things."

They both looked for a moment at the irises as if they might speak.

"Was that Loren who was just in here?" Heath asked.

"Yes," said David.

"She's very beautiful," said Heath. David didn't answer. "Are you okay? I mean, I know you're not okay, I mean, is this a bad time? Do you want me to leave?"

"No," said David. "It's nice to see you. I had just about given up on you. How did you know I was here?"

"Your friend Lillian told me. She came by the Hysteria last night. She's nice."

"I know," said David.

"I'm sorry I didn't . . . you know, return your calls and stuff. I know I've been a jerk. I was just trying to figure things out."

"Did you?" asked David.

"Not really," said Heath. "I've been kind of o.o.c. lately."

"What's that?" asked David.

"Out of control," said Heath.

"Welcome to the club."

"So what happened?" said Heath, nodding at David's infamous fingers.

"I don't want to talk about it," said David. "It's pretty embarrassing. I'm okay. I'll never play the piano again, but I'm okay."

Heath laughed, which was nice to hear. David hadn't seen him in two weeks, and he looked different somehow. Heath looked older. His forehead was troubled. David resisted the urge to touch it. He withdrew his healthy hand from beneath the sheet and lay it beside the irises, palm up, fingers splayed, near Heath's knee.

"I'm tired," David said. "They're giving me some awful drugs here."

"Do you want me to leave?" asked Heath.

"No," said David. "I just don't feel like talking. Read me something from *People*. Something funny. Read me about Burt and Loni getting married."

Heath picked up the copy of *People* that lay on David's bed. He looked through the pages of pictures, trying to find Burt and Loni. When he was little he had had a crush on Burt Reynolds. It was almost okay to have a crush on Burt Reynolds because everyone knew Burt Reynolds was sexy. Even men. Now Heath wasn't little anymore. Was Burt Reynolds still sexy? Burt Reynolds had changed. There he was, coming out of the church, beside Loni. Here I am, thought Heath. He started to read the story of Burt and Loni getting married, but when he looked up, David was sleeping. Or maybe he had just closed his eyes. Heath stared at David's hand, empty, on the bed. That's how it looked to Heath: empty. Like a bowl. You could pour water into it. You could put your cigarette out in it. You could put your hand in it.

ı ı ı ı ı ı ı

Charlotte Wallace stormed into the kitchen. "It was Lyle," she said. "The bastard."

"What?" said Loren.

"Lyle," repeated Charlotte. "He kidnapped Kate."

"Who's Lyle?" asked Loren.

"Her husband," said the cop. "He called and left a message."

"My ex-husband," said Charlotte. "Give me a break. We're having a little disagreement about child custody."

"So why did he kidnap my daughter?" asked Loren.

"He was trying to kidnap *my* Kate," Charlotte explained. "The moron couldn't even kidnap the right child."

"I'm sure when he realizes he's got the wrong kid, he'll return your child," the cop told Loren. "Listen, you don't look so good. Is there a quiet place where Mrs. Parish could sit down?" he asked Charlotte.

"My bedroom's at the top of the stairs," said Charlotte.

"Mike, why don't you take Mrs. Parish upstairs? I'll talk to Mrs. Wallace and join you in a minute. Would you like a drink, Mrs. Parish?"

"I don't want a drink," said Loren, trying to control her voice. "I want to know what's going on! I want my daughter!"

"That's what we want, too," the first cop said.

The cop named Mike took her by the arm and led her out of the kitchen.

Charlotte Wallace groaned. "Well, *I* need a drink," she said. "Can I fix you one?"

"No thank you," said the cop. "So let's get this straight. Your husband left a message saying he had kidnapped your daughter?"

"Well, 'reclaimed' is the word he used. As I said, there's been a little misunderstanding concerning custody. Actually, knowing Lyle, he probably had one of his thuggy friends do it."

"So why would they kidnap Kate Parish?" the cop asked.

"Have you ever seen twelve five-year-olds in party dresses? They do look remarkably alike. Especially in the dark. They were at the planetarium, remember. And the name tags were the same."

"Why were they wearing name tags? They can't even read."

"They were for Annmarie's benefit," said Charlotte. "The *au pair*. She took them to the planetarium."

"Your husband resides in Los Angeles?" asked the cop.

"My ex-husband," said Charlotte. "Let's get that straight."

"Is he Lyle Wallace? The actor?"

"I, myself, wouldn't call him an actor, yet some people do."

"He used to play for the Jets, right?"

"My, you're quite the fan, aren't you," said Charlotte.

"I'm just trying to keep things straight, ma'am."

"Well, that's a full-time job with Lyle."

"Do you have his address in Los Angeles?"

"Yes, although he's probably gone to Mexico."

"Mexico? Why do you think that?"

"Because we have a house there. Or rather, *he* has a house there. He got all the west coast real estate. I got this tomb."

"Where in Mexico is it?"

"Oh, Lord," said Charlotte. "I have no idea."

"Don't you have the address?"

"No," said Charlotte. "I spit on the west coast! I spit on Mexico!"

"Be that as it may, it would help us if we knew where the house is. Is it in Acapulco? Mexico City? Cancún?"

"No," said Charlotte. "It's in some awful peasanty little town. With a Spanish name. But don't ask me what. I don't remember any of it very well. Mexico was pre-Betty Ford for me. I was never very attuned to my surroundings back then, if you know what I mean."

ı  ı  ı  ı  ı  ı

Charlotte Wallace's bedroom had been designed by a manic depressive. All the furniture was wrapped in burlap, and everything that wasn't wrapped was painted black. It was like being inside a moving van.

"Maybe you should sit down," said Mike. "Or do you want to lie down? I have to ask you some questions, but feel free to lie down." He patted the bed, as if he were a mattress salesman.

Loren closed her eyes. I think I'm going crazy, she thought. This can't be happening. She could feel herself rocking back and forth. She felt very tall. I am tall, she thought. She chose to concentrate on her tallness. Tall, tall, tall, she thought. She felt Mike come over and steady her, lead her to the bed. He sat her down.

"Are you okay?" she heard him ask.

She wished he wouldn't speak. If this weren't happening he wouldn't be speaking. This isn't happening, she told herself, but she must have said it out loud because Mike said, "What?"

She opened her eyes. It was happening. She had to do something. She had to find Kate. She stood up. "I'm going to the plane-tarium," she said. "Kate must be at the planetarium."

"No," said Mike. "She isn't."

Loren turned to him. "How do you know?" she said. "Did you look?"

"No," said Mike.

"She's at the planetarium," said Loren. "I know it." She went out into the hall and started down the stairs. Mike followed behind her, and there at the bottom of Charlotte Wallace's stupidly curved staircase was the other cop, coming toward her. She must have screamed, because everyone suddenly stopped.

They all stood in their places for a second, and then the cop who wasn't Mike said, "Mrs. Parish? It's okay. We're getting this all figured out."

"I'm going to the planetarium," said Loren. "Kate is at the planetarium."

"I don't think she is," said the cop. He started up the stairs again. Loren looked past him toward the front door, thinking she could run around him, dash outside, grab a cab. It wouldn't take long to get to the planetarium. And once there, she could hold Kate, hold her hold her hold her, safe, beneath the starry, exploding vault of sky.

ı ı ı ı ı ı ı

"Hi, Kate," said Eileen, the flight attendant. "How are you doing?"

"Fine," said Kate.

"Would you like a coloring book?"

"No thank you," said Kate. "I don't like coloring books." Kate thought coloring books were stupid. She liked to draw her own pictures. "I'm going to see my dad."

"Are you? I thought this was your dad," said Eileen.

"I'm just a friend," said Jim. "Right, Kate? I'm a friend?"

Kate looked at him. She knew he wasn't Heath, but he reminded her of Heath, so he must be a friend. And she wasn't sure why she was taking a plane to see her dad—usually she took the subway or a taxi. She took a plane to see Nana, not Dad. Maybe Dad was at Nana's. But this was fun. Kate had never flown first-class before. She liked it. She had already drunk three Cokes, each of them with a cherry. And they were going to see a movie later, with things in their ears!

"I'm a friend," Jim said again, smiling at her. "Right, Kate? Aren't I a friend?"

# CHAPTER

# II

Amanda Paine was sitting in the back office of the Gallery Shawan-gunk, safe behind the velvet rope, purging the guest list, which was her favorite activity. Margot Geiger, the new gallery assistant, was going through the mail. Margot had just graduated from Sarah Lawrence.

"Here's a postcard for you," she said. She handed Amanda a picture of a fountain in the middle of a traffic plaza. The fountain had a bit of everything on it: lions, cherubs, women in togas; gargoyles drooled and fish spat, and around it small European cars drove up an avenue lined with trees and cafes. Amanda turned it over and read the caption: LA GRANDE FONTAINE, PLACE DE LA LIBERATION, AIX-EN-PROVENCE; below that was the following message, written in Anton's tiny indigo script:

Bonjour, Amanda—Solange and I are rediscovering southern France and, if your cynical heart can believe it, our love. All these lazy days, good food, and dappled sunlight make love easy. Not like New York. How is your cynical heart faring? We will be back July 7 for Dominique's wedding. Perhaps you could arrange to open the Arnot show sometime that week, before we depart for Saratoga on the 15th? I leave the gallery in your capable and shapely hands. Farewell, Amanda.

It was signed with an X and O and a splotch of red currant preserve.

"The bastard," said Amanda.

"Who?" said Margot.

"Nothing," said Amanda. "Listen, what do you think of the Heath Jackson photographs?"

"I love them," said Margot. "I think they project this wonderfully paranoiac quality, while raising important questions about focus and meaning."

Perfect, thought Amanda. If some Sarah Lawrence princess liked Heath's photographs, they must be truly awful.

"This is from Mr. Shawangunk," Amanda said. "There's been a change of plans."

"What?" asked Margot.

"We're canceling the Arnot show. We'll replace it with Heath Jackson."

"But I thought you did an Arnot show every summer," said Margot. "You said that's where you make all your money."

The little bitch, thought Amanda. Who does she think she is? Mary Boone? "Not this year. The Japanese are the only ones buying, and they don't like Arnot. We'll put up the Heath Jackson. Call Arnot and tell him. Or better yet, send him a telegram. Sign it from Anton. Then get Mr. Jackson on the phone for me, and make a reservation: two, smoking, one o'clock, Barocco."

ı ı ı ı ı ı

"Is this yours?" David asked. He was looking through Loren's bookshelves. He had been released from the hospital on Monday and had spent most of the time since then at Loren's, waiting for news of Kate. So far there had been none.

"What?" asked Loren. She was lying on the couch, the phone on her stomach, staring at the ceiling. She was trying to will the phone to ring.

David held up *Love in the Time of Cholera*. "Gregory's," said Loren.

"Have you read it?" asked David.

Loren seemed to think for a moment. "No," she said. She

didn't want to talk. Talking seemed a luxury; a decadence. How could she talk about anything with Kate gone?

Judith was scouring the bottoms of Loren's copper pans. She had been cleaning odd things all morning. She had even cleaned the coils in the back of Loren's refrigerator. A counter separated her from the living room.

For a few minutes no one said anything. David started reading the book, but he couldn't pay attention to it. The words kept swimming.

The phone rang. Loren was so tense the ringing hurt her stomach. She turned the recorder on, as the police had instructed her, and picked up the receiver. "Hello," she said.

"Hello," said a woman's voice. "This is Sonia Sanchez-Wheeler. I'm with the law firm of Agon, Mix, Broadhill, and Sanchez-Wheeler here in Los Angeles. I'm representing Mr. Lyle Theodore Wallace. Could I speak with Mrs. Parish?"

"This is Mrs. Parish," said Loren. "Where's Kate?"

"Your daughter is fine, Mrs. Parish. I'm calling to arrange her safe return to you. That's all my client wants."

"Well, what's the problem? Why hasn't she been returned already? What's taking so long?"

"We have just one problem," said Ms. Sanchez-Wallace. "But it's a small problem, and we're sure that with your cooperation—"

"Listen," Loren began, but her rage prevented her from continuing.

"First, I'd like to explain to you my client's position. We don't know what his ex-wife has told you. Were you aware, for instance, that Charlotte Wallace was denying Mr. Wallace legal custody of his child?"

"No," said Loren. "And I don't care. All I want is my daughter!"

"I know," said Ms. Sanchez-Wheeler. "Please just listen to me."

But Loren couldn't listen anymore. She threw the receiver down on the couch and started to sob. Judith went over and held her.

David picked up the phone. "Hello," he said. "This is Mr. Parish."

"Mr. Parish, hello. This is Ms. Sanchez-Wheeler. I'm contacting you to arrange the safe return of your daughter. As I was explaining to your wife, there's just one small problem."

"What's that?" David asked.

"It concerns Mr. Wallace's culpability and your intentions therewith. Let me explain: Mr. Wallace was entitled by law to regain custody of his child on May the first. He did not. He proceeded to hire a company known to me as Children Finders, Children Keepers, Inc. to regain said custody. On Saturday afternoon, May twenty-first, members of that company, armed with a warrant, proceeded to reclaim Kate Wallace from within the Hayden Planetarium while she was watching the *Sesame Street* Muppets in space. They, as you know, made a mistake. Now my question to you is, do you hold my client responsible for their incompetence, and if so, what would you propose to do?"

"In other words, do I intend to sue the bastard?"

"That's my client's concern. He hopes that you, as an anguished parent, will sympathize with his plight—you are now in his shoes, so to speak—and agree not to hold him responsible for your or your child's anguish and to direct any lawsuit toward the truly responsible party in this matter, namely, Children Finders, Children Keepers, Inc. If you are willing to sign an affidavit to this effect, your child will be released to you forthwith."

"And what if I don't?" David asked.

"To be perfectly honest with you, Mr. Parish, I don't know how Mr. Wallace would then proceed. I just hope you will have the good sense to conclude this matter as quickly and simply as possible."

"I'll have to discuss this with my wife and my lawyer," said David.

"Of course," said Ms. Sanchez-Wheeler. "Please do that. Let me give you my number, so you can call me when you've made a decision." She supplied the number.

"What about Kate?" asked David. "I want to talk to Kate."

"I'll arrange with Mr. Wallace for that to happen. Stay near your phone."

I  I  I  I  I  I  I

When Heath arrived at Barocco, he was shown to a table occupied by a bottle of champagne stuck in a bucket of ice. This confused him—he didn't know if it was a good or a bad omen. When Amanda had called him and demanded his presence at lunch, he had assumed she had changed her mind about his show. Heath had been expecting this, and on the subway he had tried to look on the bright side: He had worked hard the last month in preparation for this show, so his portfolio would be in better shape than ever. It was time to start schlepping it around again.

Amanda made her entrance, and Heath stood up as she approached.

"Please, please, sit down," she said, extending her hand so that it was parallel with the floor, as if she expected him to kiss it. Heath shook it awkwardly, and they both sat.

"It's so nice to see you again," said Amanda. "You're looking swell."

"It's nice to see you," said Heath.

"Let me apologize for the short notice," said Amanda. "I'm so glad you were free. But I have good news, and I believe good news should always be delivered promptly and personally. Don't you?"

Heath smiled and shook his head. It was all he could manage.

"Well, let's get one of these stevedores to open this bottle, and then we can toast your imminent success." She signaled to a waiter, who did as he was bid.

"So," Amanda continued, when they were both equipped with fizzing flutes. "News flash: There's been a change of plans chez Shawangunk; all, I might add, to your great good favor. As you may or may not know, we usually present a Gilberto Arnot show every July. Well, for reasons too complicated—not to mention boring—to divulge, Monsieur Arnot's work will not grace our walls this summer." Amanda raised her glass. "Instead, we'll be introducing a brilliant new photographer—Heath Edward Jackson."

Heath's combined relief and sudden joy incapacitated him. He sat there, smiling stupidly. Amanda raised her glass higher, anticipating his, which he finally supplied. "Cheers," she said. "May this be the beginning of a richly rewarding career."

They both took a sip of champagne, but Amanda had trouble

swallowing hers. She was suddenly giggling. She put her glass on the table and covered her face with her hands.

"I'm so sorry," she said through them, snorting a little in an effort to regain her composure. "This is all rather emotional for me, you see. As I'm sure it is for you."

"Yes," agreed Heath.

"Oh, my, oh, my," sighed Amanda, uncovering her face. "You see, Heath, this—your show—is a swan song of sorts for me. After lo, these many years, I am leaving the Gallery Shawangunk, and your first show will be my last."

"Really?" said Heath.

"Yes, I am afraid it is so. The time has come for me to move on. But I am not moving far. I have accepted a curatorial position at MOLTCATO."

"Mulatto?" said Heath.

Amanda laughed, a bit hysterically. "No, no, no, my darling: MOLTCATO. Museum of Late Twentieth Century Art, Toronto. You've not heard of it?"

"No," admitted Heath. "I haven't."

"They have the Schwickers' collection and money. It's an extraordinary collection. I'll be buying for them in New York."

"That sounds great," said Heath.

"I'm very excited," said Amanda. "But that doesn't mean I'm not going to devote myself to your show. I hereby pledge you my heart and soul."

# CHAPTER

# 12

Lyle Wallace, in preparing to receive custody of his daughter, had purchased a new bedroom set. It was, in fact, the same bedroom set Loren had bought for her Kate's room on Greene Street, matching Kate's original bedroom set, which remained at David's. It consisted of a small white bed carved with flowers, above which floated a star-scalloped canopy, a white bureau with knobs the shape and color of violets, and a white rocking chair.

This felicitous coincidence was lost on Kate, who by now assumed that every girl's bedroom across the country was furnished uniformly. A few nights after her plane ride, she sat up in bed, fingering the familiar flowers carved into the tiny headboard, perfectly at home in the room intended for Kate Wallace.

Lyle Wallace was sitting in the rocking chair, although he was much too big for it. He appeared to be all legs. "What are you thinking?" he asked Kate.

Kate liked Lyle, but thought that he asked odd questions. "What?" she said.

"What are you thinking?" repeated Lyle, who believed children had a keen sense of the abstract, if properly coached. "What are you telling yourself inside your head?"

"Ms. Mouse has six toes," Kate offered.

"Who is Miss Mouse?" asked Lyle.

"She's my dad's cat," said Kate.

"Do you miss him?" asked Lyle.

"Yes," said Kate. "He sleeps with me. But not under the covers. If Ms. Mouse goes under the covers, he won't breathe and die. He'll smother."

"I meant your dad," said Lyle. "Do you miss him?"

Kate traced a tulip with her finger and considered Lyle's question. "No," she decided.

"You'll see him soon," Lyle said. "Your mom, too. In a couple of days, probably."

"Okay," said Kate. "Is the light in the pool still on?"

"No," said Lyle. "We turned it off. Remember?"

"We could turn it back on," suggested Kate.

"Tomorrow night," said Lyle.

"Can I watch *Lady* tomorrow?" asked Kate.

"Don't you want to watch something else? How about *Dumbo*?"

"No," said Kate. "I want to watch *Lady*. I like dogs."

"Okay," said Lyle. "Whatever you want. But now it's time to go to bed. Do you want a drink?"

"No thank you," said Kate.

Lyle extricated himself from the chair.

"Turn the duck on," said Kate.

"It's a goose," said Lyle. He turned on a plastic goose-shaped lantern that sat on the floor, and then killed the overhead light. "Good night," he said.

"Good night," said Kate.

"Sleep tight," said Lyle. He shut the door.

Sleep tight, thought Kate. What did that mean? She snuggled down in bed and pulled the covers tightly around her. She screwed up into a tight little ball and looked at the goose. It looked back at her. Kate lay there in bed, waiting for the goose to speak.

ı ı  ı ı  ı ı ı

Gregory lay in bed, watching Loren pack. She had received a call at about ten o'clock from Sonia Sanchez-Wheeler, informing her that the Lyle Wallace impunity papers had been finalized. She and David were flying out to L.A. first thing in the morning to sign them and reclaim Kate.

Loren seemed to be packing for an extended trip. As she lay her clothes on the bed, Gregory could feel their weight accumulate across his legs. "Why are you taking so much?" he asked.

"I don't know what the weather will be like," Loren said.

"It will be hot," said Gregory. "Sunny and hot."

Loren was unconvinced. She continued to pack.

"It's funny that it's you packing to go to L.A.," Gregory offered.

"How is it funny?"

"Well, maybe not funny," said Gregory. "I mean ironic. It's usually me packing late at night for a quick trip to L.A."

Loren didn't answer.

"Just think," said Gregory. "This time tomorrow, you'll be with Kate."

Loren closed her eyes. She wished Gregory would stop talking. Talking might jinx it. She didn't want anyone to say anything until Kate was safe.

"Do you want me to come with you?" asked Gregory.

"Oh," said Loren. "I don't think so. Why?"

"I just thought you might want me there," said Gregory. I hoped you might need me, he said to himself.

"David will be there," said Loren.

"I know," said Gregory. "That's not what I meant."

"I'm sorry," said Loren. She put down her espadrilles and sat on the bed. She lay her large hand on the center of Gregory's warm chest. She felt his heart beat. "I think it would be better for Kate if it were just me and David. We want to make things as normal as possible."

Gregory put his hand on top of hers. "I could stay at the hotel," he said.

"No," said Loren. She withdrew her hand and stood up. "I think it's best if I go alone."

Gregory looked up at her. She had been so distant these past few days, and he understood that. He had felt a little of her horror and had some idea of what she must have been going through. But something else had been happening all week—this slow, cautious withdrawal from him, this refusal of any comfort he offered. "Okay," he said, "whatever you want."

Loren closed her suitcase and put it on the floor. "I'll be right back," she said. She disappeared into the bathroom. Gregory sat up and waited for her. He could feel his plan coming undone. Loren wasn't going to move to L.A. with him. They would never live together in the shadow of a palm tree, in a house with a veranda in a valley or a canyon . . . it was all unraveling, all impossible, this sunny, pacific life he had so fervently imagined.

ı  ı  ı  ı  ı  ı  ı

Henry Fank and Judith were rowing on Central Park Lake. Actually, Henry was trying, not too successfully, to row.

"I am not so very good at this," he said. "I'm sorry."

"You're getting better," said Judith. "But don't pull so much, I think. You're trying too hard."

"Do you know, at breakfast this morning, who was there?" Henry asked. He was a breakfast chef at the Parker Meridien Hotel.

"No, who?"

"Lee Iacocca," said Henry. "He had some blueberry pancakes."

"I like blueberry pancakes," said Judith. "Sometime I'll come for breakfast."

"Yes, you must," said Henry. He seemed exhausted from his rowing.

"Why don't we just drift for a while," suggested Judith.

"Drift?"

"Yes," said Judith. "Stop rowing, and we'll just float. Here," she said, showing him how to rest the oars across the top of the boat. "Now relax," she said.

Henry removed a white handkerchief from his pocket and wiped his brow. "I sweat," he said, "I'm sorry." He carefully folded and replaced the handkerchief. "So your husband is in India," he said.

"Yes," said Judith.

"Why don't you go with him?"

Judith put her hand in the water, but then removed it when

she remembered where she was. Not Lake Arthur. "Well," she said. "For many reasons, I suppose."

"You did not want to visit India?"

"No," said Judith. "I would have liked to go to India. It's just that, well, you see, we've been married a long time, and we wanted to spend some time apart. So Leonard went to India, which was something he wanted to do, and I came to New York, so I could do some public health work, which I wanted to do."

"And how long will you spend this way?"

"About a year," said Judith.

"A long time," said Henry. "Don't you think?"

"Yes," said Judith. "I guess it is."

"Myself, I cannot imagine such a thing. It is very odd to me. To spend time away from someone you love, when there is so little time. That is what I realized when my wife died: How little time is."

"When was that?" Judith asked.

"She died two years ago, when I came here. We travel on a boat that was not a good boat, and too many people on it. She got sick and there was no way to make her better. There was no doctor such as you. Many people die. Her sister, she die, too."

"That's very sad," said Judith.

"I think so," said Henry. They drifted for a moment and listened to the shushing noise of the water. "I'm sorry," he said. "This talk makes you sad, and that is not . . . it is too bad. Not my intention. Shall I row some more?"

"No," said Judith. "Let me."

"You can row?"

"Of course," said Judith. She stood up. "We must do this very carefully, or we'll tip the boat over."

"Oh, please," said Henry. "I am not good swimming, I think."

"We won't tip," said Judith. "Stand up. Give me your hand."

Henry rose and held onto Judith's hands with a terror that she found delightful. "Now slowly," she said, "you turn this way and I'll turn that." They began to rotate and as they did, Judith looked over Henry's shoulder, glimpsing the lake and the trees and the gorgeous skyline of Central Park South, and felt for a second curiously euphoric. She gripped tighter to Henry's hands and guided him safely to his seat.

i i i i i i i

If 72428's sperm, which had been introduced to Lillian's reproductive system several weeks ago, had made itself at home there, the ensuing results would have manifested themselves in a chemically detectable way. But Lillian had decided not to use a home pregnancy test. She wanted the baby—if there was to be a baby—to announce itself with natural harbingers.

It was Saturday. Lillian had cleaned her apartment, and then gone to the office and caught up on some work. She took a nap on the couch in the reception room, and awoke, disoriented, late in the afternoon. She lay still and let her life filter slowly and disappointingly back into place. She felt solitary, knowing that at that moment she was in no one's thoughts. How little my life sticks to anything! she thought.

On the way home she stopped and sat in the park. As the light faded, people collected their blankets and magazines, their coolers and Frisbees, their children and lovers and dogs—all the accoutrements of a day in the sun—and walked either east or west to the lighted noisy avenues. Lillian stayed behind. As she sat in the emptying park, a feeling awoke inside her, a feeling that she was at the end of something, that these were the last moments in this era of her life. And so it was in this way, by sensing that something had ended, that Lillian realized something—or everything—was about to begin.

# PART

# II

LEAP YEAR, (otherwise bissextile), the name given to the year containing 366 days. The astronomers of Julius Caesar, 46 B.C., settled the solar year at 365 days 6 hours. These hours at the end of four years made a day which was added to the fourth year. The English name for the bissextile year is an allusion to a result of this interposition; for after Feb. 29 a date "leaps over" a day of the week.

Of the custom for women to woo during leap year no satisfactory explanation has ever been offered. In 1288 a law was enacted in Scotland that "it is statut and ordaint that during the rein of hir maist blissit Megeste, for ilk yeare knone as lepe yeare, ilk mayden ladye of bothe highe and lowe estait shall hae liberte to bespeke ye man she likes, albeit he refuses to taik hir to be his lawful wyfe, he shall be mulcted in ye sum ane pundis or less, as his estait may be; except and awis gif he can make it appeare that he is betrothit ane ither woman he then shall be free." A few years later a like law was passed in France, and in the 15th century the custom was legalized in Genoa and Florence.

*Encyclopaedia Britannica*

# CHAPTER

# 13

Amanda Paine and Heath Jackson were sitting in the office of the Gallery Shawangunk, selecting the pieces for his show. Actually Amanda seemed to be doing the selecting. She sat with Heath's portfolio on her lap, leafing through the pages of prints. A friend of Amanda's, Kennedy Cooley, a tall black woman in a sea-green sundress, stood looking over her shoulder. Amanda paused over some photographs, but none of them moved her to speak. She was smiling a small, cryptic smile. Kennedy Cooley would periodically glance over at Heath, as if trying to match him up with a particular photograph.

"Well," said Amanda, "they look wonderful."

"Yes," agreed Ms. Cooley. "Much nicer than Arnot's paintings. You were right to bump him."

"You're really not doing an Arnot show?" Heath asked.

"No," said Amanda. "We're doing you instead. As a surprise to Anton. Don't you think he'll be surprised?" she asked her friend.

"Yes," said Kennedy. "I think he will. If I were he, I would be surprised."

"I see you've been working," Amanda continued, before Heath could ascertain the nature of Anton's surprise. "Some of this new stuff is rather good. I especially like"—she opened the book and flipped—"this," she said, showing him the picture of Ms. Mouse eating the noodle out of David's eye.

"Yes, I liked that too," said Kennedy Cooley. "It's very sexy."

"And I like how it goes with the show's name. We're calling it 'Simultaneous Organisms: The Photography of Heath Edward Jackson.'"

"I wanted to ask you about that," said Heath.

"Oh," said Amanda. "Ask what? Ask away."

"Well, it's just that . . . I just wondered if that name was, you know, final."

"Why?" asked Amanda. "No you like?"

"Well," said Heath, "to tell you the truth, I don't like it. I mean, the 'Simultaneous Organisms' part."

"Well," said Amanda. "I don't want you to be unhappy about the name of your show. That would be . . ."

"*Quel* tragic," suggested Kennedy.

Amanda shot her a glance. Heath had the feeling she was trying not to laugh. He suddenly felt very uncomfortable. This is getting weird, he thought.

"It would be unfortunate," Amanda decided. "And I want Heath's entree to the art world to be nothing less than perfect."

"Well, it's no big deal," said Heath.

"You're right," said Amanda. "It's a detail. But details are important. If we don't take care of the details, the details will take care of us." She paused, stunned by her pithiness. Then she continued. "What do you think, Kennedy?"

"I agree with Mr. Jackson. I think a less . . . ambitious name would better serve the photographs."

"Well," said Amanda. "Thank God I haven't printed the cards yet! So be it: 'The Photography of Heath Edward Jackson.' Is that unambitious enough for you?"

"Could we skip the 'Edward'?" asked Heath. "I really hate my middle name. I never use it."

"No," said Amanda. "Middle names are hot. Is there another name you prefer?"

"What about 'Tiger'?" said Kennedy. "I'd buy a photograph by someone named Heath Tiger Jackson."

ı ı ı ı ı ı

Every Wednesday morning the Galton siblings—Lillian, Adrienne, and Julian—gathered in Julian's office for a weekly meeting. Julian had the biggest office. He was the founder and president of Galton Enterprises, Inc. Both Adrienne and Lillian were vice presidents, and they constantly argued over who should get the second biggest office. Luckily the smallest office had the best view, so they switched on and off. Presently Lillian had the room with the view.

"Peter Boyde from SATAN called again," Julian began.

"Can't you even say it?" said Lillian. "Say it. Say South Africa Tourist Authority Network."

"South Africa Tourist Authority Network," said Julian.

"Shut up, Lillian," said Adrienne. "I have a headache. Does listening to a Walkman give you a headache? I always get a headache when I do."

"You only listen to it so you won't hear the phone ring," said Lillian. "I know all your tricks."

"Not all," said Adrienne.

"What about South Africa?" said Julian.

"I thought we decided that last week. I said I'd quit if we represented them."

"Lillian, if you quit every time you said you would, you'd be dead from exhaustion. It's an idle threat. Besides, this is a very big account."

"I think that's immaterial," said Lillian. "We all know it's a moral rather than a financial question."

"But it's not like we're forcing people at gunpoint to vacation in South Africa," said Julian. "We're just making them aware of their options. People should be aware of their options, wouldn't you agree?"

"Oh," said Adrienne. "Speaking of options. Mom called this morning. She wanted to know if anyone was coming home for the Fourth."

"You can count me out," said Lillian. The thought of barbecues and potato salad nauseated her.

"South Africa," said Julian. "South South Africa Africa."

"Julian," said Lillian, "we're not doing South Africa. You know it. You're just scared of Peter Boyde. I'll call him if you want. Do you want me to call him?"

"Okay," said Julian, who was, in fact, scared of Peter Boyde. "Now, what's new?"

"Mom also said the Loessers want to rent their summer house. She thought one of us might be interested."

"I meant what's new business-wise," said Julian.

"Where is it?" asked Lillian.

"I'm not sure," said Adrienne. "Upstate somewhere. One of those hot counties people are talking about. It's supposedly very nice. It's on a pond or something."

"How much is it?" asked Lillian.

"I don't know. You should call Mrs. Loesser. Mom gave me her number."

Julian stood up. "You're both fired," he said.

"What?" said Adrienne.

"I said you're fired," said Julian.

"If I'm fired, I won't call Peter Boyde," said Lillian.

"All right. You call Peter Boyde. Adrienne's fired."

"Talk about idle threats," said Adrienne, inserting the humming prongs of her Walkman into her ears.

ɪ  ɪ  ɪ  ɪ  ɪ  ɪ

Several thousand miles away, Sonia Sanchez-Wheeler threw open the glass doors and strode into the lobby of Agon, Mix, Broadhill, and Sanchez-Wheeler, where Loren and David sat on a tangerine-colored leather couch.

"Welcome!" Ms. Sanchez-Wheeler brightly proclaimed.

Loren and David stood up. Ms. Sanchez-Wheeler shook both their hands. "Why don't we go to my office?" she said. "It's more comfortable there."

They followed her down a long hallway of glassed-in offices. "Is this your first visit to Los Angeles?" Ms. Sanchez-Wheeler asked over her shoulder.

Loren and David looked at each other in disbelief. "Where's Kate?" Loren asked.

"Here we are." Ms. Sanchez-Wheeler directed them into the office at the end of the hall, a large corner office filled with sunlight and trees and wicker furniture. "Could I get you something to eat or drink? Have you had breakfast yet?"

Loren repeated her question.

"She's on her way," Sonia Sanchez-Wheeler said. "I just talked to Lyle. They're stuck on the freeway. It's a wonder you got here from the airport so quickly. Are you sure I can't get you anything? A croissant? Some o.j.? It's fresh-squeezed."

"No thank you," said David.

"Well, then, please sit down."

Loren and David sat. "We'll get right to business, then," said Ms. Sanchez-Wheeler, picking up her phone. "Antony? Could you bring in the Lyle Wallace agreement? Thanks." She hung up. "I hope you're keeping track of your expenses. As we agreed, my client will reimburse you for all the costs you incur. How long are you staying out here?"

"Just a day or two," said Loren. "We're taking Kate to Disneyland. We thought it might be a good way to ease her out of this ordeal."

Ms. Sanchez-Wheeler laughed. "If I'm not mistaken, Lyle's beat you to it. He took her to Disneyland yesterday. They stopped in on their way. Kate's a lovely child! Have you ever thought of having her tested?"

"For what?" David asked.

"Screen-tested," said Ms. Sanchez-Wheeler. "I think she has a very appealing quality. You might consider it, as long as you're out here."

"We're not interested," said David.

"Of course. You've other concerns presently. I understand. But let me give you my husband's card. Donovan Wheeler. He's with CAA." She opened her desk and extracted a business card, which she offered them.

"We're not interested," David repeated.

"Oh," said Ms. Sanchez-Wheeler. "I'm sorry." She looked at the card for a second, then laid it on her desk.

An awkward silence was interrupted by the arrival of Antony. "Here you are," he said, handing a folder to Ms. Sanchez-Wheeler.

"Thank you, Antony. Well," she said when he had departed,

"I think these forms are pretty straightforward. They're the exact ones that have been vetted and approved by your lawyer, but let me leave you alone with them for a moment. I'll go find out where Mr. Wallace and your daughter could be. If you need me, I'll be right next door."

"She's the one I'd like to sue," said Loren when they were left alone. "She's horrible."

"She's a lawyer," said David.

Loren shuddered. "I'm not signing a thing till I see Kate. What if she's brainwashed or something? Remember Patty Hearst? Maybe he's turned her into some militant starlet."

"I think it would be tough to brainwash Kate," said David. "Her mind is pretty much her own."

"Well, I'm not taking any chances." Loren stood up and looked out the window. She seemed to be in the very center of the city: It spread out in smoggy sunshine as far as she could see. She was standing like that thinking, I'll never live here, not for a minute, when the skin along her spine began to effervesce, and she turned to see Kate running down the hall, her arms outstretched, straight toward her mother and the plate glass wall.

# CHAPTER
## 14

The morning Loren left for Los Angeles to retrieve Kate, she had woken up at five-thirty to find she was holding Gregory. They were stuck together with a thin sheet of sweat. She couldn't tell if it was his back that had been sweating or her stomach—probably a combination of both. She also couldn't tell if he were awake. She guessed not, got out of bed, and took a shower. Her plane was at eight a.m. David was coming by in a cab for her at six-fifteen.

As she dried herself, she could hear the whine of the coffee bean grinder. The bed was empty. She got dressed and took her suitcase into the living room.

"Do you want some coffee?" Gregory asked. He was standing in the kitchen, naked.

"No," she said. "I better get going."

Gregory looked at the clock to indicate he was aware of the time—she had plenty of time for coffee—but was kind enough not to mention this fact.

"I want to make sure I'm there when David comes," said Loren. "I don't want to keep the cab waiting." She was meeting him on the corner of Houston and Greene.

"Right," said Gregory. He put down the grinder and came out from behind the counter. He wasn't naked; he was wearing boxer shorts. "Do you want me to come down with you?"

"No," said Loren. "Why don't you go back to bed? It's still early."

Gregory just smiled. He picked up her suitcase. "It's heavy," he said. It was a comment rather than a condemnation. Loren took it from him, then put it down while she unfastened the locks. She opened the door.

"Listen," said Gregory. "Will you call me tonight? Just to let me know everything's all right?"

"Of course," said Loren.

They stood for a moment by the open door.

"Okay," said Gregory. "Go." He reached out and touched her shoulder, lowered his face to kiss her.

Loren put down the suitcase and embraced him. She started to cry. "I'm sorry," she seemed to be saying.

Gregory held her and stroked her hair. It was still damp from her shower. It smelled clean. "It's okay," he said. "It's all okay."

"No," said Loren. "I'm sorry."

After a while they pulled apart. "Call me tonight," Gregory said. "Tell Kate I said hi."

Loren nodded and picked up her suitcase. Gregory closed the door behind her. He heard the elevator's loud ascent, its door clang open, and then its retreat.

He stood for a minute beside the front door, leaning against the wall, and then went over to the window. He was just in time to see Loren turn the corner. Across the street a man was sitting outside of a produce market, chopping the green shocks off carrots. A dog watched him. A woman came out of the store. She inserted a straw into a small carton of Tropicana and drank some. She stood in the sun for a moment talking to either the man or to the dog. Then she headed in Loren's direction. Gregory tried to picture Loren. Was she still standing on the corner? Or was she already speeding toward the airport? He wasn't sure. What he was sure of was that she was gone.

ı ı ı ı ı ı

"Why is it," asked Solange Shawangunk, "that the road from the airport to the city always takes the ugliest route possible?" She peered out of the limo's windows, whose green tint gave Queens a particularly ornery glow. Then she turned to Anton. "Why do you think that is?"

"I don't know," he said.

"It's true for every city," Solange continued. "Think of it: Paris, London. They should hand out blindfolds at the airport."

They had been away for six weeks, and in that time their apartment, on the thirty-eighth floor of the Trump Tower, had forgotten them. So while Solange perused the mail that had accumulated, Anton moved about, turning on lights, flushing toilets, sitting briefly in all the chairs, reasserting the Shawangunk presence.

"Look at this," said Solange. She handed him a postcard. On one side was a black and white photograph of a cat eating a noodle out of a man's eye socket, and on the other side the following message was printed:

OUT OF CONTROL:

PHOTOGRAPHS BY HEATH JACKSON

THE GALLERY SHAWANGUNK

JULY 13–AUGUST 27, 1988

OPENING RECEPTION WEDNESDAY, JULY 13

6:00–9:00

And below that, the following message was scrawled: I'VE CANCELED ARNOT! SURPRISE! XO AMANDA.

"What's going on?" asked Solange. "You told me you had fired Amanda."

"Did I?" asked Anton.

"Yes," said Solange. "As a matter of fact you did."

"Well," said Anton. "It was a tricky situation. I decided it would be best if we let her stay on—you know: Humor her."

"Anton, darling, we had an agreement. *Comprends?*"

"Yes," said Anton. "It's just that . . . well, maybe it's a joke."

"In my short, unhappy acquaintance with Ms. Paine, she did not strike me as being a humorous woman. I doubt it's a joke. And here she's canceled Gilberto's show—Gilberto, who I hasten to remind you is our only economically profitable client—and replaced him with pictures of bestiality!"

Anton took another look at the photograph. "I don't know," he said. "This looks kind of interesting. Amanda has an excellent eye."

"I hadn't thought it was her eye that made an impression on you."

"Oh, Solange, don't get nasty. You know it's over between Amanda and me. You know that."

"I know we had an agreement, and I know I kept my half of it. I'm not so sure what I know about you and Miss Paine."

"Well, listen, don't worry. I'll take care of it. I'll call Amanda and find out what's going on."

"I think not," said Solange. "I think, my darling, I will proceed from here, as I should have proceeded long ago. Give me that postcard."

"No. What are you going to do with it?"

"Give it to me," said Solange. She held out her hand.

Anton gave her the postcard. She smiled at it, and then she spat, quite neatly, onto it. "You too," she said, holding it out for him.

"No," said Anton.

"Spit," commanded Solange.

Anton complied.

Solange rubbed their spittle together with her finger, all the while making low, guttural noises in her throat. Then she ripped the postcard into tiny pieces, which she divided into two piles. She gave half of them to Anton. "Here," she said. "Bon appetit, my love."

"No," said Anton, but he knew it was futile. He watched Solange and did as she did: He put the moist fragments of card into his mouth and chewed them. Their eyes were locked. Solange was smiling. She leaned forward and kissed her husband. Chewed paper and tongue mingled in their mouths.

I  I  I  I  I  I

Lyle Wallace was sad to be losing Kate. Though their acquaintance had been short—a little less than a week—it had been long enough for Lyle to grow fond of his ward. In fact, he found he preferred her to his own Kate, who seemed by comparison rather a dull child.

On the morning of her departure, he awoke with a sullen heart.

He bathed Kate and carefully dressed her in the party dress she had been wearing on her arrival.

"Guess who you're going to see today?" he asked her as he unpinned the name tag from her frilly chest.

"Who?" wondered Kate.

"Your mom and dad," said Lyle. "They're back from their vacation."

"They went on vacation?"

"Yeah. Remember, I told you: They asked me to take care of you while they went on vacation."

"Where did they go?" asked Kate.

"Portugal," said Lyle.

"Did Gregory and Heath go too?"

"I don't think so," said Lyle. "But maybe."

In the car Kate seemed preoccupied. She stared out the window at the traffic stalled all around them.

"Are you going to miss me?" Lyle asked.

Kate looked over at him. "Why?" she said.

"Well, we'll probably never see each other again."

"Oh," said Kate. She played with the clasp of her seat belt.

"Keep it buckled," Lyle said.

"Maybe if they go on vacation again, you'll take care of me," Kate said.

Lyle looked down at her and smiled. "Maybe," he said.

Sonia was waiting for them in the lobby.

"Finally," she said to Lyle. "They're foaming at the bit. Talk about uptight New Yorkers."

"Well, here she is," said Lyle.

Sonia knelt down and smoothed Kate's hair. "Hi, Kate," she said. "How was Disneyland?"

"Good," said Kate.

"You look so pretty. Are you ready to see your mom and dad? They want to see you!"

Kate didn't answer. She was looking over Sonia's shoulder, down the long hall, to where Loren stood in Sonia's office, looking out the window. She started running toward her mom. She was halfway down the hall before Lyle realized she didn't see the glass wall. He didn't know how he knew it, he just suddenly knew—it was in the way she ran. Kate ran like you run when you want to run as fast as you can so that nothing can stop you, and that's how Lyle ran after her.

At first Sonia didn't realize what he was doing. She thought Lyle had freaked out and tried to grab him, but only managed to rip his shirt. Then she understood what was happening and tried to scream. She could see Loren at the other end of the hall trying to scream, too. But everything was quiet.

When Kate was a few feet from the wall, Lyle sensed that he wouldn't catch up with her. He hadn't tackled anyone in five years, but suddenly that's what he was doing: He dove forward, sailing through the air, his large body surprisingly agile. He remembered it perfectly; he knew just what to do. He grabbed Kate from behind, curled his body around hers, and, shielding both their faces, somersaulted into the glass.

# CHAPTER
## 15

Gregory flew to Los Angeles and took a taxi to the hospital. He arrived to find Loren sleeping, watched over by David and Kate.

"Hi," he said.

David stood up, and they shook hands.

"Hi, Kate," said Gregory.

"Hi," said Kate. "I was kidnapped. I didn't see the glass wall but Lyle saved me, only the wall crashed on Mom. She's going to have plastic surgery!"

"Wow," said Gregory.

Kate was glad to see Gregory. She had a lot to talk about, and her dad had been a distracted audience. "Being kidnapped was fun," she continued. "I went to Disneyland and learned how to swim under water, with a mask. When Mom gets better, we're going back to Disneyland. Mickey Mouse isn't really Mickey Mouse. He's just an actor dressed up as Mickey."

"Why don't we go get some lunch, Kate?" David asked.

"We had lunch," said Kate.

"We'll have a snack," said David. "Then I'll take you to the hotel, and you can show me how you swim."

"I need a mask," said Kate.

"Okay. We'll stop and get one."

"How is she?" Gregory asked David. He nodded at Loren.

"She's okay," said David. "They won't know how bad the

91

scarring will be till they remove the stitches. She had seventy-four. She lost a lot of blood, but they gave her a transfusion. I don't know if she'll wake up. But listen, I'll leave you alone."

"Thanks," said Gregory. "Where are you staying?"

"The Sheraton Townhouse," said David. "On Wilshire."

"I'll give you a call," said Gregory.

"Let's go," David told Kate. "Say good-bye to Gregory."

"Bye, Gregory," said Kate.

Gregory leaned over and kissed Kate. "It's good to see you again," he said.

They left. Gregory sat by the bed and watched Loren sleep. Actually there wasn't much to see: Her face was covered in bandages. He felt he should hold her hand or touch her or something, but he was afraid of hurting her. After about an hour a nurse came in and told him he had to leave, but that he could come back at three o'clock.

Gregory went out and had a Caesar Salad because he liked them and he didn't order them in New York anymore because of the egg disease. On his way back to the hospital he bought a copy of *HG*. It was an odd choice—Loren wasn't particularly interested in either houses or gardens, but it was the only happy looking magazine he could find.

Loren was still sleeping. He sat down beside her and waited. Suddenly she said, "I think I'm blind."

"What?" Gregory asked.

"Gregory?"

"Yes," he said.

"Oh," said Loren. "I thought it was David."

"No," said Gregory. "It's me."

"I think my eye . . . " She paused while she tried to think of which eye it was. "I think my eye toward you is blind."

"No," said Gregory, "it's just bandaged."

"I know that," said Loren. "But underneath—I think it doesn't see."

"I'm sure it's fine," said Gregory. "The doctor said it was fine," he added, although he had spoken with no doctor.

They sat there for a moment. "Are you here for work?" Loren asked.

"No," said Gregory. "I'm here to see you."

After a minute Loren said, "If I believed God punished people for behaving badly, I'd believe I was being punished."

"But you don't believe that," Gregory said.

"I don't believe the God part," said Loren.

ı   ı   ı   ı   ı   ı

"You see," said Judith, "I would have been perfectly safe alone." She and Henry were riding the N train back from Queens. Judith had been invited for dinner with Henry's family: his daughter Joan and his grandson Kyle. Henry was escorting her back as far as Manhattan; from there on she would venture home via taxi.

"But maybe not," said Henry.

They were silent for a moment, as the subway crawled across the 59th Street Bridge, awed by the view of Manhattan.

"It's so beautiful," Judith said. And Henry, who had never thought the city particularly beautiful, was surprised to find himself nodding in agreement, for he suddenly felt the beauty—it was a palpable, pulsating thing. He kept his eyes on it but moved his hand for Judith's and was not surprised, when he touched it, to feel it open and clasp his own.

At 59th Street he came through the turnstile behind her, ignoring her orders to cross the platform. He would not leave her, he said, until she was safe in a taxicab. So they stood on Third Avenue, close but not touching, silent, aware of the wonderful tension between them.

"It was nice of you to come so far for dinner," Henry said.

"You really must stop being so polite," said Judith. "It's I who should thank you."

"Oh," said Henry, "I'm sorry."

"And you shouldn't apologize for being too polite," said Judith.

Henry was about to apologize for apologizing but stopped himself by laughing. Judith laughed too. They stood there, letting the taxis speed by. And then Judith said, "I should go."

"Are you sure it's safe for you to go alone? I could come with you and take the subway back."

"No," said Judith. "You've already gone far enough out of your way."

"But being with you . . . "

"What?" asked Judith.

"Being with you is not going out of my way," Henry said.

They looked at each other. He has such a beautiful face, Judith thought. It was all she could think. When they kissed, it was just a matter of mutual inclination: No one had to bend down or lean up; they just moved their faces forward.

"I am a happily married woman," said Judith, when the kiss was completed. "You know that, don't you?"

"I know that you are a married woman," said Henry.

"I am a contentedly married woman," said Judith, as if there were some subtle, complicated hierarchy between loving and being in love.

ı ı ı ı ı ı

The day after Loren was released from the hospital she and David and Kate went to Disneyland. The night before their visit, they stayed in a hotel, in two adjacent rooms on the top floor. Kate and Loren slept in one and David slept in the other. Each bedroom had a tiny terrace, from which the turrets of Cinderella's castle could be seen.

Both David and Loren lay awake in their cool, clean beds, listening to the hum of the a.c., wondering what would happen next. It was as if the cards they had been playing with had been tossed back up into the air and were flurrying all around them.

Though the drapes were drawn, Loren could sense the light growing behind them. She got out of bed. Kate slept in the exact middle of the second king-sized bed. She lay on her stomach, her face smashed into a pool of drool on the pillow. Loren sat down and touched her. She wondered what Kate was dreaming. It's all so secret, Loren thought, that world inside.

After a while she got up and drew aside a corner of the curtain to see the day. It looked hot and gray—a little greenish at the corners. Or was that the tint of the glass? She opened the sliding doors and stepped out onto the terrace, pulling the door shut behind her.

"Good morning," someone said. It was David; he was sitting on his terrace, a few feet away.

"Hi," said Loren. "How long have you been out here?"

"About an hour," said David. "I couldn't sleep."

"Neither could I," said Loren. "What time is it?"

"About six," said David. He stood up and moved to the railing of his terrace. If they both reached out, they could have touched each other. "So," he said, "what do you think?"

"About what?"

"Anything," said David. "If you've been awake, you must have been thinking something."

"I was thinking lots of things."

"How's Kate?" asked David.

"She's sleeping," said Loren. "She's dreaming."

"I want to see her," said David.

"Wait," said Loren. "And we'll wake her up, later."

"That will be nice."

Loren smiled. She looked down at the pool, which lay like a turquoise lozenge on the earth.

"Loren?" David said.

"What?"

"What are you going to do?"

"What do you mean?"

"I mean, are you still moving out here with Gregory?"

"No," said Loren. "I think I've left Gregory."

"Oh," said David.

"What about you?" Loren asked. "What about you and Heath?"

"I don't know," said David. "I think it's all over, too."

"That's too bad," said Loren.

David shrugged.

For a moment neither of them spoke, and then Loren said, "Do you remember that night we slept together? After Lillian's party?"

"Of course," said David.

"I think about that a lot," said Loren. "Why do you think we did that?"

"I don't know," said David. "It was your idea."

"Do you think it was a bad idea? Do you wish we hadn't?"

"No," said David.

"Do you think we loved each other then?"

"I think so," said David.

Loren looked out at the Magic Kingdom. The sky was getting brighter and bluer. "Listen," she said, her voice shaking. "I feel like we have this chance, and we can't blow it. I mean, we have to at least talk about it."

"About what?"

"About getting back together," said Loren. "We've fucked up. At least I have. And all this, this stuff with Kate and this"—she touched her bandaged cheek—"I think, you know, for Kate's sake, but also for ours, too, I think, I mean, I'm not sure how you feel, but I'd like to try to make it work again."

"Do you think we can?" David asked.

Loren didn't answer. She was looking down at the pool. Suddenly it seemed to come alive. The water began to pitch and roll, with tiny waves spilling out.

"Look," said Loren, pointing far below them. "It wasn't doing that a moment ago."

"Maybe they just turned the filter on," said David.

"No," said Loren. "It's an earthquake. It's how they start. We've got to get downstairs!" She ran into her hotel room to wake Kate.

David ran through his room and out into the hall. He tried to open Loren's door, but it was locked. He pounded on it. And then he stopped pounding, because he thought he could feel the floor shaking.

# CHAPTER
## 16

Heath and Gerard were in the penthouse at Barney's, trying to find something Heath could wear to his opening that night. Several good-looking salesmen were lurking around, trying to make them feel cheap and doltish. They were having more of an effect on Heath; Gerard was impervious to other people's fucking with his self-image. He was a dancer.

Heath was trying on a pair of black and white checked pants and a black T-shirt.

"That looks kind of cool," Gerard said.

"What do you mean, 'kind of'?"

"It needs a belt," said a salesman. He unlooped one from a belt corral. "Try this," he said. "It's genuine unborn calfskin."

"Does that mean it's from a cow fetus?" asked Heath.

"My motto is, 'The fewer questions asked, the better,' " the salesman said. "This is the ultimate in leather. Just feel it."

"No thanks," said Heath. "I have some belts at home."

The salesman rolled his eyes: He could well imagine Heath's belts. "The wrong belt could ruin everything," he said. "Accessories are key, you know."

"We're aware," said Gerard.

"How much is this shirt?" asked Heath.

"It's one eighty," said Gerard. "But forget the price. How many times in your life do you attend your first SoHo opening?"

"Whose opening are you going to?" asked the salesman.

"His," said Gerard.

"Really? What kind of art do you do?"

"Photography," said Heath.

"Oh," said the salesman. "That's funny. I thought photography was dead."

· ı · ı · ı · ı

Amanda was terrorizing the caterers when the phone rang. She excused herself and went into the office. "Gallery Shawangunk," she said. "Out of Control."

"Hi, Amanda. It's Anton."

"Hi, baby. What can I do for you?" asked Amanda. She was looking out through the window at the waiters, who were setting up tables. They weren't as attractive as she had hoped. In fact, a few of them were downright ugly. What was the world coming to?

"I just wanted to warn you," Anton was saying. "We'd better be careful. Solange is on the warpath."

"What do you mean?"

"Well, I'm not sure. But we'd better play it cool with her tonight."

"Is there any other way to play it with a block of ice?" asked Amanda. "Don't worry about me. I can handle Syringe."

"I'm not so sure. Also, I told her I fired you. I think it would be good if we got our stories straight, so she doesn't get suspicious. So could you consider yourself fired?"

"And I told you I quit. I got the job at MOLTCATO starting September first."

"I know, I know, but could you, just for tonight, be fired? And act kind of destitute and tragic. It may help soften Solange up."

"Soften her up? Who are you kidding? A blow torch wouldn't soften her up."

"You don't know Solange like I know Solange."

"Just one of the many things I'm eternally grateful for," said Amanda.

ı · ı · ı · ı · ı

Amanda had instructed Heath to bring a woman—a beautiful woman—to the opening as his date. He decided to ask Tammi, his waitress friend from the Wisteria. They arrived at six-thirty in the car Amanda had sent for them. Heath looked through the tinted glass into the gallery window. A lot of people he had never seen before were standing around inside, drinking. No one seemed to be looking at the photographs.

"I can't do it," he said. "I can't go in there."

"Unfortunately you have to," said Tammi, a practical woman. "Maybe you should have another drink."

"I don't know," said Heath. "I already feel a little schlitzed."

"Well, maybe a smoke then," said Tammi. "Just to relax us." She opened the rhinestone-studded clutch she had borrowed from the lost-and-found box at the Wisteria for this occasion and fished out a joint. She lit it and handed it to Heath. "Relax," she said.

They sat there smoking, watching the crowd in the gallery. Who are all those people? Heath wondered. He thought he saw the salesman from Barney's go in, but then realized that all the men looked like Barney's salesmen.

"I feel ugly," he said.

"You're gorgeous," said Tammi. "Everybody in there wants to fuck you." She laughed. "A friend of mine worked as a dresser for some summer stock theater—you know the kind where all the alcoholic has-been actresses play Blanche DuBois or Maria Von Trapp? Anyway, she'd have to get them out on the stage, you know, but every night they'd choke. So she'd tell them, 'You're gorgeous. Every man in that audience wants to fuck you,' over and over again and then push them out into the lights."

"That's a real encouraging story," said Heath. "Thanks."

ı  ı  ı  ı  ı  ı  ı

"Here he is!" exclaimed Amanda, when Heath finally made his entrance. "Darling," she said, kissing both his cheeks, "congratulations! There are so many people I want you to meet."

"This is Tammi Bullota, a friend of mine," said Heath.

"Hello there, Pammy," said Amanda.

"Tammi," corrected Heath, but Amanda took no notice. She slunk her arm through Heath's and maneuvered him away.

"Anton," she said, "you remember Mr. Jackson?"

"Of course," said Anton, and shook Heath's hand.

"And this is Anton's lovely wife, Solange," said Amanda. "The two of them jetted back from France just for the opening."

"Oh," said Heath, "that was very kind of you."

"Kindness had nothing to do with it," said Solange, smiling brightly.

"Will you excuse us?" said Amanda. "I want to introduce Heath to our friends from the media. Listen," she whispered to Heath, as she steered him away from the Shawangunks, "let me do the talking. And stop smiling like that. Try to look a little bored. Relax."

"Okay," said Heath.

"Let's schmooze," said Amanda. "Jon, darling," she said to the man who looked most like a salesman from Barney's. "I'd like you to meet Heath Jackson. Heath, this is Jon Cadogan. Jon's with *ARTnews.*"

"Hi," said Heath.

"Greetings," said Mr. Cadogan.

"And Heath, this is Leonora Trumpet. And where are you now, Leonora? It's always someplace new!"

"I'm the Tuscan correspondent for *OM.*"

"*OM?*" said Amanda. "I've not heard of it."

"It's the new magazine for old money," explained Leonora. "It's the magazine for people who didn't make their money yesterday."

"Speaking of which, any sales yet?" asked Jon.

"Just a tremendous amount of interest so far," said Amanda. "Heath's vision is new. We don't expect it to be immediately embraced."

"I beg to differ," said Leonora. "I find Mr. Jackson's vision extremely embraceable. If you know what I mean."

This debate was interrupted by the arrival of Solange. "Amanda, my dear," she said. "Are you ready for the little talk you wanted?"

"Later," said Amanda. "I hardly think these good people are interested in our affairs."

"I'm all ears," said Leonora.

"*Moi aussi,*" said Jon.

Solange smiled. "Perhaps you're right," she said. "There's a time and place for everything. And it is time, I think, that I become better acquainted with our artist. Will you allow me to steal Mr. Jackson from your clutches? I promise I'll return him."

"He's all yours," Leonora said.

"Go for it," said Jon.

Heath followed Solange through the crowd into the gallery office. She closed the door and lowered the shade over the window. "There," she said. "Alone at last."

Heath was feeling nervous, and he wished now he hadn't smoked that joint with Tammi. He decided to sit down.

"Yes, make yourself at home," said Solange. "Would you like a cigarette?"

"No thanks," said Heath.

"Do you mind if I . . . "

"Uh, no," said Heath. "Go ahead."

Solange extracted a pack of Galoise from her purse and lit one. She inhaled, exhaled, and then looked at the cigarette, as if it were malfunctioning. "So," she said. "You haven't said much. Do you know what's going on?"

"Going on? What do you mean?" asked Heath.

"Poor boy," Solange murmured. "Amanda"—and she gestured with her cigarette toward the gallery proper—"is not a nice woman. I hope you have at least figured that much out."

"She's been nice to me," said Heath, although 'nice' didn't seem to be the best word to describe Amanda's behavior.

"In fact she hasn't," said Solange. "Just because people do nice things *for* you doesn't mean they are being nice *to* you."

"Oh," said Heath.

"Amanda is using you. She is making a fool out of herself, but she is also making a fool out of you."

"Oh," said Heath. He was finding it difficult to concentrate. He wished this woman would go away. "How so?" he managed to say.

"Did you not find it surprising that Amanda was willing to show your work in this gallery, given the fact you have not shown else-where, given the fact that you are incredibly young, unknown, and given the fact that your talent is, shall we say, unproved?"

"Well, sure I was surprised," said Heath. "But . . . "

"Why look a gilt horse in the mouth?"

"Gift horse," said Heath. He felt himself sweating.

"Whatever," said Solange. "Here is my point: Amanda has been using you. She has purposefully mounted a laughable show to embarrass the gallery, Anton, and myself. Not to mention Heath Jackson."

"Laughable?" said Heath. "I don't hear anybody laughing."

They were quiet for a second, and, as if on cue, a gale of laughter arose from behind the wall. Oh, God, thought Heath. I hate you, God. I hate myself too. I hate photography. I hate art. "I hate art," he said aloud. He stood up.

"It's Amanda, not art, you should hate."

"I hate them both," said Heath.

"Hate is a powerful emotion," said Solange. "It is a creative emotion. It is, personally, my favorite."

"Why would Amanda want to embarrass the gallery? And us?"

"For an artist, you are curiously unintuitive. But then perhaps you are not an artist. We shall see."

"I am an artist," said Heath. He had to sit down after saying that, because he had never uttered those words, not even to himself, before. I am, he thought. I am an artist.

"Why do people misbehave?" asked Solange. "Why are people petty? Why are they vindictive?

Heath knew the answer to that one. "Because of love," he said.

Solange smiled. "Because of love gone wrong," she corrected.

There was a knock on the door.

*"Entrez,"* said Solange. It was Anton and Amanda. They came in and closed the door behind them.

"Excuse us," said Amanda. "But we needed something in here."

She went over to the desk and opened the top drawer. She was wearing a pair of gloves. "Ah," she said, removing an object from the drawer, "here it is." She turned around. She was holding a gun. She pointed it at Solange and fired it once. It made no noise. Solange looked surprised for an instant, crumpled up, and fell to the floor.

"Hey, Tiger, think fast," said Amanda, throwing the gun to Heath.

Your natural instinct, when something is thrown at you, is to catch it. There was so little time to think. Heath caught the gun, and when he looked up, Amanda and Anton had disappeared.

# CHAPTER
# 17

Dear Leonard,

Since I haven't heard from you in such a long time, I'm not sure where to address this letter. I'll send it to the address I have, with the assumption that you're still there. I assume that if you've moved on, you would have let me know.

The first thing I have to tell you is that Kate is safe and sound. Loren and David are with her now in Los Angeles, and they say she is fine. Unfortunately, Loren was in an accident involving a glass wall. She was in the hospital for several days with 74 stitches but she's out now. She says it sounds worse than it actually is—I wanted to fly out but she told me it wasn't necessary. So I'll be glad to see her—they come back to New York after a quick trip to Disneyland.

To tell you the truth, I'm worried about her. She is usually so tough, you know, but this ordeal—Kate being kidnapped and then this accident—well, I don't know how she's stood it all. And things with Gregory do not seem to be going well. Although she doesn't talk about it (at least not to me). I just hope this doesn't drive her and David back together. Sometimes I think they will never learn.

I suppose the same could be said of me. Oh, darling, I wish

you were here, so I could *talk* to you! Anyway, this next bit I've debated telling you, and I've decided I should. You see, I've fallen in love, I think. Or I have fallen into something like love. I don't know. It all happened rather oddly and unexpectedly (as you well know, I am hardly a candidate for this sort of thing). It seems pointless to burden you with a detailed description of him—suffice it to say he is hardly the lover you would imagine for me, if you can imagine such a thing. I certainly couldn't, and that's why I didn't resist—because I never thought it would develop. You see, I never thought I was capable of this. But I've discovered, to both my fear and my delight, that I am capable. I've surprised myself, and I'm sure I've surprised you, too. So far it is all very innocent. I don't know what, if anything, will come next.

It may be wrong of me to write and alarm you, to spoil your precious (and I mean that sincerely) solitude. So I suppose I am writing for my sake, for I can't continue without this confession to you. It *was* all your idea, this year apart. I know I agreed to it, but I realize now I feel betrayed by it—by your need for it. I should have told you that sooner but I have only just realized how I feel. I tried so hard to embrace the idea that I was dishonest with myself. You may think this liaison I mentioned is motivated by that feeling of betrayal, but I don't think it is. Who knows what's motivated me to behave in this very uncharacteristic fashion? Whatever it is I'm experiencing, I think it's separate from what I feel for you. All those feelings are intact. They wait for you.

Darling, if you receive this letter, will you write me? Please. Just to let me know it found you, and more if you would. Do you still plan to return at Christmas? Perhaps this is all about missing you. I feel it very keenly now, at this moment: missing you. I feel confused and lonely. Please write to me.

With love,
Judith

I I I I I I

## OUT OF CONTROL:
## PHOTOGRAPHS BY HEATH JACKSON
### The Gallery Shawangunk, New York

What at first seems to be yet another portfolio of standard New York City images, evolves, upon closer inspection, into something considerably more exciting. Although the subject of these photographs may be clichéd, Jackson's rendering of each image is very much his own. His vision is menacing, yet narrative: Objects within the frame, seemingly unrelated, conspire to tell us something, and if the scenarios here are not clear, the mood, at least, is. A snarling dog watches a woman nurse a baby on a park bench; a flock of stilleto-heeled shoes seem to hover above a rabbi's head; and in the signature image, a cat delicately sucks a noodle off a man's face. Within a single photograph, there are several fields of focus, as if each object is moving at its own select speed. If some of these images seem too artfully posed, the best of them transcend artfulness and announce a vision that bears continued attention. —Jon Cadogan

ı ı ı ı ı ı

Dear Loren,

I'm going to call you to talk about this but I decided to write this letter because all afternoon, as I've been packing, I've been thinking about—well, about us and what happened, and I know if I don't write it down I'll forget it. You know me.

I've decided to move out to L.A. early. There doesn't seem much point in hanging around here. Anyway, when I get settled and everything, I'll give you a call. I just thought it might be good if I'm gone when you get back. It will be one less thing you have to deal with, right?

One of the things I've been thinking about was why this happened—why it didn't work out. Things seemed so great about a month ago, when we decided to move to L.A. together.

That seems so long ago now, and almost impossible. But I'm glad I had that moment with you—when I believed it would all happen for us. I wonder what you thought then. In retrospect I have this feeling that you were never very convinced by the idea. I think it was lousy timing on my part—I wanted everything to happen very quickly for us. It was because I was so happy with you that I fucked up. I see now that if I had just chilled out we'd probably still be together. Or at least I like to think that.

Loren, the other thing I want to say is about what you said in the hospital. About your being punished. If you meant it then (and I hope you didn't), I hope by now you know it's not true. I'm not sure what you meant by 'behaving badly' but please know that I don't think you've behaved badly as far as I or anybody else is concerned. I think that under the awful circumstances of the last few weeks you've behaved very well. I guess what I'm trying to say is that I'm not bitter about any of this. I'm sad, but I'm not bitter. This had been the best year of my life.

Of course I'll be thinking about you all the time. I hope you can forget this mess and be happy. I want you to be happy. You're so great when you're happy. I'll call you like I said, okay? I know that after all this shit you probably never want to set foot in L.A. again, but if you do, know that you have a good friend nearby. Okay?

Love,
Gregory

ı ı ı ı ı ı ı

## SOHO SLAUGHTER: OUT OF CONTROL AT ART GALLERY

**A Post Exclusive**—Brooklyn photographer Heath Jackson was charged with the attempted murder of Solange Shawangunk, the owner of the Gallery Shawangunk on Broome Street. The incident took place last night at an opening reception for the SoHo show "Out of Control: Photographs by Heath Jackson."

Witnesses told police Jackson and Shawangunk were alone in an office at the gallery when the shooting occurred. Moments later, Shawangunk was discovered shot once through the stomach. She remains in a coma and is listed in critical condition at St. Vincent's Hospital.

Jackson, 27, who has no police record, pleaded not guilty and has been released from custody on his own recognizance. No motive was given for the attempted murder, although it appears that Jackson and Shawangunk may have been romantically involved. Amanda Paine, the gallery's director, told the *Post* that Jackson and Shawangunk disappeared into the office halfway through the reception. "There was obviously some sort of emotional tension between them," she said.

Margot Geiger, a spokesperson for the gallery, informed the *Post* that Jackson's photographs were selling "incredibly." "We've sold out the show and are taking orders for new work," she said.

Mr. Jackson could not be reached for comment.

ı  ı  ı  ı  ı  ı  ı

(Dictated to Loren)

Dear Lyle,

Thank you for taking care of me while I was kidnapped and for catching me before I crashed. It was fun. I swum at the hotel without a mask. I closed my eyes. I like it better with a mask. We were in an earthquake and Mom threw up. Were you in an earthquake? It was fun but I was sleeping.

It's hot in New York. At daycare I can drink soda, but not Coke. Only the kind with fruit in it. And I get Frozade on the way home. Do you like Frozade? Ms. Mouse lives with Mom now. So does Dad. No one lives at Dad's. He said some night we can go sleep there if I want.

Love,
Kate

**Fertility Association of New York, Inc.**
660 Broadway
New York, NY 10012
*Meeting Your Fertility Needs Since 1987*

Dear Mr. Jackson:

We have just concluded our semi-annual sperm supply inventory. Our records indicate that material donated by you (#72428) is in low supply. We hope that as a charter member of FANY you will continue to play an active role in our growth. As you know, we offer competitive rates, and we have recently introduced a bonus system for frequent donors. The more you give, the more you get!

To discuss these programs, or to schedule a follow-up screening, please call Gudrun Skalo at NYC-BABY. We look forward to hearing from you and welcoming you back to the FANY family.

Sincerely yours,
Ursula Tabor-Schwicker,
President and Founder

# CHAPTER
## 18

"Did you have to go to jail?" David asked. Before Heath could answer the waiter appeared. They both ordered salade nicoise and iced tea. It was a hot day, and they had met for lunch in the garden of a restaurant.

"I spent one night in jail," said Heath. "My hearing was the next day."

"Is there anything I can do? Do you have a lawyer?"

"No," said Heath. "I'm defending myself."

"You are?"

"Jesus," said Heath. "Of course not. This isn't a joke, you know. I could go to jail for fifteen years."

"I know it's not a joke," said David. "Is he a good lawyer?"

"It's a she," said Heath, "and I hope so."

"You seem pretty glib about all of this."

"Glib? I'm scared shitless. If Solange doesn't come out of her coma, I'm dead meat. She's the only one who can save me."

"There wasn't anyone else around?"

"Just Amanda and Anton, but they swear they weren't. And Amanda's assistant and this creepy Trumpet woman are giving them an alibi."

"How is Solange? I mean, what are her chances?"

"About fifty-fifty. But that's assuming Amanda doesn't get to her again. I wouldn't be surprised to hear she's checked out at any minute."

"When's the trial?"

"Sometime in the fall."

"And what are you going to do till then?"

"I don't know. I can't leave New York. I've got to find a job. The Hysteria fired me, for security reasons."

"Jesus. Do you need money?"

"No. Listen, I don't want to talk about this. It's demoralizing. Let's talk about something else, okay?"

"Sure," said David.

"Let's talk about us," said Heath.

David didn't say anything. Their teas were delivered. The glasses were sweating.

"Or is that equally demoralizing? I guess so. Why don't we talk about you. That should cheer us up. I gather you're back with Loren. That you've renounced your corrupt lifestyle and have returned to the straight and narrow path. With the emphasis on straight."

"It's not that simple," said David.

"It seems pretty simple to me," said Heath. "You are back with Loren, right?"

"Yes," said David. "But there are . . . circumstances. I wish I could explain it."

"You could try," said Heath.

David sipped his tea.

"Start from the beginning," Heath prompted.

"When I met you?"

"No," said Heath. "When you met Loren. This is about her, isn't it?"

"It's about you, too," said David.

"But mostly about her," said Heath.

David leaned back and looked up at the sky. Bird sounds emerged from stereo speakers hidden in the trees.

"I met Loren on Cape Cod. I was there with my sister and Loren was there with Lillian. We met on the beach. It turned out we were both going to graduate school at U Penn. Loren was going to Wharton and I was getting a master's in botany. We fell in love. We got married, moved to New York, and lived on Cornelia Street.

I got my job editing garden books at Wilson Watson, and Loren got her job at the girl's bank. When Kate was born we moved uptown. That's when things began to go wrong. Uptown. We started to have trouble sexually—I mean, I started to have trouble sexually—and Loren met Gregory. We got divorced. Loren moved to Greene Street. I lost my job at Wilson Watson and got my job at *Altitude*. Lydia went home to Costa Rica for Christmas. You came to be my secretary. I fell in love with you."

Heath looked at him for a moment and then looked away.

"Everyone was happy then," David continued. "Loren and Gregory, me and you. At least I think you were happy. For a little while?"

Heath nodded.

"One night, last spring, Loren and I met at a party. We slept together. It was the night you went to Lar Lubovitch. Remember? Then everything bad started to happen, very quickly: Loren decided to move to California with Gregory. I burned my fingers. Kate was kidnapped. Loren and I went to L.A. A glass wall crashed on Loren. We thought we were going to die in an earthquake, but we didn't die." David paused. He was aware of Heath looking at him, listening to him, poor, beautiful Heath. He didn't look back at Heath because he couldn't bear to. He knew if he looked at Heath for too long he would betray Loren. And betraying Loren seemed, somehow, to be betraying Kate.

"The man who kidnapped Kate taught her to swim. She wrote him a thank-you letter. She told me she that she misses him, that she loves him. And under the circumstances, why shouldn't she? I guess that's the point: We love the people perhaps we shouldn't. We don't love the people we should."

"Meaning that you love Loren," said Heath.

David nodded.

"Meaning you don't love me," said Heath.

"No," said David. "It's not that I don't. It's more like I can't. I have this second chance to make things work with Loren, and I can't turn it down."

"You could, if you wanted to. It's just a question of what you want."

"It's a question of what's the right thing to do," said David.

"And the right thing to do is to live with Loren, who you don't really love?"

"I love Loren," said David. "In a way."

"Who would you rather sleep with, Loren or me?"

"It's not a question of sex," said David. "There are all these other factors, like—"

"I know, I know," said Heath. "But who would you rather sleep with?"

"I don't know," said David.

"You don't know? Of course you know. It's not a hard question."

"Okay, then," said David, "you. But sleeping—I mean, you know, sex—it's important, I know it is, but there's a lot of other stuff that goes on. I mean, you have to consider the total picture."

Their salads arrived. The tuna glistened with oil and sunlight. The string beans were steamed to a violent green. The all of it was crowned with a ring of hairy anchovies.

Heath felt sick. He looked at David. "Do you think you'll be happy with Loren?"

"Not how you mean happy. You're very young. You don't realize there are other things, other feelings worth having."

"Such as?"

"Security," said David. He tried to sound convincing. "Contentment."

"Well," said Heath. "I guess that's the difference between you and me."

"I guess so," said David.

Heath stood up. "I think you're pathetic," he said. "I pity you." He went inside the restaurant. It was dark and cool. His eyes had to adjust. He could feel his irises expanding, or maybe it was the world shrinking. He could feel the horrible motion of living. He stood in the restaurant's tiny bathroom, the light turned off, in perfectly sealed darkness. He wanted to cry, but he couldn't. He wanted to cry for everything.

Outside, the street was sunny. People were walking back to work from lunch. Everyone was tan and sated. Cars drove past with the windows rolled up tight. Air conditioners drooled onto the sidewalks. Trees moved their limbs, to no effect, overhead. Heath stood on the corner. I should go back inside, he thought. I shouldn't have just walked out like that. Then he thought: Fuck it.

He had just started to walk toward the subway when David appeared at his side. For a moment neither of them spoke. Then Heath said, "I'm sorry I walked out like that."

"It's okay," said David.

"I'm very messed up right now," said Heath. "I mean, I don't know what's going on, I don't know what I'm saying."

"Listen," said David, "if you need anything, anything, if there's anything I can do, I want to help you, but I understand if, well, if you don't want to stay in touch. But call me if you need anything. And I'm sorry. Okay?"

"Okay," said Heath.

"I'm sorry . . . I'm sorry I'm not different. Braver, or something. Because you're right, I think. I know you think I'm bad a person, but I'm not. I don't have bad intentions." David touched Heath's arm. "I just love badly," he said. "I'm just bad at love."

ı  ı  ı  ı  ı  ı  ı

One hundred miles north, Lillian leaned out of an upstairs window in a strange house. Below her, hummingbirds hovered above a bed of mango-colored irises. She had taken the day off and driven upstate to see the Loessers' house, which she was considering renting for the last two weeks in August. She had found the key, hidden beneath the moss-stained brick on the patio, and wandered through the cool, quiet house. The rooms were full of books and wooden chairs; fabrics had faded, doors creaked. The sun shone through the latticed-paned windows, casting warm, patterned carpets of light on the slanting wooden floors.

She drew her head inside the bedroom but left the window open. Except for the hum of the birds and ticking clock, everything was quiet. Well, of course, Lillian thought, these beautiful places do exist. People spend days here, eating and sleeping, cutting flowers, arranging them. Reading in the shade, drinking cocktails on the terrace. Cool nights in old beds. Stars and frogs. The slow procession of days.

She lay down on the bed, a narrow bed with a white metal

frame, a bed she could imagine in a French children's hospital. She lay still and tried to feel the life quickening inside of her. Maybe I will never leave here, she thought. I will gestate and give birth on this bed. I'll raise my child in the house . . .

She awoke an hour later, hot, her clothes and skin damp. The pond, she remembered, there is supposed to be a pond. She got up and looked out the window. There seemed to be a glossy glint of water through the trees, at the bottom of the lawn. She went downstairs and out through the French doors, crossed the patio. The hummingbirds dipped and flew away. She walked through the garden, inhaled basil and mint. The lawn was hot and dry. She trod on the ceilings of gopher tunnels and followed a path into the forest of birch and pine trees, toward the coolness of the pond. It was small, rock-ringed, the water green. Lillian removed her sandals and waded into the weedy shallows. Fish appeared and nibbled her flesh. She kicked them away. She wished she had brought her bathing suit, and then, realizing that she was perfectly alone—the woods seemed to stretch away forever, there wasn't another house around for miles—she decided to go in anyway. She undressed, laying her clothes on the grassy bank, and in what she hoped was a fish-frightening maneuver, charged into the pond and dove into the green water.

It felt wonderful. She swam out to the middle, where icy currents bubbled up from some primordial spring. She lay on her back and floated, spinning under the sun. She kicked a little when fish nibbled. Then she let herself sink into the water, as far as she could fall into the dark coolness. When she surfaced she saw a man standing on the bank, next to her abandoned clothes, watching her.

# CHAPTER
## 19

"Are you drowning?" the man asked. "Do you need help?"

"No," said Lillian. She sunk back under water. She stayed submerged as long as she could, hoping he would go away, but he was still there. In fact, he had moved closer—he had waded out a ways into the water.

"What are you doing?" he asked.

"Swimming," answered Lillian.

The man seemed to ponder this response and find it acceptable. "I came to water the garden," he said. "I come every day when the Loessers aren't here."

"I want to get out," said Lillian.

"Out of what?"

"The pond."

"Oh," said the man.

"I can't do it while you're standing there."

"Why not?"

"I'm naked," said Lillian.

"Oh," said the man. He looked down at her clothes. Her bra lay like a dead bird, shot from the sky, fallen to earth. He looked back at Lillian and smiled. "I'll go up to the house," he said.

"Go anywhere," said Lillian. "Just go away."

"Do you want me to go home?" he asked.

"Where do you live?"

The man pointed across the pond, into the woods. "Over there," he said.

"Yes," said Lillian. "Go home."

"You must be Lillian. Mrs. Loesser told me you'd be coming."

"Yes," said Lillian.

"If I go home, what about the garden?"

"I'll do it," said Lillian.

"Oh. After I water the garden, I usually have a cocktail, on the terrace. A gin and tonic."

"I'm getting cold," said Lillian. "The fish are eating me."

"I'm sorry," the man said. "It's just that you look so pretty."

Lillian didn't respond to this compliment. She didn't reject it, either.

"Maybe we could have a drink together."

"I don't drink," said Lillian.

The man looked perplexed.

"I mean, I don't drink alcohol."

"There's cranberry juice."

"No," said Lillian. "I've got to get back to the city. Lickety-split," she added, for some unknown reason.

"Why?"

"I have things to do," said Lillian.

"Oh." He stood there for a moment, looking dejected. He was rather sweet, Lillian decided, in an odd, dim sort of way.

"What do you do?" asked Lillian. "Over there?"

"Where?"

"Over there, where you live. What do you do?"

The man looked into the woods. He thought for a moment. "I'm learning to play the piano," he said. "I'm teaching myself." He held his hands in the air and fingered an imaginary keyboard. He seemed to lose himself in this charade. He stood there, transfixed, in the pond's shallow water, caressing the air.

"Fine!" shouted Lillian after a moment, in an effort to awaken him. "Very good!"

The man opened his eyes. "Do you know what I was playing?" he asked.

"Mozart," Lillian guessed.

"Yes." He smiled. "Are you sure about the drink?"

"Yes," said Lillian.

"Yes, you mean no?"

"That's right."

"But you won't forget the garden?"

"No," said Lillian.

"Okay," the man said. He began to walk around the pond, to the far side, where a path disappeared into the woods. Lillian watched him. From the back he didn't look half so dim: He had a groovy little pony tail and a great ass. He paused and looked back at Lillian. "Are you going to rent the house?" he asked.

"Yes," said Lillian.

He smiled. "Good," he said, and disappeared into the trees.

When she was sure he was gone—she listened to the sound of him fade—Lillian swam to the bank, tried to dry herself by shaking like a dog, and dressed. She sat on a rock, in the warm leafy sunlight. It was time to go, she knew, but something detained her. If she could have articulated what this something was, she would have said to herself, He may come back, but this thought remained cloistered, unacknowledged, one of those fish that skulk at the bottom of ponds, far from daylight, waiting.

ı ı ı ı ı ı ı

Henry Fank was sleeping. He made quiet, not unpleasant snoring noises. Judith lay awake beside him on her waterbed in the dark bedroom. She was feeling a little desperate. Simple—or not-so-simple—desire had carried her through much of the evening; it had flooded her body, possessed her, wavelike, and then retreated. And here I lie, she thought, high and dry. For now that it was over she could not embrace Henry. He had been a strong, sweet lover, but now, afterward, he was not someone she could lie down with. That was the pity of it. She wanted someone who knew her to hold her, wanted to hold someone she knew. Ultimately, she realized, it is not about love: It is about knowing and being known. And it was Leonard, and Leonard only, who knew her. How wonderful that was, but also how confining. And how impossible to escape.

Henry woke up. Or perhaps he had never been sleeping, the transition was that graceful. He leaned on his elbow, above her.

"Are you thinking of your husband?" he asked.

How could he have guessed that? Judith wondered. "Yes," she said. Her voice sounded odd, broken. Unused. She tried to smile up at him, without success. He lowered himself and embraced her, but she did not make it a mutual gesture. He sensed this, unfixed himself from her, and got out of bed.

"I'll go," he said.

He began to dress in the darkness. Judith lay quiet, paralyzed. I should say something, she thought, anything—I can't let him leave in silence. But she could not speak. He dressed quickly and paused for a moment, looking down at her. She forced herself to meet his gaze. The look they exchanged meant nothing. It was mute.

He walked out of the room, into the kitchen. She heard him turn on the tap. She got out of bed, found her robe. He was sitting at the kitchen table, drinking a glass of water. She sat down beside him. Neither of them had turned on a light.

"Do you feel remorse?" he asked.

Remorse, she thought. What a complicated word. "How do you know that word?" she asked.

He glanced at her, then looked away, out the window. A woman was walking a dog down on the street and paused while it sniffed a tree.

"When I came here, when I learned English, I was very unhappy. As I told you, my wife, she died on our way here. So I think I learned all the sad words first."

The woman walked away with her dog. Judith stood up. "Please," she said, holding out her hand, "come back to bed."

ı   ı   ı   ı   ı   ı

"Meet me at the polar bears," Amanda commanded.

"I don't think they have polar bears," said Anton.

"Of course they do. What's a zoo without polar bears?"

"Well, what if they don't? What if they phased the polar bears out?"

"Then we'll meet at the largest white mammals. Can you handle that?"

"I don't think the zoo is a good idea. Why don't we just have lunch?"

"No," said Amanda. "The zoo is perfect. No one we know will be at the zoo. Everyone we know goes out to lunch."

"That's true," said Anton.

"Plus I'm wearing a disguise," said Amanda.

"How will I recognize you?"

"I'll be the beautiful woman at the polar bears," said Amanda.

There were, in fact, polar bears—two—who sat on rocks looking hot. Amanda was wearing sunglasses and a picture hat. Her face was powdered white. Her lipstick was the color of blood.

"What kind of disguise is that?" asked Anton.

"Finally," said Amanda. "What took you?"

"The doctor called. They think Solange may be coming out of her coma."

"Then we have to act fast," said Amanda. "Let's sit down. Those bears give me the creeps." Little did she know the feeling was mutual.

They found a bench in the shade. "What did the doctor say?"

"A lot of doctor talk. You know. About her vital signs. And brain waves. Stuff like that."

"I can't believe I didn't kill her. All that target practice for naught. I should sue them."

"I just want to get this over with," said Anton.

"As do I. So we've got to move fast."

"What do you mean?"

"Baby, when Solange wakes up from her coma, it's good night for us. You realize that, don't you?"

"Yes," said Anton.

"So it's imperativo that she doesn't wake up. That's your job."

"I don't know," said Anton. "Maybe we can reason with her, or something. Maybe she'll go along with the Heath Jackson story."

"Darling, don't be stupid. You've got to send Solange to dreamland, pronto."

"Me! Why me? This was all your idea. You're the one who started it."

"And you'll finish it. I can't visit her in the hospital. That would look too suspicious. You're the only one who has access to her."

"What am I supposed to do?"

"I don't know. It shouldn't be so very difficult. She's in a coma, for God's sake. She must be tube city! Just, you know, unplug something."

"I can't," said Anton.

"Baby, you have to. We haven't much time. I know it's hard. But it's, well, it's worth it! If Solange dies, you'll be a very rich man. And I'll make you a very happy rich man. I promise you."

"Yeah, but if Solange lives, I'll still be rich."

"Darling," said Amanda, "look at me. We've been through all this. We made a decision. We acted on that decision. We can't have second thoughts now. That's how things get fucked up. We have to stick to the plan."

"But the plan's not working."

"It will work. It's just taken a detour. An intermission. Think of this as intermission. And the next act depends on what you do this afternoon. It can be a good ending or a bad ending. It's up to you."

Anton looked around. "I liked the old zoo better," he said.

# PART

## III

And yet one must be reasonable and remember that falling in love is never ordinary to the people who indulge in it. Indeed, it is perhaps the only thing that is being done all over the world every day that is still unique.

Barbara Pym, *Crampton Hodnet*

# CHAPTER
## 20

| | |
|---|---|
| ORCA: | Good afternoon, and welcome to "The Orca Show." Some of the most interesting shows we've done in the past have been with celebrities, and today's guest is New York's newest and most controversial addition to that category. You've heard about him, you've seen him on the news, and this afternoon we'll have the chance to chat with him—we'll even take some of your telephone calls. So stay tuned, because when we come back we'll be talking with Heath Jackson, the talented and handsome photographer accused of the point-blank shooting of his patron, the wealthy and influential Solange Shawangunk. We'll be speaking with him right after this important message. |

## FIRST COMMERCIAL BREAK

| | |
|---|---|
| ORCA: | Okay, welcome back. Ladies and gentleman, it's my great pleasure to introduce to you, in his first talk-show appearance, Mr. Heath Jackson. Hi, Heath! Welcome to "The Orca Show!" |
| HEATH: | Thanks, Orca. |

ORCA: Heath—may I call you Heath?

HEATH: Sure.

ORCA: It's such a nice name. Anyway, Heath, before we proceed, I think it might behoove us to nail down some facts about your case. Are you game for that?

HEATH: Sure, that's what I'm here for.

ORCA: Good. Now, you've been accused of the point-blank shooting of Solange Shawangunk. The story, as I understand it, goes like this: During the opening reception of your show of photographs, "Out of Control," at the Shawangunk Gallery in SoHo, New York City, witnesses claim you disappeared into an office with Ms. Shawangunk and were found moments later, holding a gun, standing above the woman's crumpled body. Is this true, Heath?

HEATH: Well, it's true, but it's not the whole truth.

ORCA: Well then, by all means, tell Orca, the live studio audience, and our several million home viewers the whole truth.

HEATH: Well, Ms. Shawangunk had asked me to accompany her to the office.

ORCA: For what purpose?

HEATH: To talk.

ORCA: Talk? Come on, Heath! A good-looking guy like you? Talk? Why would she want to talk to you, in the middle of the reception? Witnesses claim there was some 'tension' in the air.

HEATH: She wanted to warn me about Amanda Paine. She thought Amanda was . . . misusing me.

ORCA: Misusing you? How so? Sexually?

HEATH:     No. As I told the police, before Solange could explain it to me, Amanda burst in . . .

ORCA:      It's your assertion that Amanda Paine shot Solange Shawangunk?

HEATH:     Well, Orca, my lawyer has discouraged me from making any specific accusations. We feel that's best left up to the police.

ORCA:      Are you aware that witnesses say Amanda was at the reception at the time of the shooting?

HEATH:     Yes, but she wasn't. She and Anton came into the office.

ORCA:      Heath, we have a surprise for you. Let me welcome Leonora Trumpet, the well-known lifestyles expert. Welcome, Ms. Trumpet.

LEONORA:   That's Trom*pay*.

ORCA:      I'm sorry: pay. Welcome to "The Orca Show." Now tell us, you claim Amanda was speaking with you at the time of the shooting?

LEONORA:   Yes. I had been introduced by Ms. Paine to Mr. Jackson. We were chatting when Solange—Mrs. Shawangunk—appeared. There was obviously something stewing between her and Mr. Jackson. And I mean stewing as in hot!

HEATH:     Hey, wait a minute . . .

LEONORA:   Well, they excused themselves and disappeared into the office. Amanda and I continued talking—we were, in fact, discussing the alleged murderer's photographs. A short while later, she wanted to show me slides that were located in the office. We entered that room to discover the scene you described: Mr. Jackson holding the gun, and Mrs. Shawangunk lying on the floor, moaning and bleeding. It was awful.

HEATH:       This lady's out of her mind.

*(Leonora weeps; Orca holds her hand.)*

ORCA:        Let's hear from one of our viewers. Mike, are you
             ready with a phone call? Go ahead.

VIEWER:      Hi, Heath. I think you're great, and I really like
             your work. My question is: what speed film do you
             use?

HEATH:       It depends what I'm shooting.

LEONORA:     What if you're shooting Solange Shawangunk?

ORCA:        We'll be back with Heath Jackson after this
             important message.

## SECOND COMMERCIAL BREAK

ORCA:        Heath, it seems to me that like many of these
             crimes of passion, there are questions here that
             won't be resolved until the case comes to trial. Far
             be it from me, Orca, to try to answer those
             questions at this time. So let's turn our attention
             away from the specifics of the case and talk about
             your personal life. Tell me, Heath, were you
             sexually abused as a child?

HEATH:       No, I wasn't.

ORCA:        It helps to talk about it. It's nothing to be
             ashamed of. Are you sure you weren't sexually
             abused?

HEATH:       Not that I recall.

ORCA:        I understand the content of your photographs is
             controversial. Is it true that many of your
             photographs depict sexual relationships between
             people and animals?

HEATH:       No.

| | |
|---|---|
| ORCA: | No? What about this one? Mike, can we get this on the monitor so the people at home can see? Great. Tell us, Heath, what's this a picture of? |
| HEATH: | That's my boyfriend and his cat. |
| ORCA: | Your boyfriend? |
| HEATH: | Well, my ex-boyfriend. |
| ORCA: | Are you trying to tell us you're gay? I thought you were having an affair with Solange Shawangunk. |
| HEATH: | That affair is a fabrication of sick minds. |
| ORCA: | Heath, are you bisexual? Or is it multi-sexual? Men, women, cats? How about children, Heath? Little boys? Do they turn you on? |
| HEATH: | Sorry, Orca, I'm just gay. |
| ORCA: | Well, Heath, I'm afraid our time is up. I do thank you for joining us today. You folks at home, don't go away. We'll be back after this brief message, with Dr. Kelli Loe, author of *Whence This Rage: Working Women in Love* . . . |

Solange heard the TV go off. Anton came and sat down beside her. She could smell him. She tried to speak, but the words she made sounded, even to her, like gibberish. Faraway gibberish. She wasn't even sure what she was trying to say; maybe that's why it came out so distorted. She could sense Anton leaning over her, the warmth of him, his smell. She could smell his fear. Or was it hers? What does Anton have to be afraid of? She tried to raise her hand to touch him, but it wouldn't move. For some reason, all she could see was the hotel room in Aix: the doors to the terrace open, the curtains blowing back into the room. It was raining, and they were making love, for the first time after so long. . . . She could smell the rain. The traffic on the wet street. Her head was hanging off the bed, her neck hurt, the ceiling so far away, so beautiful, Anton above her, between her and the ceiling, like now, only. . . . She felt his hands on her arms—what was he doing? And then she knew. They were both afraid. The rain was coming in the windows, falling on them. The wind had turned cold. The curtain flapping. . . . No. She shut it all out, stopped, thought of what to say, concentrated, forced talk to bubble up from deep inside her, words she could not hear, but kept repeating, over and over, Darling, don't kill me, darling, don't kill me, no, darling, no, don't kill me, please, my darling, no. . . .

# CHAPTER
# 21

"Is Gregory stronger than Daddy?" asked Kate.

"Well, Gregory is bigger," said Loren.

"But is he stronger?"

"Maybe," said Loren. "Just a little."

"Gregory used to threw me up, when he put me to bed. He'd threw me up and catch me."

"Throw me up," said Loren. "What book do you want to read?"

"I don't want to read," said Kate. "I want Gregory to threw me up and catch me."

"He can't," said Loren. "He doesn't live here anymore."

"Is he on vacation?"

"No," said Loren. "Maybe Daddy will throw you up. Should I go get him?"

"No," said Kate.

"Daddy used to throw you up. When you were little. You're getting too big for that now."

"No I'm not. It's because Daddy's weak."

"Daddy's not weak."

"He's weaker than Gregory."

"Daddy does other things for you. He took you to see *Bambi*."

"Bambi's mother died," said Kate.

"I know," said Loren. "That was very sad, wasn't it?"

"Did you almost die, when the wall crashed on you?"

"No," said Loren. "I just got some bad cuts. Some booboos. But I'm all better."

"You have scars," said Kate.

"Yes," said Loren. "But scars are okay. They mean you're better. Now, are you sure you don't want to read a book? What about *Bambi?*"

"No," said Kate. "If Daddy threw me up, would he drop me?"

"No," said Loren. "Of course not. He'd catch you. And throw you up again. Should I get him?"

"No," said Kate.

"Daddy loves you. He would never drop you. I love you, too. Do you want me to throw you up?"

"No," said Kate. "Is Daddy your boyfriend?"

"Yes," said Loren. "I suppose he is."

"What about Gregory?"

"Gregory is my friend. He's not my boyfriend anymore."

"Why not?"

"Because you can only have one boyfriend at a time."

"So you take turns?"

"No," said Loren. "Well, sometimes. But the idea is to find one person, forever."

"Oh," said Kate. She thought for a moment. "Is Gregory homeless now?"

"Of course not," said Loren. "He lives in California."

"He has a house there?"

"Yes," said Loren.

"How do you know?"

"He told me."

"Does it have a pool?"

"I'm not sure," said Loren.

"Can I go visit him?"

"Maybe," said Loren. "Someday."

ı ı ı ı ı ı

Amanda Paine found orchestrating a cover-up a not unpleasant task. She had a flair for it. Perhaps I should run for public office, she thought. Or better yet, be appointed to public office. Something with the New York State Council on the Arts. Someone would eventually have to replace Kitty Carlisle Hart.

The future of the Gallery Shawangunk was uncertain. Heath's show had sold out, and Amanda was planning to curate for MOLT-CATO come September. In the interim, she visited the gallery infrequently. Margot Geiger was there every day and had proved herself adept at handling the curious crowds who came to gawk at Heath's work.

One particularly dead August afternoon, when Amanda had stopped in the gallery to see about cleaning out her desk, Margot appeared in her office doorway, seeking an audience. Amanda bade her sit. "What is troubling you, my child?" she asked, à la the Mother Superior in *The Sound of Music*. Unfortunately she had the feeling that Margot would prove to be a less malleable novitiate than Julie Andrews.

"Well, it's about this murder stuff," Margot began.

"Attempted murder," Amanda corrected.

"Whatever," said Margot. "It's just that . . . well, I feel . . . you know what I told the police? About seeing you and Anton in the gallery when it happened? Well, I've been thinking, maybe I shouldn't have said that."

"Why ever not?"

"Because I don't think I did."

"Did you see us in the gallery before the . . . the event?"

"Yes."

"And after?"

"Yes."

"Then doesn't it follow, my dear child, that we were there *during?*"

"Well, not really," said Margot.

Amanda sighed. How exasperating people could be! "Margot," she said, "the police do not believe you were a private detective. You were a young woman at a very crowded, very happening social event. As I recall you had been drinking."

"I had a glass of champagne."

"Exactly," said Amanda. "Of course you did. That is my point: You were at a party. And it is in that social context that you gave your statement to our friends the police. I hardly think they expected you to be scrutinizing the crowd, noting every single appearance and disappearance."

"Well, maybe I should have made that clearer—that my statement was, you know, not professional. My mother thinks—"

"Your mother!" exclaimed Amanda. "Really, Margot, let's leave our mothers out of this."

"But I needed advice."

"All the more reason to avoid one's mother. Darling, listen to me. If one wants advice, one talks to one's hairdresser. One's therapist. The salesgirls at Agnes B. In a pinch, perhaps to one's friends. But darling, one does not consult one's mother! Call Mathilde Krim, call Ivana Trump, but for God's sake let your mother enjoy her golden years in peace."

Margot was offended. Her mother was only forty-four. "What about you?" she asked Amanda. "May I ask you for advice?"

"Of course you may," said Amanda. "I would be delighted to advise you."

"What do you think I should do? Should I see the police about modifying my statement?"

Amanda pretended to ponder this. "No," she decided. "I think not. The less you have to do with the police the better. Further contact with them, altering your statement—which we have agreed is acceptably accurate—will only draw attention to yourself. There are times, of course, when women benefit from attention, but I assure you that this is not one of those times."

"So you are thinking of my best interest?"

"But of course I am," said Amanda.

"I wonder, while you are considering my best interest, if you could tell me who will succeed you as gallery director in September?"

"Well," said Amanda, thinking, The little bitch. The revolting, scheming little wormette. "That is Solange's decision. It is, after all, still her gallery. If she were to die—God forbid"—and here she paused to cross herself, unpracticed heathen though she was—"it would become Anton's decision. In that case, I would use my influence with him, negligible though it is, to help chose my successor."

"Have you any candidates in mind?" asked Margot.

"I haven't given it much thought," said Amanda. "But I see

now that it is time I did. Let us be perfectly honest with each other, Margot. You have proved to be an excellent assistant, but you must know that it would be highly unlikely for you to be appointed director."

"But do you think it an impossibility?" asked Margot.

"I like to think," said Amanda, "that nothing is impossible."

"So do I," said Margot. She stood up.

"Then we have an agreement?" asked Amanda.

"Yes," said Margot. "I think we do."

# CHAPTER
## 22

Lillian stood, transfixed by a landscape of Rubenesque red peppers. She was at Davenport's Farm Stand, buying produce, one of her favorite bucolic activities. She came every day and lingered in the cool, shaded shed, shaking cantaloupe, peeling back the leaves of corn, sifting through the bin of tomatoes, seeking the reddest, firmest, loveliest specimens. Hers was a quest for perfection, and it was a quest with many easy rewards, some of them sublime. Is there anything more perfect than the perfect peach?

"What's wrong?" asked a voice.

Lillian looked up from the peppers. The man from the pond was standing in the next aisle, behind a landslide of lemons and limes.

"Oh," said Lillian. "Hi. I was just . . . uh, you know . . ."

"Vegging out?" the man said.

"No," said Lillian. "It's just the peppers, they looked so incredibly beautiful, it was weird for a moment."

"What, is this 1968? Are you tripping?"

"No," said Lillian. "I'm just easily . . . "

"Stimulated?" the man suggested. He came around and looked in her basket. "You need a lemon," he said, dropping one in. "You've got to maintain a careful balance of colors." He was standing close enough so that Lillian could smell him. He smelled a little of sweat and a little of cut grass.

"Are you a food stylist?" Lillian asked.

"Kind of," he said. "I run a restaurant."

"Oh," said Lillian. "I thought you were learning the piano."

"Well, that's true. That's what I really do. This restaurant thing is just a hobby."

"Where is it?" asked Lillian. She had no idea where these questions were coming from. It suddenly occurred to her that she was flirting. This realization almost stunned her—it had been ages since she had last indulged in this sort of behavior, but somehow she managed to collect her wits.

"Down the road." He gestured. "Aways."

"What's it called?" It was really quite easy, once begun.

"Chez Claude."

"Is it French?"

"I try."

"Can I come to it?"

"I don't think I can stop you."

Nothing could stop her. "I'm Lillian," said Lillian.

"I know. Mrs. Loesser told me all about you."

"I didn't know Mrs. Loesser knew all about me."

"She thinks she does."

"Well, she didn't tell me anything about you."

The man raised his eyebrows. "That puts you at a disadvantage."

"Yes," said Lillian.

"How do you like country life?"

"Aren't you going to tell me your name?"

"Oh. Claude. Get it: Chez Claude?"

"But of course," said Lillian.

"So what else do you want to know?"

Lillian smiled. She looked down into her basket. "What else do I need in here? To maintain the balance?"

Claude peered into the melange of fruit. He considered. "Blueberries," he decided.

It was the middle of the afternoon. Lillian had gone to buy corn for dinner. Loren was reading *The Bonfire of the Vanities* on the terrace. Kate and David were floating on a raft in the middle of the pond. Kate was all on the raft and David was half on—his legs dangled in the water. They ate cherries and talked.

"Can you swim backward?" Kate asked.

David said he could, and demonstrated.

"Can you swim upside down?"

"How do mean?"

"With your head down in the water and your feet sticking up."

"I don't think so," said David.

"Try."

David tried, and failed. "That's hard," he said, sputtering, having swallowed some water in the attempt.

"Heath can do that," said Kate.

"Can he?" said David. "How do you know?"

"He told me. He told me he was a swimmer on TV but he was on after my bedtime."

"Heath told you that?"

"Yes. But Mom told me Heath isn't your boyfriend anymore."

"She's right," said David.

"Do you hate his guts?" asked Kate.

"No," said David. "I like Heath. I'm just not . . . he's not my boyfriend anymore."

"How do you know?"

"Because . . . well, I realized I didn't love Heath anymore. That I love Mom instead."

"So you stopped loving Heath?"

"Yes," said David. "I guess so."

"Maybe you'll stop loving me," said Kate.

"No," said David. "I'll never stop loving you. Never ever ever."

Kate thought for a moment. She spat a cherry pit into the water. It sunk slowly and was mouthed by fish the whole way down. "How do you know?" she asked.

"I just know," said David. "I could never not love you. It would be impossible."

"Impossible?" asked Kate. "What's that mean?"

"It means it can't happen. Like, it's impossible for fish to fly."

"Fish can fly," said Kate. "They're called flying fish. We saw a movie at daycare."

"But they don't really fly," said David. "They just jump out of the water. They're really swimming."

"No," said Kate. "I saw them. They were flying."

⏐  ⏐  ⏐  ⏐  ⏐  ⏐

Heath had spent an exhausting and discouraging morning in mid-town Manhattan trying to register with a temp agency. It seemed no one wanted to employ alleged murderers. Even Debbie Cusack, his counselor at Temp Around the Clock, the agency that had sent him to David at *Altitude*, told him she could do nothing for him until he was "one hundred percent clean."

Heath had become a little desperate for money despite the fact that his grandmother, who had never forgiven him for "turning queer and not going to medical school," had surprisingly volunteered to pay his legal fees. Apparently the idea of a convicted criminal in the family was more than she could bear. Heath had made about twenty thousand dollars from the sale of his photographs, but for some complicated legal reason this money was being held in escrow. Now that the temp agencies had refused him, his only hope was to wait a couple of weeks and try the Hysteria again.

Heath arrived home to find Gerard lying on the living room floor, naked, surrounded by a posse of fans. Most of these fans had been salvaged from the street and rejuvenated. Gerard was curiously mechanical. Heath took off his shirt and sat on the couch. A soap opera silently unraveled on the TV.

"Any luck?" asked Gerard, who was being uncharacteristically understanding and helpful about everything.

"No," said Heath. "And I thought temp agencies would take anyone. I mean, they cater to losers."

"Maybe you should have given them an assumed name."

"Everyone recognizes me. I have to wear my sunglasses on the subway."

"You and Jackie O."

"I don't think Jackie O rides the subway," said Heath. He went into the kitchen for a beer. It was only two in the afternoon, but he felt he deserved it. When he came back into the living room, Gerard was sitting up. Gazing down at the floor, with his arms resting on his knees, he looked like a Robert Mapplethorpe photograph, sans pedestal.

"Do you want some more bad news?" he said.

"No," said Heath. He stood there with his beer. Then he said, "What?"

"Sit down," said Gerard.

Heath sat. "What?" he repeated.

"Solange Shawangunk is dead," said Gerard.

# CHAPTER
# 23

### Solange Hatier Shawangunk, 44

Solange Hatier Shawangunk, a gallery owner and international socialite, died yesterday at St. Vincent's Hospital, New York, of complications resulting from a gunshot wound she sustained in a shooting that occurred in the Gallery Shawangunk last July 13. She was 44 years old.

A nursing supervisor at the hospital, Laleel Bundara, said that although Ms. Shawangunk had been in a coma since the shooting, she had made excellent progress and not been expected to die.

A doyenne of the downtown art scene and a luminous presence at cultural events on two continents, Ms. Shawangunk was born in Port-au-Prince, Haiti. She was educated at St. Therese de l'enfant Jesus, Belle-Anse, Haiti, and at the Sorbonne. She lived in Europe for several years, and moved to New York in 1976, with her husband, Anton Shawangunk. They opened the Gallery Shawangunk the following year. One of the first galleries to be located in SoHo, it exhibited the work of the then fledgling photographer

Holly Pierson and maxi-expressionist Gilberto Arnot. In 1983 Ms. Shawangunk resigned as director of the gallery but remained an involved owner.

Heath Jackson, a photographer whose show, "Out of Control: The Photographs of Heath Jackson," opened at the gallery in July, has been accused of the attempted murder of Solange Shawangunk. His trial is scheduled for the fall.

Ms. Shawangunk is survived by her husband, Anton Shawangunk, a half-brother, Marco Hatier of Mustique, and a half-sister, Leonora Hatier Trumpet of New York City and Volterra, Italy.

SHAWANGUNK, Solange. The staff and artists of The Gallery Shawangunk mourn the passing of our dear friend and guiding force on the sad occasion of her tragic death. Our sympathy goes to her devoted husband, Anton. A memorial service will be held at the gallery on a date to be announced.

Amanda Paine, Director,<br>
and Margot Geiger, Assistant Director<br>
The Gallery Shawangunk, New York

ı ı ı ı ı ı

Neither Loren nor David was sleeping. They lay awake, not touching, on the bed. It was Sunday night—their last night in the country.

After a long while Loren said, "Why can't we fall asleep?"

"I don't know," said David.

"I know," said Loren.

David did not reply. He was staring at the ceiling; Loren was looking out the window. She could see the tops of trees and stars. She thought she could see shooting stars, but she did not trust herself to see such beautiful, extraordinary things.

"You're sad," said Loren. She watched the stars and waited for

David to answer. When he did not verify or deny her observation, she rephrased it. "Why are you sad?"

"Kate thinks I'm going to stop loving her."

"Oh," said Loren. She paused. "Kate is very confused. I told you about my talk with her."

"Yes," said David.

"Is that what you're sad about?"

"I didn't say I was sad."

"But you are."

"You're sad too."

"No," said Loren. "I'm not."

They were silent for a moment, and then David said, "I wish we could go back to the beginning. Isn't that awful?"

"The beginning of what?"

"The beginning of us."

"There are more awful things to wish," said Loren. She turned away from the window. David lay, naked, uncovered, and she stared at his body. In the dark it looked familiar and unprotected and a little pitiful. If you look at anything closely enough, long enough, Loren thought, it will break your heart. She looked away. "Everyone wants to go backward," she said. "It's universal. But you have to resist it. You have to realize there are good things behind you, sure, but there are bad things, too. And there will be good and bad things in front of you. You just don't know them yet."

"I wasn't talking about life in general."

Loren touched his arm. "I think what I said still applies."

"You think there are good things ahead for us?"

"Yes," said Loren. "Of course I do. You have to believe that."

"I think I'm sad because I don't believe that," said David.

"Oh," said Loren.

For a long time neither of them spoke. They had come as close as they would come to acknowledging that it was over. It seemed pointless to talk about it—they both knew they both knew it.

"I can't stand this," Loren finally said. "I'm going for a swim. Do you want to come?"

"What about Kate?"

"If she wakes up, Lillian's here. She knows where to find Lillian."

"Okay," said David, "I'll come."

They got out of bed and put on some clothes. On their way downstairs they stopped to check on Kate. Kate slept beautifully. David and Loren watched her for a long time because it made them feel better about themselves, about everything. Loren thought, If we could always stay here, watching Kate sleep, if this were all, we would be fine. But of course it was not all. It was the tiniest part. It was just a few minutes, late at night.

They walked through the dark house, out the French doors, across the terrace. The garden was poised, stunned by the heat. The dry lawn bristled underfoot. In the woods Loren took David's hand, and they walked silently through the trees to the pond.

They stood for a moment looking at it. It was so still. Do fish sleep? They seemed to be—even the water seemed to be sleeping.

"I'm sorry," said David.

Loren let go of his hand. "Forget it," she said. "Okay?"

"Okay," said David. He sat down on the bank. Loren took off her clothes and waded out. The noise she made seemed ridiculously loud. She sunk slowly under water, surfaced, and swam out toward the middle. She swam far enough out so she could not see David squatting on the bank. She treaded water and gazed up at the stars. They were shooting, ever so slowly, one after the other, losing their niches and falling.

David watched Loren swim out into the darkness. He could hear her, but he could not see her. He was thinking of the beginning of them, the first time they had met, on the beach at Cape Cod. They had gone back to the beach that night. David remembered how Loren had peeled off her clothes and charged into the dark water, dived under the waves, then reemerged, run up the beach like a huge, wet goddess and grabbed his hand; how she had pulled him into the surf, how they had swum close together, kissing underwater; how his mouth had found different salty-tasting parts of her; how later they had lain on the wet sand, just below the high-tide mark, making love; how he did not know if he were licking shells or the coil of Loren's ear, kissing seaweed or her wet tangle of hair. David remembered how when it was over, Loren had pulled him on top of her, held him tightly, ran her large hands up and down his spine. How she had said to him, "Make me warm. Keep me warm."

# CHAPTER
# 24

Amanda entered the salon. She teased off her gloves and lifted her veil. "I'm so awfully sorry," she said. "Please accept my most sincere condolences."

"Thank you, Miss Paine," said Anton. "Thank you so much for coming."

"Will you excuse me?" said Dominick Carlisle, the funeral coordinator. "I think it's time I opened the chapel."

"Of course," said Anton.

"I'll come get you when we're ready, Mr. Shawangunk. May I freshen your drink?"

"I think not," said Anton.

"May I have a drink?" said Amanda.

"Certainly," said Mr. Carlisle. "What could I get you?"

"Vodka," said Amanda. "Just the teeniest splash."

"Ice?"

"Please."

Mr. Carlisle levitated a bar from the depths of a credenza. He splashed some vodka in a tumbler full of rocks.

"Perhaps a tad more," said Amanda.

Mr. Carlisle complied. Splash, splash. Splash. He handed Amanda the drink and concealed the bar. "I'll be back for you in about half an hour," he said to Anton.

They were left alone. There was a moment of silence, and then Amanda let out a small, ecstatic whoop. "We did it," she said, raising her glass. "Or rather, *you* did it. You did it, my darling: to you!"

"I did nothing," said Anton.

"What do you mean? Didn't you—"

"I did nothing. I couldn't do it."

"Well, she died," said Amanda. "That's the main point. Our problems are over."

"We have a new problem," said Anton.

"What? Tell me!" Amanda sucked the last splash of vodka from her rocks and sat beside Anton. "There is no problem I can't solve, my darling."

"Don't be so sure. Solange's corpse has . . . disappeared."

"Disappeared?"

"The body that was delivered here . . . is not hers. And her body cannot be found at the morgue. I've made some inquiries, but far be it from me to navigate through New York City's bureaucracy."

"So what's in the coffin? What are we burying?"

"Sandbags," said Anton.

"Do they know? I mean, our henchman-friend here, does he know?"

"Of course."

"And they'll do it? They'll have a funeral for sandbags?"

"If you pay them enough, they'll have a funeral for a piece of dog shit."

Amanda stood up and began pacing the room. She drew aside a curtain and looked down on Madison Avenue. The first limos and taxis had arrived. A black-clad crowd milled. It looked a little like the East Village. "It's her friends," Amanda announced. "Her voodoo friends. They've stolen her body, for their sicko voodoo rituals. It's probably in Haiti by now. I'm sure there is nothing for us to worry about."

"Did you see the paper? They mentioned Leonora in the obit."

"I saw that," said Amanda. She tried to access the bar. "How did they know? I thought no one knew they were related?"

"Nobody did. Except for our friends at the *Times*. Apparently they know everything."

"Well, I don't see the problem there. I never understood why we had to pretend Leonora was an Italian journalist, anyway."

"Because witnesses that stand to inherit a couple million are not always best believed."

"I don't understand that either." Amanda abandoned her attack on the recalcitrant bar. "They were only half-sisters. Why should she inherit anything? Anyway, baby, you worry too much. The secret is not to worry."

"I'm worried now," said Anton. "I think we've fucked up."

"Darling," said Amanda, "I never fuck up. It's not in my vocabulary. It's beyond my ken. It's—"

"I wish you'd be quiet," said Anton. They were both silent a moment, and then Anton said, "I can't believe we can't even bury her without hassles."

Amanda reseated herself. "Baby," she said, "listen: She's dead. Who cares where her body is? Let them make potpourri from her fingernails and hair! Let them roast her on a spit and dance around it! Let them perform their vile deeds. It's over, darling. It's all, all over. I promise you."

Anton looked at her.

"Kiss me," said Amanda, kissing him.

The door opened. Mr. Carlisle stood at attention. He cleared his throat. "Excuse me, Mr. Shawangunk," he said. "It's time to begin."

⌐ ⌐ ⌐ ⌐ ⌐ ⌐

"Here's one for you," said Judith. "Southeast Asia River. Six letters. The first letter is M."

"Mekong," suggested Henry.

Judith and Henry were sitting up in bed doing the Sunday *Times* crossword. Actually, Judith was doing it, and Henry was watching. His vocabulary was quite good, but it was ill-suited to the intricacies of Eugene Maleska. This was fine with Judith, who was territorial where crosswords were concerned. It was the bane of her marriage: She and Leonard were constantly fighting over who got first crack. It was heaven to have it all to yourself.

"M-E-K-O-N-G," said Judith, writing it in. "Of course. Thank you."

Henry beamed, and lay back in bed.

They had established the pattern of their relationship. They met every Saturday evening at the upper tiers of the New York State Theater, from which they watched the brightly colored spectacle of opera combust far below them. They had dinner and took the A train up to Judith's. They spent the night on the waterbed. Sunday morning began with the crossword, followed by breakfast, after which Henry made his complicated way back to Queens, from which he would call Judith midweek, wondering if she wished to get together again? Yes, she would say, that would be nice.

They took nothing for granted. Each week Henry sweated while dialing Judith's phone number, which he had taken the liberty of memorizing. He repeated it to himself at odd times, mantralike. But when it came time to call her, he would think, This time she will say no. And each week Judith waited for his call, an anticipation that gave answering the phone a sexual thrill she hadn't experienced in years. Decades.

A six-letter word for malodorous. Smelly, thought Judith. Putrid. Rancid. This litany was interrupted by the caw of her door buzzer.

"Is that your buzzer?" asked Henry.

"It must be a mistake," said Judith. "I'm expecting no one. What time is it?"

Henry leaned out of bed and fished his watch from the floor. Judith admired the taut brown boyish skin of his back. She kissed his spine. "Nine-thirty," he said.

"They pushed the wrong buzzer, I'm sure. It often happens." Judith returned to the puzzle, but the buzzer persisted. She got out of bed and gave the puzzle to Henry. "Finish this up," she said.

In the kitchen she pushed the TALK button. "Who is it?" she asked.

She pressed LISTEN. First she heard a roar of traffic and static, and then she heard a voice quite clearly. It was a voice from her past. A voice she knew well. It said, "Judith? It's Leonard."

# CHAPTER
# 25

After a moment of pure shock, Judith recovered sufficiently to press the TALK button. "Leonard?" she croaked.

"Yes," said Leonard. "Let me in."

"Who is Leonard?"

Judith turned to see Henry standing in the bedroom doorway. The realization that he did not know Leonard was her husband startled her. "Leonard?" she said into the grill.

"Yes, it's me. Let me in!" His patience seemed to be waning.

"I'll be right down," Judith found herself saying. "Stay there."

By cleverly not pushing the LISTEN button she managed to avoid hearing Leonard's response to this order. But Henry was repeating his unnerving question. She found it was time to lie.

"Leonard is my cousin," she said. "I'll go down and see what he wants."

"Why don't you let him up?"

"Because . . . because, well, look at us: We aren't dressed. It wouldn't be decent, you know. Leonard is something of a prude, you see, and this being Sunday . . ." Judith found lying to Henry almost impossible. The look on his face told her he believed none of what she was saying, yet he listened with a maddening politeness. What does it mean, thought Judith, that I can't lie to him? She had always managed to lie (when absolutely necessary) to Leonard.

This thought was interrupted by an insistent buzzing. "Leonard," she shouted, "I'll be right down!"

"Who's up there with you?" Leonard shouted back.

"No one," Judith lied.

"I heard him," said Leonard. " 'Who os Leonard? Who os Leonard?' "

"Oh," said Judith, "it's just a friend. I'll be right down."

"Do me no favors," Leonard said.

Before she could respond to this suggestion, Henry was standing beside her, fully dressed. "I think Leonard must be your husband," he said.

"Yes," admitted Judith, "he is. But I don't know what he's doing here now. He's supposed to be in India."

"Well, maybe there is something bad happened. I think you should let him up, and I will go." He reached his hand toward her face. For a moment Judith thought he was going to touch her cheek in some tender gesture, but his hand kept moving. He pressed the DOOR button. "You can call me, maybe, when this gets discovered, the reason of Leonard being here, and so forth. I will go now." He opened the door.

"I'm sorry," said Judith. "I don't know . . . I mean, yes, I'll call you. I'm sure it's . . . well, I'll call you, I promise."

Henry bowed his head in farewell, and then disappeared down the hall. She heard him descend the stairs, avoiding the elevator. She stood in the open doorway, frozen and confused, waiting for her husband's appearance.

But the elevator was suspiciously quiet. Where could he be? She returned to the intercom and paged him, but Leonard no longer seemed to be in the lobby. Her mind began to fill with wild thoughts: maybe he had intercepted Henry, and had caused a scene. She immediately pictured a fist fight in her tranquil lobby. Forgetting her keys, she vacated the apartment and followed Henry's trail down the stairs, only to find the lobby empty. She ventured timidly out onto Bennett Avenue, but found it was as still as a diorama: there was no sign of Leonard, no sign of Henry.

Judith was perfectly alone. She stood there for a moment,

trying to make sense of what had just happened. She then tried to think of what she should do next. At this, too, she failed.

ı ı ı ı ı ı ı

"Do you know what an experiment is?" Loren asked Kate. They were having breakfast at Aggie's.

"Yes," said Kate. "We did an experiment at daycare. With Miss Coco."

"What did you do?"

"We cut a worm in half. It was supposed to grow two worms but it didn't."

"Oh," said Loren. "Well, what happened?"

"It died," said Kate.

"Well, that wasn't a very successful experiment. Miss Coco should have known better."

"Known what better?"

"That it's not smart to cut worms in half. Perhaps some worms you can do that with, but not all."

"We cut a leg off Jiffy to see if it growed back."

"Who's Jiffy?"

"Our hamster," said Kate.

Loren shuddered. "Well, that was very cruel and naughty," she managed to say. "Did Miss Coco know you did that?"

"Yes," said Kate.

"Well, I hope she saved Jiffy."

"No," said Kate. "We had to sacrifice him."

Miss Coco has gone too far, thought Loren. She made a mental note to pursue the matter at work on Monday. Or perhaps a phone call as soon as she got home. "Well," she said to Kate, "that is what is known as an unsuccessful experiment."

"What?"

"The experiment didn't work, did it?"

"No," said Kate.

"So you learned something from it."

"I don't know," said Kate.

"Of course you did. You learned not to cut legs off hamsters. That's bad."

"But it was good to sacrifice it."

"No. Sacrificing things is naughty. I hope you know that."

"It brings good to the world," said Kate.

"No it doesn't. Miss Coco is wrong about that!" Loren paused for a moment, trying to think of a way to return the conversation to the matter at hand. Kate picked at her eggs. "What's the matter?" Loren asked. "Don't you like your eggs?"

"They taste funny."

"Here, let me taste." Loren forked a bite of Kate's omelet. "They taste good, honey. That's basil. You said you liked basil. Remember we had it at Lillian's house in the country?"

"No," said Kate.

"Well, we did. With tomatoes, remember?"

"There's Grandpa."

"Where?"

"Outside. He was walking."

"Grandpa's in India, honey. You know that. Now eat your eggs."

"I don't like them."

"Do you want mine? We can switch. Mine has nice cheese in it."

"What kind?"

"Goat cheese. You like goat cheese."

"No, I don't. Can I have a muffin?"

"Eat some of your eggs first. Eat five bites."

"Four."

"No," said Loren. "Five. And then you can have a muffin."

"Do they have chocolate chip?"

"No. They have blueberry. Anyway, so you know what an experiment is?"

"Yes," said Kate.

"What is it?"

"It's where you cut something off."

"No. It's when you try something, to see if it works. I mean, cutting the hamster's leg off was an experiment in a way, but it was a cruel experiment. It was a naughty thing to do, you see: You hurt the hamster, and that isn't nice."

Kate was frowning down at her omelet.

"But the idea is the same," Loren continued, more gently. "You wanted to see if the hamster would grow another leg, so you cut it off. And you found out he wouldn't."

"Couldn't, not wouldn't," said Kate.

"You're right: couldn't. He would if he could, I'm sure. Anyway—two more bites; I'm counting—Daddy and I did an experiment. When we decided to live together again. We wanted to see what would happen. If it would make us happy."

"You should cut Daddy's leg off."

"No I shouldn't. Stop being silly. We thought we knew how the experiment would end. We thought it would make us happy to live together. But we were wrong. Just like Miss Coco was wrong about the worm and Skippy."

"Who?"

"The hamster."

"Jiffy," said Kate.

"Oh, yes, Jiffy. Poor Jiffy. But it's good to do experiments, if they're not cruel and stupid ones like Miss Coco's, because you learn things from them, even if they don't work out the way you thought they would. In fact, that's how you learn, when things don't work out."

"I had five," said Kate.

"I know."

"Are you crying?"

"No," said Loren.

"You look like you are."

"I'm just a little sad," said Loren.

"Can I have a muffin now?"

"Yes," said Loren. "Of course you can."

# CHAPTER
# 26

**THE NEW YORK BANK FOR WOMEN**

**INTER-OFFICE MEMORANDUM**

TO:   Esther Ploth
DATE: October 3, 1988
FROM: Loren Connor
RE:   Voodoo at Daycare

My daughter, Kate, recently told me a rather alarming story about activities that were taking place at the NYBW daycare center. According to Kate, a hamster by the name of Jiffy (possibly Skippy) was mutilated in the guise of an "experiment" by Miss Coco. Kate claimed Miss Coco cut a leg off the hamster with the purpose of seeing if it would "grow back." When the leg showed no signs of reappearing, the animal was (according to Kate) "sacrificed."

While I believe that the dissection of certain already dead animals can be a valid educational experience, I think such experiments, even if properly conducted, are inappropriate at the daycare level, to say nothing of what was in effect a vivisection. Kate seems to have taken this grotesque event in stride, but I was not pleased to hear about it and think an end should be put to such activities. I confronted Miss Coco (is Coco her first or last name? I don't see her listed in the employment directory), who denied Kate's entire story. She told me Kate was a troubled child with a vivid imagination and that perhaps "her head should be shrunk." (I found that remark threatening and unprofessional.) I do not believe Kate was lying. I believe Miss Coco, or whatever her name is, was. I asked to see the hamster—assuming if it had not been sacrificed it would still be inhabiting the Habitrail. Miss Coco showed me a gerbil, claiming it was a hamster. Esther, I know a gerbil when I see one, and this animal was most certainly a gerbil. Miss Coco continued to insist it was a hamster.

I found her most uncooperative about the whole matter, which leads me to believe that she should be at least more closely supervised, if not dismissed. I know it isn't easy to find qualified daycare practitioners, but our record hasn't been very good. It seems that if Kate isn't singing insipid Jesus songs (remember Mrs. Betty?) she's performing satanic rituals. I'm all for progressive education (we're planning to send Kate to the Little Red School House), but I feel that activities in the daycare center may be getting out of hand. I hope you agree with me and will look into this matter. Perhaps we should schedule a meeting to discuss this.

I I I I I I I

"What can you do?" the man asked Heath.

"Well, I can mix just about any drink known to man. I'm good with people. And I've had lots of experience: I've worked for two years at the Cafe Wisteria—that's in Tribeca—and before that I worked in a restaurant in Charlottesville."

"Can you do tricks?"

"What do you mean?"

"You know, tricks. Like in that movie."

"What movie?"

"The one with Tom Cruise. *Cocktail.* Have you seen it?"

"No," said Heath. "I heard it was awful."

"Awful? It was great. You should have seem him. He could . . . well, he and this other guy, they threw bottles around and danced a lot and shook drinks behind their backs. He also recited poems, but I wouldn't want you to do that. I don't like poetry."

"Well, I'm just a normal bartender. I mix the drinks, you know, without messing around."

"Anyone can do that. I can do that. What I want is someone who can dance around and throw stuff. Juggle, I mean."

Get me out of here, thought Heath. Colette Menzies, his lawyer, had told him he had to find a job: He couldn't be unemployed when his case came to trial, especially now that Solange was dead. Colette didn't appreciate the fact that he had been trying but that no one wanted to hire someone accused of attempted murder. She told him if worse came to worst, he would have to go to McDonald's. A few days earlier he thought he had found a job as a Party Animal. He would have had to dress up like a dog or something and go to children's birthday parties and act stupid. The person doing the hiring thought it would be okay to use him because he'd be in a disguise, but then she called back the next day to say the boss had said no. A cow Party Animal had recently molested a birthday girl, so they were being unusually careful.

Heath hadn't slept since he heard Solange had died, at least not at night. He slept a little during the day in front of the TV, but it was hard to tell how much he slept because he watched soap operas and time seemed very skewed on them. He also noticed how nobody had windows in their houses on the soaps. Or if they did, their curtains were always drawn.

He had called David a couple of times and listened to his machine, trying to think of some clever, pithy, and hurtful message to leave. But he thought of nothing. Once David had picked up, which was odd, since he was living downtown with Loren.

It was horrible just waiting to be found guilty. Sometimes he thought about killing himself. All he knew was that he didn't want to go to prison. The one night he had spent in jail had been awful. One of the men in the cell with him—a thin drunk man with very few teeth—kept trying to hug him. For luck, he said. I'll hug you for luck. Come here and I'll hug you. I'll hug you good. Heath couldn't face fifteen years of that.

Solange woke up in the hotel room in Aix. It was evening. The room had gone dark. It was still raining. Someone—Anton—was closing the terrace doors, drawing the drapes. He came and sat beside her on the huge tousled bed.

"Darling," he said, stroking hair off her forehead, "you've slept for ages. Was it nice?"

She looked up at him. In the gloom she could just make out his face, peering lovingly down at her. "I've been dreaming . . ." she said.

"Lovely," he said. He lifted back the blankets from her throat, tucking them under her breasts, which lay uncovered, quivering slightly in the cool air, like something at the bottom of a river. He touched them both. "You're shivering," he said.

"You didn't kill me," she said.

He smiled, leaned down, touched his lips to her sternum. "Not quite," he whispered into her skin.

She reached her hand out from under the blankets and stroked the back of his head, tangling her fingers in his silky hair.

"I thought you were going to kill me," she said.

He lifted his head, brought it close to her face. "Was I too rough, darling?" he asked.

"No," she said, confused. "It's . . . I thought I was . . . I thought you were . . . it was an awful dream." She lifted her face toward his, kissed him, long and slow. She closed her eyes and reached out in the dark to embrace him, to pull him down alongside her, but her hands, however far out they reached, remained empty. . . . She opened her eyes.

A large smiling woman sat beside her, patting the soles of her bare feet. "Well, you finally come to," she said. "We was beginning to wonder."

Solange closed her eyes.

"Whoah," said the woman, cradling her face. "Open up. You ain't going back now you come to. We was worried about you, I'll say. I got to call Coco. I promised I'd call her moment you come to. I'm Coco's ma."

"Coco?" said Solange.

"She's my daughter," the woman said. "She brung you here. You been staying with me."

"How long?" Solange asked.

"Almost two weeks. You was down real deep. We thought you might never come up. I got to call Coco."

Solange looked around the room. She was lying on a couch, swaddled in an afghan crocheted from fluorescent synthetic yarns. There was an open tin of sardines on the coffee table before her and beyond that a mammoth console TV set on which flickered news.

"You must be starving. You want a fish?" the woman asked, stabbing a sardine with what looked like a fondue fork. She held it toward Solange, dripping bile-colored oil on the afghan.

"No," said Solange. "Where am I?"

"This is Teaneck, New Jersey, darling. Now I'm going to call Coco. You look real peaky, so hunker back down, you hear. I'll be right back."

# CHAPTER
# 27

By the time Coco's mother returned from her phone call, Solange had recovered her wits and some of her natural color.

"Coco say she'll be out to fetch you tomorrow night," Coco's mother said. "You hungry?"

"No," said Solange.

"You should eat something. You ain't et for two weeks. I could fix you some eggs. How about that?"

"No thank you," said Solange.

"You don't remember me, do you?"

"I think not," said Solange.

"I'm Jewel," said Coco's mother. "You don't remember Jewel?"

"No," said Solange.

"You remember anything? Maybe your head messed up."

"My head," said Solange, "is just fine."

Jewel smiled. "Well, I was a maid of your ma's. Way back when in Port-au-Prince."

"I didn't think Coco had a mother," said Solange.

"Sure she do. I just . . . I got myself married to this white man, off a cruise, see, and come up to the U.S.A. Coco stay down with you. Your ma took care of her for me."

"I thought she was an orphan," said Solange. "She never told me."

"She's a strange one, but I don't blame her. We're all strange is how I figure. I mean, look at you, talk of strange. You gonna tell me how you come to be a zombie?"

"It's a long story," said Solange.

"Time's one thing I got."

"Are they sardines?" Solange, overcome by a sudden, lunging hunger, nodded to the tin of fish on the coffee table.

"Best thing for you after a trance. That fish oil warms your blood. Here," Jewel handed the tin and the fork to Solange, "eat them all, baby."

While Solange devoured the first tin of fish, Jewel fetched another and a tall glass of water into which she dropped some fizzing pellets.

"What are those?" asked Solange, reaching out for the glass.

"Just something to perk you up," said Jewel. She watched as Solange's thirst was slaked. "So," she prompted, when her patient had returned to the sardines, "you gonna tell me your story?"

"Well," Solange began, picking a grizzly bit of fish from her teeth, "my husband, Anton, has this mistress named Amanda."

"That's a bad name, Amanda. You got to always watch out that way."

"Anyway, she—Amanda—tried to murder me, to get Anton and my money, I suppose. She shot me, but I didn't die, I just went into a coma."

"Good for you."

"They blamed the murder on an innocent young man. I'm the only one who knew Amanda really shot me, except for this man, who has no witnesses. So you see, if I came out of my coma, Amanda was in . . ."

"I know what she be in," said Jewel.

"Exactly," said Solange. She wiped some fish oil from her chin and then licked her fingers. Delicious. "So when I started to regain consciousness, Anton tried to smother me, but he stopped at the last minute. He couldn't do it."

"Most men can't," said Jewel.

"That night I did come up, and I knew that Amanda would be back to finish the job. So I decided to do it for her, pretend to be dead until I could figure out how to deal with them. Luckily, Coco was there. She had been coming to see me, trying to get me out with . . . well, you know, and there was this nurse, Laleel Bundara, who Coco and I know from the church. They put me into the death trance, Laleel had me declared, and then they snuck my body out . . ."

"And that's how you come be zombie in Teaneck."

"That's my story," said Solange. "What about you? What are you doing in Teaneck?"

"I'm selling real estate," said Jewel. "I'm with Century 21."

i i i i i i

Pleasant as Jewel was, Solange found being conscious in Teaneck a fate worse than assumed death. So, on the morning after her reawakening, she borrowed twenty dollars and a raincoat from Jewel and took a bus to the Port Authority. She belted the raincoat as chicly as she possibly could, taxied to the Carlyle, registered under an assumed name (Rowena Stronger), and gave her last few coins to the bellboy, promising him more later if he would fetch her up some breakfast. She took a long shower of the type that can only be enjoyed in a clean, luxurious hotel room and emerged from it, swaddled in terry, to find her breakfast delivered. Eggs Florentine had never tasted— No. Nothing had ever tasted this good. She stood by the window, smiling down at the elegant avenue. Raising her glass of fresh-squeezed, she toasted her new life and then set about structuring it.

"Daycare, Miss Coco," was how Miss Coco answered the phone.

"Guess who?" said Solange.

"Baby mine," said Miss Coco. "Where are you?"

"Back where I belong. I've managed a suite at the Carlyle."

"The who?"

"A hotel. But I need to get into the apartment. I need clothes and money. And I want my jewelry, if that bitch Amanda hasn't already made off with it."

"Well, go get them, baby," said Miss Coco. "They're yours."

"I can't," said Solange. "I can't be seen. I've got to lay low for a while. That's why I need your help. Can you go to the apartment for me?"

"Well, I can't go now," said Miss Coco. "I'm at work, lady. And I can't leave. One bitch is already on my case, trying to get me fired."

"Why don't you come by here after work, say, five-thirty? And bring me a wig."

"A wig? Where am I going to find a wig?"

"There's a place on Madison, about 61st or so. Enny of Italy. Charge it."

"What color do you want?"

Solange thought for a moment. "Red," she decided.

' ' ' ' ' ' '

"It gets dark so early now," said David.

"Yes," said Lillian, "but you know, I like it. What I really love are those evenings in December when you leave work at five and walk home, and it's like the middle of the night. The headlights and shop windows. It makes the city seem almost European. Like Paris. Or how I imagine Paris, never having been there."

"How come you don't travel more? Don't you get a lot of free trips through work?"

"Yeah, but I don't really like it. Traveling confuses my life."

"That's funny," said David. "I feel just the opposite. I feel like my life is confusing and it's only when I go away that I have any perspective."

"But you hardly ever travel."

"I know. That explains a lot, doesn't it?"

They stood on the corner of Madison Avenue, waiting to cross over toward the park. A short black woman clutching what appeared to be a hatbox bumped into them, excused herself, and hurried away into the ambered dusk.

"That was Miss Coco," David said. "She works at Kate's daycare."

"She looked a little strange," said Lillian. They entered the park and walked in silence. "Guess who called me the other day?" Lillian finally said.

"Who?"

"Heath."

"Heath called you? He doesn't even know you."

"Yes he does. I met him last spring, when you burned your fingers, and I went down to the Cafe Wisteria and told him. My errand of mercy, remember?"

"Oh, yeah. I forgot about that. Why did he call you?"

"He wanted some PR advice. Apparently he had a really terrible experience on 'Orca.' "

"He was on 'Orca'?"

"Yes. So I'm going to try to get him some simpatico interviews. We're having lunch next week. Do you want me to tell him about you?"

"What about me?"

"About you and Loren. That you've split up."

"No," said David. "I mean, I don't care. It doesn't matter. It's over between Heath and me. Let's sit down."

"No," said Lillian. "We should keep walking. It's getting awfully dark. Where are we?"

"We're . . . if we keep walking this way, we'll come out near the Museum of Natural History."

"We're walking west?"

"Yes. Is that okay? Do you want to turn around?"

"No, this is fine. I'll take the bus back across."

"We could have dinner."

"I can't."

"Why not?"

"I just can't. Are you sure you know where we're going?"

"Yes. Isn't that the San Remo? We're just a bit farther uptown than I thought. I think."

"As long as you know where we're going."

"Are you feeling any better?"

"Yes. I haven't been sick in weeks."

"You don't look different."

"I'm starting to bulge a little. Here, feel."

"I don't feel anything."

"Yes. Here. Feel that?"

"That's your pelvis."

"No, it's not. It's my baby."

"It's an awfully hard baby. Is it kicking?"

"Not kicking, really. More like . . . undulating."

"Tell me again about the father."

"I don't know much. He's young—twenty-six, I think. Smart, handsome, and creative. He's tall and has green eyes. Brown hair."

"He sounds great."

"Let's hope so."

"Maybe we aren't walking west. Maybe we're going uptown."

"Are we lost?"

"No. I mean, this is Central Park. How lost can we be? I just think maybe we should be walking, well, maybe more in that direction. I think that's west."

"So we are lost."

"We're a little lost," said David. "At least, *I'm* a little lost. I shouldn't speak for you. You may be exactly where you want to be."

ı ı ı ı ı ı ı

"Greetings," said Amanda Paine to the concierge.

"Good evening, Madam," he replied. "May I help you?"

"In fact you could. I'm here at Mr. Shawangunk's request—Anton Shawangunk, 38C—he's alerted you, I'm sure."

"On the contrary, I'm afraid. Mr. Shawangunk is out of the country."

"But of course, I know that. That is precisely why I am here. He's asked me to collect his mail, water his plants, and feed the cat."

"I didn't know Mr. Shawangunk had a cat."

"I was speaking metaphorically," said Amanda.

"Well, he left no word with us. What company are you with?"

"Oh, goodness, no," laughed Amanda. "Unlike you, I am not employed in the service sector. I am merely doing Mr. Shawangunk a favor."

"I'm so sorry."

"Mr. Shawangunk and I are colleagues, you see."

"I thought you looked familiar."

"Yes . . . I've stopped in before—on business, of course."

"Of course," said the concierge. "Well, you're in luck. Mrs. Shawangunk's sister is up there now. She's come to sort out Mrs. Shawangunk's things. Mrs. Shawangunk is no longer with us."

"She's broken her lease, so to speak," muttered Amanda, as she hastened toward the elevator. Once safely ensconced in its ascendant shell, she reviewed the situation: Anton was due back from a week in Mustique later that evening. After the gaffe at Solange's funeral, he had decided they should avoid each other until after Heath's trial. But a week's separation was more than Amanda could bear, and on the assumption that Anton must be feeling similarly, she had decided to surprise him in his bed that night. How annoying that Leonora had picked this particular evening to come and meddle! Well, she would just have to be gotten rid of.

The apartment door was locked. Amanda knocked and was ignored. "Hello!" she called, knocking again. "Leonora? It's Amanda. Let me in!"

The door opened a few inches, exposing a slice of Miss Coco's rather unfriendly face.

"Greetings," said Amanda. "Are you helping Mrs. Trumpet? Is Leonora here? Who are you?" Apparently some maid who doesn't speak English, Amanda thought. She tried to speak more distinctly. "I am here to help. Let me in."

"But . . ." Miss Coco protested, to no avail. Amanda forced herself through the crack in the door.

"Have you started? Leonora's in the bedroom, I suppose? Follow me." The bedroom was adrift in clothes. The mess seemed to originate on the bed, which was covered with dresses, lingerie, and jewelry, and explode out across the floor. Leonora was nowhere to be seen. "My, my," said Amanda, standing in the doorway, "you must learn to respect clothes, my dear! I think perhaps you are not qualified for this particular job." As she spoke, Amanda unlocked a cavernous armoire and peered inside. "Oh, dear God," she cried, clutching the heavy wooden doors for support.

# CHAPTER
## 28

A train left Grand Central Station later that night. It crept into the dark tunnel, emerged briefly into the illuminated backyards of the Bronx, and then descended to the shores of the Hudson. It slipped beneath the canopy of the Tappen Zee and sped north, into the tight sleeve of night. Lillian sat by the window, staring through her reflection at the fluid darkness of river. She was going to see Claude for the weekend.

Years later, she would think: Remember that midnight ride, racing toward Claude, who I knew very little but hoped I might love very much? Remember the beginning and how happy I was then? But now, as the train slowed to stop in Rhinecliff, this happiness was unfelt, furled deep inside her. It would be recognized only in retrospect. How dangerous life would be if it were otherwise, and we felt our greatest happinesses as they occurred! The world would be undone by joy: Cars would speed off roads, planes drop from the sky, and trains hurtle ecstatically off their tracks.

ı ı ı ı ı ı ı

As Amanda stood gaping into the open armoire, she vaguely sensed the horrid little maid come up behind her, but she found herself unable to move, unable to speak, unable to do anything but stare. She was overcome with longing. The armoire was full of the most beautiful shoes in the world. Amanda was a woman of many and complex desires, yet her lust for shoes was of epic proportions. Oh, how she wanted to touch them all, wear them all, but most of all she wanted to *own* them all! Life was so unfair. . . . Perhaps if she tried on just one pair. Those pumps upholstered in watered silk—what color were they? An iridescent lavender? She leaned down to get a closer look and tumbled forward into the dark. She heard herself scream, felt her head hit one of the shelves, and then fell into a flurry of falling shoes.

ı ı ı ı ı ı

"We have blackberry and strawberry-rhubarb," the woman in the aqua pantsuit said.

"We'll try a slice of each," said Claude, "and a bowl of vanilla ice cream. Are the pies warm?"

"I could nuke 'em up for you."

"Skip it," said Claude.

"Skip the pies?"

"No, just skip the nuking."

"Whatever you say."

Lillian and Claude were sitting in a diner booth. Lillian was looking down at her placemat, which depicted different styles of covered bridges. Claude's featured an illustrated catalog of desert plant life. The combination was a little disorienting. She looked up at Claude. They both smiled. Neither of them knew quite what to say. They were at the stage where it was hard to talk. They both knew they liked each other better than any conversation they could have at this point would indicate.

"So," said Claude, "how was the train ride?"

"Nice," said Lillian. "Although I almost missed it. I was walking in the park with David, and we got lost."

"Is he the one who was up here? David and Loren?"

"Yes, although they're not a couple anymore."

"That's too bad," said Claude.

Lillian shrugged. "I don't know," she said. "I think it's better this way. I think it was a mistake for them to get back together."

"What do you mean, back together? I thought they were married."

"They were. And then they were divorced, about a year ago. Well, longer now. And then Kate—remember Kate, their daughter? Well, she got kidnapped, and they both went out to California to get her, and Loren was crushed by a glass wall, and they were in an alleged earthquake, all of which made them decide to get back together. But it didn't last very long."

"You have weird friends," said Claude. "Do you know that?"

Lillian laughed. We're all weird to someone, she thought. She wondered whom she was weird to. Then she thought, I should tell Claude about the baby. It's wrong not to. I'll tell him when the pie comes.

"How are things at Chez Claude?" she asked.

"Slow," said Claude. "We're only open two nights a week now that summer's over."

"What do you do the rest of the week?"

"I don't know. I hang out. Play the piano. I'm teaching a sauce course at the Culinary Institute."

"Don't you get bored up here?"

"No," said Claude.

"You don't miss Manhattan?"

"Not at all."

"How long have you lived up here?"

"A year. Almost just. I left New York right after the crash. I wasn't always a chef, you know. I worked as a stockbroker for twelve years."

"You did?"

"Uh huh. Although it's hard to believe now. I finally decided it was time to forget it and come up here. If I'd stayed in New York, I think I would be dead by now."

"How would you have died?"

"Any number of ways," said Claude.

An aqua arm lowered two plates of pie between them, followed by a dish of vaguely yellow ice cream. "Enjoy," a voice said.

Now, thought Lillian. Say it now. Say: "Oh, by the way, I'm five months pregnant with a complete stranger's baby." Just say it.

"Do you want ice cream on your pie?" Claude asked.

"I'm five months . . ."

"What?"

"I haven't eaten pie in five months," said Lillian. "I'd love ice cream on it."

ı ı ı ı ı ı.

"This is my room," said Claude, opening a wooden door. A big black dog jumped off the bed and looked at them. "That's Pushkin."

Pushkin allowed Lillian to pet him. She sat down on the bed. "He's lovely," she said. "What kind is he?"

"He's a Briard. Come, Pushkin, let's go out. I'll just let him out for a minute. I'll be right back."

"Okay." Lillian heard them go downstairs and out the front door. She stood up and looked around. A large platform bed was at the center of the room. A desk piled high with cookbooks and magazines faced it. The bed was neatly made. Pushkin had been sleeping on a towel that was covered with dog hair. Lillian could hear Claude outside, talking to the dog. It sounded as if he were singing. She looked at her reflection in a mirror and saw a woman in a man's bedroom, sitting on a man's bed, waiting for the man to return, waiting for . . . that's me, Lillian thought. That woman waiting is me.

ı ı ı ı ı ı ı

"Good evening, Bernard," said Anton.

"Welcome home, Mr. Shawangunk. How was your trip?"

"Very nice, Bernard . . . considering."

"Of course. I still expect to see Mrs. Shawangunk walk through the door. It's very sad. Her sister came by this evening to remove some of her things. She thought it would be less painful if she did it while you were away. And another woman, too, come to water the plants."

"Really?" said Anton. "How strange. I trust you didn't let them up."

"But I did. They both had keys."

"They've departed, I take it?"

171

"The sister, yes. I saw her come through about an hour ago with several suitcases. The other woman was a colleague of yours, I remember now: someone from the gallery. I think she's still up there."

"I'm sure she is," said Anton. "Good night, Bernard."

"Good night, Mr. Shawangunk."

Sometimes Anton felt as if he didn't have sufficient energy to live his life. Just the thought of Amanda exhausted him. There was a light on in the bedroom, which looked to have been burgled. Clothes were strewn about, drawers and closets flung open, leaking their contents onto the floor. Anton sighed, put his bags down, and went to find a drink. He was emptying a bottle of tired seltzer down the kitchen sink when he heard an awful thumping and his name being called. He followed the sound to Solange's shoe chateau.

"Amanda?" he called.

"Let me out!" she shouted back.

"The key's gone— No, wait, here it is." He unlocked the heavy wooden doors. Amanda rolled out at his feet. "Are you all right?" he asked, helping her up. He pushed aside a flouncy LaCroix and sat her on the bed.

Amanda responded by kissing him, long and hard, pulling him back on top of her.

"Amanda, no," he said. "What's happened here? Why were you in the armoire?"

"Darling, it's been the most awful evening. What I go through for you, my love! You see, I came to surprise you. I planned to be in bed—there's a bottle of champagne here somewhere, if we can find my bag, and something, well, you'll see later, but something naughty you rather like, darling. Anyway, after I finally convinced his royal fucking highness downstairs that he could let me up without endangering national security, I find the most horrible little woman here rummaging through all of Solange's clothes, just pawing everything. I didn't know what was going on. Bernard had said Leonora was here . . . well, I was just about to dismiss her when I opened that . . . that thing. Well, you know me and shoes, darling, I queased out for an instant, and before I knew it, I had been pushed inside and the doors were locked."

"You've got a nasty bump on your head."

"Do I? Kiss it and make it fabulous, will you?"

"Amanda, I thought we had an agreement. I thought we weren't going to see each other until this was all over."

"But, Anton, I missed you! And I've been so miserable. You know that job with MOLTCATO? Well, it's gone kaput! They tell me now I have to be a Canadian citizen. Can you imagine anything more revolting? As if I'd be Canadian for a second! So it looks like we're partners again; we'll just have to get rid of that horrible girl, somehow, because I refuse to work with her—"

"Amanda, I think you'd best go home. Come, and we'll find you a ride."

"Darling, what are you saying? You can't send me home, now, this late and with this awful bump on my head."

"I'm perfectly serious. I find I can trust you rather less than I thought."

"Darling, you can trust me implicitly . . . to the grave."

"Which is exactly where we both shall be, if you don't start behaving. Now, come. Let's find your coat." Anton began rooting through the mess on the floor.

Amanda watched him. "I have the distinct feeling," she said after a moment and in a somewhat different tone of voice, "that I am not the only person in this room who has been misbehaving. Have you been naughty, Anton?"

"Amanda, don't start that."

"Because, you know, if you had been, if you'd been naughty, I'd have to punish you. You know that, don't you, darling?"

"Please, Amanda. No. Not now—"

"You've been a naughty boy, I can tell. Are you listening to me, Anton? You've been a big bad sexy naughty boy, and it's my job to punish you. Do you see my bag there? There's something in it Mommy needs. Bring it to me, Anton. That's a good baby. That's my naughty little big bad sexy boy . . ."

# CHAPTER
## 29

"Keith Jackson is here to see you," Roger said.

"Okay," said Lillian, "send him in."

"Oh, I forgot to tell you, your mother called. And somebody named Mister . . . well a Mister Something, and somebody named Clyde."

"Why didn't you put them through?"

"I don't know how."

"I showed you. You just push my extension. Number ten."

"You're number ten?"

"Yes," said Lillian. "Next time I get a call just put it on hold and then push number ten. But not while I'm meeting with Mr. Jackson. Now go get him."

"Who?"

"Mr. Jackson. The man who's waiting to see me."

Eventually Heath found his way to Lillian's office. "I'm sorry I had to cancel lunch," she said, "but as you've probably noticed I have a temp in this week who's somewhat less than incompetent. I think it's best that he's not left alone. Are you hungry? I could send him out for some sandwiches. God knows what he'd return with, but we could try . . ."

"No," said Heath, "I'm fine."

"Then sit down," said Lillian, sitting herself. She hadn't seen Heath in months—not since her trip to the Wisteria. He looked older but no less attractive. "Well," she continued, "I'm sorry to hear about all this trouble. I hope I can be of some help."

"Thanks," said Heath. "I appreciate your making time to see me."

People who don't work in offices always think people who do work in offices are incredibly busy, thought Lillian. But then the thought occurred to her that some people who worked in offices really were incredibly busy. Periodically Lillian suffered an overwhelming desire to be one of those women who catapulted, perfectly coiffed and costumed, from bed to breakfast meeting, spent their twelve-hour days trotting in and out of conferences, pearls jangling down the front of their Chanel suits, juggling sheaves of messages with mugs of coffee, constantly jotting cryptic notations in Filofaxes, grabbing a quick bite to eat at the Grill Room before lashing themselves into Burberrys for night flights to the coast. But these urges quickly passed, leaving Lillian exhausted and a little nauseated.

"Have you had any luck finding a job?" she asked Heath.

"That's one thing that's finally worked out. The Hysteria just called me and asked me if I'd check coats. It's a step down, but I don't really care. It will be nice to be back there. So come check your coat sometime."

"I will," said Lillian. "Anyway, as I explained on the phone, Galton Enterprises specializes in helping foreign tourist agencies with PR. But I think whether it be countries or people, PR is PR. You said you'd been on 'Orca'?"

"Yes," said Heath. "I brought you the tape. It was really awful." He fished a videocassette from a Tower Records bag and placed it on the desk.

"Well, why don't we take a look at this," said Lillian, "so I'll have some idea of what you've been up against."

"The wall," said Heath.

Lillian swiveled in her seat and slipped the cassette into a VCR behind the desk. While she watched Heath and Orca and Leonora Trumpet skirmish, Heath stood by the window, watching the rain fall onto 57th Street. New York City had never seemed less glamorous to him. Everybody down on the sidewalk was walking around as if they were extras in a movie about the end of the world—a TV movie about the end of the world.

"Well, I don't think you came off so terribly," Lillian said, as the video rewound. "They just caught you a little unawares is all. Surprise witnesses can do that."

"I looked like a jerk," said Heath.

"No you didn't. You looked fine. Just a little underdirected. Have you done any other interviews?"

"No. I was just on the news a few times, right after it happened, you know, the mike shoved in my face, and then when Solange died, these reporters came to my house, but I just said, 'No Comment.' That I can do."

"Have you had any interest from other shows?"

"Yes. The 'Today' show and 'Live at Five' both want me on the week before the trial. And some photo editor at *US* magazine said they're interested in me for their Lookout section. They're doing a special Crimes of Passion issue."

"Well, my motto is, 'There's no such thing as bad publicity, *if* you know what you're doing.'"

"Which I don't."

"You know, if you're going to do this stuff, you should consider hiring yourself a PR agent. Someone who can really help you. Do you have any money for something like that?"

"No," said Heath. "Right now, I'm broke. My grandmother's paying my legal fees, and I doubt she'd spring for a PR person."

"Well, then, the important part, the only thing you should remember, is that when you make an appearance—any appearance—it's an opportunity for you. It's not an opportunity for them. What you want to do, at least in terms of PR, is to project the most sympathetic image of yourself possible. You want people to think you're a nice person. I mean, obviously you are, so that shouldn't be such a problem. But you have to be specific. Is there anything you've done, or do—you know, nice things for the benefit of mankind?"

Heath thought but apparently without result.

"Do you ever do charity work?"

"I worked for the Gay Men's Health Crisis, visiting men with AIDS, and shopping for them and stuff. And I was in the AIDS walk."

"That's good," said Lillian. "See, this is the sort of thing people who murder don't generally do. What else? What about donations?"

"I give money to people on the street. But I don't have a lot of, you know, excess cash. The only other thing I've donated . . ."

"What?"

"No, it's nothing." Heath laughed.

"What? What's so funny?"

"I donated sperm once," said Heath.

"What?"

"I donated sperm. That wouldn't count, though, because they pay you for it."

"Where did you donate sperm?"

"The Fertility Association of New York. I went with my room-mate. He does it all the time, to help support his coke habit."

"How long ago was this?" demanded Lillian, trying to disguise the hysterical edge she heard in her voice. She tried to speak more calmly. "Think. This could be a very useful angle. You know: He taketh life away, but he also giveth life."

"But I didn't taketh life away," protested Heath. "It was a while ago. Anyway, I'm really embarrassed. I shouldn't have told you. I just needed some, well, some darkroom equipment, and . . . Gerard was going and he talked me into it. I only went once. I'd never do it again."

"How old did you say you were?"

"I'm twenty-seven. Why?"

He's probably had a birthday, thought Lillian. She tried to see the color of his eyes—they looked brownish in the depressing rainy light—but then she realized how absurd she was being. There were millions—well, maybe not millions; thousands—of sperm donors. The chances of her choosing Heath's sperm, well, the chances of that were probably as good as the chances of she and Heath getting it on together in real life.

ı ı ı ı ı ı ı

Down the block, around the corner, and up the avenue, Hannelore Green, president of the New York Bank for Women, was presiding over the Tuesday Morning Management Meeting.

"I have the results back from Gloria Mitchell and Associates, whom we consulted at Loren's suggestion about updating our slogan,

'The Institution Whose Time Has Come.' If you'll remember, Loren convinced us that an institution whose time had come in 1972 can hardly pretend to be on the cutting edge today. Ms. Mitchell has come up with three suggestions for us. I'd like to discuss them now. The first is 'The New York Bank for Women: Tomorrow's Bank for Today's Woman.' "

"I thought we want to avoid a gender bias," said Charlotte Wallace.

"We do," said Hannelore.

"But who wants tomorrow's bank today?" asked Loren. "It doesn't make much sense. Wouldn't one want today's bank today and tomorrow's bank tomorrow?"

"But it connotes that we're ahead of the times," said Hannelore. "At least that's the idea."

"But we aren't really," said Charlotte.

"We were the first bank to distribute free condoms with all ATM transactions," said Maureen.

"Maureen, we were the *only* bank to do that."

Maureen shrugged. She had thought it a great idea.

"Well, here's the next," said Hannelore. " 'The New York Bank for Women: As You Change, We Change.' I like this one. I like the way it suggests we're constantly evolving."

"It makes it sound like we're going through menopause," said Charlotte.

Loren laughed, but was silenced by a look from Hannelore, who said, "I don't think the changes implied are biological ones."

"Once again," said Loren, "I think it's a question of semantics. What if it weren't 'changes'—which I agree suggests the biological—what if it were 'As You Evolve, We Evolve'?"

" 'Evolved' makes it sound like it's a bank for monkeys," said Charlotte.

"Well, there's one more: 'The New York blah blah blah: The Bank with the Perfect Fit.' "

"All I can think of is diaphragms," said Charlotte.

"Why this sudden predilection with the gynecological?" asked Hannelore.

"I don't know," said Charlotte. "It's just what comes to mind."

"It makes me think of bras," said Maureen. "Or shoes."

"Enough free-associating. This isn't a joking matter," said Hannelore. "We paid three thousand dollars for this consultation."

"Consultants are always a waste of money," said Charlotte. "When you can't make it in your chosen field, you become a consultant. Everyone knows that."

"Well, this was all your idea, Loren. What do you think?"

They all turned to Loren, who did not answer. She was looking at one of her pink telephone messages. It was from someone she had not talked to in more than two months.

GREGORY CALLED, Stacey had written. CALL HIM ASAP.

# CHAPTER
## 30

"And then what happened?" asked Loren. She stood in the bathroom doorway, wrapped in a towel, fresh from the shower. Lillian sat on the bed, paging through a copy of *New York Woman*. They had a dinner date: just the two of them.

"It was all very weird," Lillian continued. She was telling Loren the story of her weekend in the country chez Claude. "He came in with the dog, and everything seemed fine, and I was just about to tell him about Lillian, Jr., when he said, 'I've made up the bed next door for you.' "

"Oh, God," said Loren.

"Exactly. I didn't know what was going on, so I just went along with it. We went next door, into this little tiny guest room where there was this little tiny bed that had been painstakingly made—you know how you can tell when someone's labored over something like that? He went back to his room. And I got in the little bed."

"He sounds like a louse." Loren stood in front of the mirror, toweling dry her mane of hair.

"That's just it: He isn't a louse. I mean, he wasn't. It was all so sweet: the pie, the ride home, the little bed. Even the dog was sweet, and you know how I am about dogs."

"Well, maybe it's just a matter of time. Why the rush to hop in the sack, anyway? It's all downhill from there, believe me."

"God," said Lillian. "I'm ready for some downhill. Some slalom, so to speak. I've been traveling the uphill road of celibacy for two years."

"Two years? I thought you broke up with Evan three years ago."

"I did," said Lillian.

Loren raised her eyebrows.

"It was nothing," said Lillian.

"But you never told me," said Loren.

Lillian stared down at the magazine. "Forget it," she said. "It was just, you know, just a thing."

"What was his name? I want to know his name at least."

"Carlos," said Lillian.

"Good for you," said Loren. "Everyone should fuck a man named Carlos once in their life."

"Anyway, getting back to the problem at hand. What should I do?"

"Did you make it obvious you wanted to sleep with him?"

"I thought I did."

Loren came into the bedroom and began dressing. She was thinking. "Well," she said, "it could be any number of things. Is he gay?"

"I don't think so," said Lillian. "I mean, he certainly doesn't seem to be, and he's been, well, let's just say he's pursued me in a very hetero way."

"This gay thing is a tough one," said Loren. "You can never be too sure, believe me. Anyway, let's assume he's not gay. Maybe it's physical. Is he, you know, all right . . . down there?" As she hooked her bra she nodded toward the floor.

"Down where?" asked Lillian. "His feet?"

"Lillian! Does he suffer from le maladie de Jake Barnes?"

"Who? What?"

"Jesus, you're so illiterate. Is his penis functioning?"

"Well, I didn't give him a goddamm physical. I mean, doesn't one assume a man's penis works? Have things gotten that bad?"

"Assume nothing," said Loren. "It just sounded, you know, if he came across as being interested and then backed off, maybe he has some sort of physical problem. Does this look all right together?"

"Yes," said Lillian. "Where are we going?"

"I don't care. Wherever you want."

"What about Spring Street Natural? Since we're down here?"

"Anywhere but there."

"Why?"

"That's where David had his little accident."

"Oh, I forgot. I know: Have you ever been to the Cafe Wisteria?"

"No. Where is it?"

"It's on Church Street. Let's go there."

"The Cafe Wisteria . . . isn't that where David's old boyfriend worked?"

"Actually, yes," said Lillian. "I saw him this week."

"Who? David?"

"No. The boyfriend. Heath."

"Really? Where?"

"He came by the office. I'm helping him with some publicity. His trial's coming up."

"Do you think he did it?"

"No. He was framed. While we're talking about men, can I ask you something else?"

"What? I think I'll put my hair up. It will just take a second."

"If a man is gay, I mean, if you know it, can he still be seduced?"

"Why do you ask me?"

"Well, because of David . . ."

"You want to sleep with David?"

"No," said Lillian.

"Who do you want to sleep with?"

"Heath," said Lillian.

"Heath? Why?"

"You'll laugh."

"I'm already laughing," said Loren. "Why?"

"I think he's the father of my child."

Loren stopped laughing when she saw Lillian's face. She came and sat beside Lillian on the bed. "Lillian," she said, "why would you ever think that?"

"He told me he donated sperm. And he matches my donor profile exactly."

"But, Lillian, thousands of men in New York must match that profile. Did he donate the same place you were inseminated?"

"Yes," said Lillian.

"I still think . . . I mean, it's absurd! You must see that. And even so, I mean, even if it were true—which it's probably not—why do you want to seduce him?"

"It's just that. . . ." Lillian said. "I know it's stupid. It's hard for me to explain. I feel . . . not, you know, well, perfect about this pregnancy. I mean, how it was brought about. How it happened. And I thought, well, if Heath was the father—which I think he is, I really do, and I know that may sound insane, but I do have this feeling—but if he is, or was, and if I slept with him, then, well, then, even if my baby wasn't conceived in love, if there was that union between us, it would be . . . oh, God, you know: closer than what. . . . " Lillian seemed to be crying.

Loren held her. "Lillian," she said. "There's nothing wrong with how your baby was conceived. In fact, it was conceived in love: yours. And anyway, what matters is not how babies are conceived but how they're raised. You know that, don't you?"

"I suppose," said Lillian.

"Don't suppose," said Loren. "Know."

| | | | | | |

Margot Geiger, Class of '88, is now the Director of The Gallery Shawangunk, one of SoHo's most prestigious institutions. She joined the gallery last June as Administrative Assistant, and was promoted to her present position of Director in October. Margot, who pursued a self-designed course of study exploring the Cultural Evolution of Latin American Women welcomes the opportunity to consider the work of Sarah Lawrence artists. Please send your slides to her, care of The Gallery Shawangunk.

That'll fix the bastards, thought Margot, gleefully extracting the alumni news form from the typewriter. All those ugly girls in the Intro Painting Crits who said nasty things about her work, and especially Magda Bish, that commie lesbo teacher who called her series of one hundred self-portraits "decadent." She could hardly wait till Bish came groveling:

Dear Magda,
Thank you so much for sending in your slides.
Unfortunately I felt these new paintings lacked a certain—

"Excuse me."

Margot looked up to see a short man in a business suit standing behind the velvet rope. She waited a delicious moment before acknowledging him. "Yes?"

"I was wondering . . . are there any Heath Jackson photographs available?"

Margot looked at the man again. He seemed vaguely familiar. "As you can see, that show's come down."

"Yes," said the man, "I can see. I just wondered if there are any photographs that haven't sold . . . that I might look at."

"We close at eight," said Margot. It was seven-thirty.

The man looked at his watch and shrugged. "Is it too late? I could come back."

Margot roused herself with apparent great effort. "No," she sighed. "I think there are a few dupes that we're holding for MOMA. They haven't made a decision yet. I could maybe show you those."

"Please," said the man. "If you would."

"Wait there," Margot said, and disappeared into the back room. She returned moments later with a large black portfolio, which she lay on a table. "Okay," she said, "you can come back now."

The man unhooked the rope and entered the sanctum. "You look familiar," she said. "Have you been in before?"

"No."

She unzipped the portfolio and flipped it open. The first photograph was the cat/man/noodle. The man in the photograph was the man standing beside her. He gazed down at himself, and something in the way he looked at the photograph made Margot Geiger's tiny, prunish heart swell.

Lillian and Loren walked by the Gallery Shawangunk on their way to the Cafe Wisteria. They looked in the big windows at sculptures assembled from tree trunks and shopping carts, and walked on.

An Italian woman in a black lace bra and purple leather miniskirt checked their coats. She stood in a little foyer at the top of the basement stairs. "Good evening," she said. Loren and Lillian handed over their coats. She put them on a table behind her and handed them a chit. "Enjoy your deener," she said.

"Is Heath Jackson here?" Lillian asked.

"Heath ese downstairs," the woman said. "He brings the coats oop and down for me. You know heem?"

"Ah, no," said Lillian. "We just wondered . . ."

"I spleet my teeps with heem," the woman said.

Anita, the hostess, approached. "Welcome to Cafe Wisteria," she said, shepherding them away.

Heath overheard this exchange from his post behind a little curtain at the top of the stairs. When he wasn't lugging coats up or down, he stood there, intoxicated by that lovely amalgam of music, talk, and laughter. Sometimes he longed to pull the curtain aside and walk toward the euphoria, take his proper place at the bar, and resume his life. But this reverie was invariably interrupted by Gina's slender naked arms, thrusting either chits or coats back through the chink in the curtain.

# PART
# IV

leap  1: to spring free from or as if from the ground  2 a: to pass abruptly from one state or topic to another  b: to act precipitately

*Webster's New Collegiate Dictionary*

# CHAPTER
# 31

"This is a voice from your past," said Solange. She waited, but there was no response. "Anton?" she said.

"Solange?"

"*Oui,*" she said. "*C'est moi.*"

There was another, shorter pause. Then Anton said, "I'm not totally surprised. I had a feeling you weren't dead."

"That's odd," said Solange. "Considering you killed me."

"But I didn't kill you. Amanda did."

"In fact she didn't, but I find that beside the point. I find rather a lot beside the point nowadays. I suppose being dead has that effect on one."

Anton was silent.

"Darling," said Solange, "ask me how I am."

"How are you?"

"I've never been better. Now ask me what I want."

"What do you want?"

"Many things. But I think it's only polite to make one's demands in person."

"Well," said Anton. "I'm at your disposal."

"I'm glad you see it that way," said Solange.

I I I I I I

For a while after David and Ms. Mouse had returned to the Upper West Side, Loren had considered calling Gregory. She wanted to talk with him, but she felt a little ashamed, and this shame, combined with her pride, made her mute. His unexpected telephone message empowered her.

"I'm sorry," she said when she finally reached him. "I should have called sooner."

"Why didn't you?" Gregory asked in his wonderfully familiar voice.

"I don't know. I was trying to figure out what to say. And I felt bad."

"I told you not to feel bad. Remember, in my letter?"

Loren smiled. "How are you?" she asked. "How's L.A.?"

"It's okay. Living here is just like what you'd imagine. Actually, it's a bit more like what you'd imagine than you'd imagine, if that makes any sense. How's New York?"

"Fine," said Loren. "Cold."

"How's Kate?"

"Kate's fine. I've just put her to bed. She misses you."

"And David?"

Loren paused. She didn't know what to say about David.

"I heard a rumor about you and David," Gregory said.

"What?"

"That you split up. Is it true?"

"Who did you hear that from?"

"Lyle Wallace."

"Since when do you associate with kidnappers?"

"He's starring in the show I'm producing."

"Is he? What kind of show is that?"

"It's a pilot about an ex-football player who inherits his brother's Italian restaurant and falls in love with his brother's widow. It's kind of a cross between *Moonlighting* and *Moonstruck*."

"It sounds awful," said Loren.

"It's actually not bad. Lyle can act, believe it or not. He's a nice guy."

"What did he say?"

"He said he heard from Charlotte that you and David had split up. Is it true?"

"Yes."

Neither of them spoke. They both held their phones more tightly to their ears, as if the feeling that was flowing between them might leak.

l l l l l l l

"Let's walk," said Judith. "We can bring the dog."

She and Leonard were going down to the high school to vote. After their oral confrontation in New York, Leonard had returned home to Ackerly, Pennsylvania, and bought a dog. In the interim, he and Judith had shared several inconclusive telephone conversations. Judith had decided that voting was a good ulterior motive for spending some time with him.

The charm of animals had always eluded Judith, and she found this puppy a particularly obstreperous creature. But under the circumstances she was trying to fake some enthusiasm.

"He's not very good on a leash," Leonard admitted.

"I'm sure it's just a matter of time," said Judith. "A little practice will do him good."

After a brief skirmish in the foyer, Leonard managed to snare the prancing beast, and the three of them set off. They rounded the corner and walked aways in silence. "Heel, Agra," Leonard commanded, to no visible effect.

"I was thinking," Judith said, "that this is the eleventh presidential election I've voted in."

Leonard, who hated idle observations, ignored this comment.

"I must say it seems to get more and more pointless, doesn't it? I don't understand this country anymore. Do you?"

"No," Leonard mumbled, his eyes dogward.

"It's bewildering," said Judith, "not to mention depressing."

"I have other things to be bewildered and depressed about," said Leonard.

"Such as?"

Leonard attempted to pause and strike a pose of utter defeat, but Agra would not cooperate. "I'm disappointed," said Leonard, "in you."

"Why are you disappointed in me?"

"Isn't it obvious? The moment I got your letter I made plans to return. I kept thinking, oh, this letter is a joke of some sort, because this cannot be true. And I arrived home to find that it was true. And you ask me why I'm disappointed."

It was Judith's turn to study the dog. For a moment she said nothing. "I still don't understand," she finally said.

"You have fallen in love with somebody else."

"But I still love you. I thought I made that clear in my letter."

"I don't feel loved," said Leonard. "I feel excluded."

"Then you don't understand. What I did . . . it was something that was separate from our love. You went away, Leonard. That didn't include me, but I don't resent that."

"My going away was a neutral act that was mutually agreed upon. What you've done is neither."

"How can you say that? Who are you to decide what is neutral and what is mutual? I'm the one who should know. It's my heart, after all."

"But I never thought of it as your heart. Or *my* heart. I thought it was a heart we shared."

"I think you've been in India too long: 'a heart we shared.' That's mush, darling. That's *West Side Story.*"

"Please don't be sarcastic," said Leonard.

"I'm sorry," said Judith. "I'm just trying to be realistic."

They arrived at the high school and performed their civic duties in silence. It began to rain as they walked home. Judith wondered if it was raining in New York.

"So what are your plans?" Leonard asked. "Are you home for good?"

Oh, Judith thought, why isn't life simpler? Of course it's a matter of choice: I could say, Of course I'm home for good, I'm never leaving.

"No," she said.

Leonard shrugged. They both watched the rain accumulate in a soggy stripe along the dog's spine. "I just want things to be normal again," Leonard said.

Judith touched his arm. "Darling," she said, "don't you remember? You were the one who was so restless . . . who hated how things had become. It was you who said we had to get away from here, and each other, or we would die. You were very unhappy when things were normal."

"But that's the whole point," said Leonard. "You see, I've found out I wasn't really. I *was* happy. It's what I want. I want to be home with you."

"I want that too, but there are things . . . my job, and my apartment, and being near Loren and Kate . . . things I want to finish in New York."

"What about your Chinese friend?" Leonard asked.

"He's Vietnamese," said Judith. "I have to finish that, too."

"Then go to New York," said Leonard.

"You'll be all right here?"

"Of course," said Leonard.

"I'm glad you understand," said Judith, knowing he didn't really understand.

"Just promise me you'll come back," Leonard said.

ı ı ı ı ı ı ı

"Death becomes you," said Anton, when his eyes had adjusted to the dim light. The bedroom of Solange's suite was illuminated by an altarlike arrangement of flickering candles. Solange lay in bed. Anton stood at the foot, looking down at her.

"And I rather like you as a redhead," he continued, a little desperately. "It's sexy."

Solange ignored these compliments. She gazed up at the wavering shadows on the ceiling.

"May I sit down?" asked Anton.

Solange nodded. He drew a chair up to the bed and sat. "I'm sorry," he said after a moment, when he realized she was waiting for him to speak. "I suppose that sounds absurd, but nevertheless . . . it's the truth."

Solange looked at him. "Do you love Amanda Paine?" she asked.

"No," said Anton.

"You told me that once before. In Aix. Remember?"

Anton nodded.

"Were you lying then?"

"I don't know. I don't think I ever really loved her, but, well . . . I got carried away."

"That is true," said Solange.

"I'm not carried away anymore," said Anton.

"What are you now?"

"I'm penitent," said Anton. "I'm devoted to you." He got out of the chair and knelt beside the bed. He looked up at her.

Solange smiled. She slowly pulled back the bedclothes, revealing the spot beside her. Something that looked very much like a heart lay there, leaking blood onto the sheet. She reached out and touched Anton's cheek. Her fingers were hot.

"What I want," she said, "is you."

# CHAPTER
## 32

"Is Corsica the same as Crete?" Susan asked.

"What do you mean?" asked David.

"You know, like Holland and the Netherlands are the same." Susan sat on the couch in David's office. She lit a cigarette. "I don't really smoke anymore," she announced, and thus excused, proceeded to drag.

"No," said David. "They're two separate islands."

"But they're real close, right?"

"What's all this about?"

"You know the March piece on Crete? Well, I think I fucked up. I told the photographer Corsica. Anyway, I just got the film back and it looks a lot like Crete, or at least how I picture Crete. Do you think we could fake it? Or maybe we should do Corsica instead?"

"It's got to be Crete," said David. "And we need pictures of Crete."

"If I hadn't told you, you'd never have known."

"Then you shouldn't have told me."

Lydia came in. She was dressed entirely in black, as she had been since the election. Unfortunately this somber attire made her appear more fashionable than mournful. "There's a Colette Menzies on three for you," she told David.

"I'll talk to research," said Susan. "There must be some pictures of Crete floating around."

When David was left alone, he picked up the phone. "Hello," he said.

"Mr. Parish? This is Colette Menzies. I'm with the law firm of Farrell, Calegari and Lopez. I'm defending Heath Jackson. I believe you know Heath?"

"I do," said David.

"Well, as you know, Heath is accused of murdering Solange Shawangunk."

"I know," said David.

"Of course you do. I'm calling to ask you a favor in regard thereto. It's come to my attention that the prosecutor believes—or at least contends—that Heath was having an affair with Mrs. Shawangunk and killed her in a jealous rage upon hearing she had been reunited with her husband."

"That's absurd," said David.

"I know it is. And it's my job to convince the jurors of that absurdity. I wondered if I might enlist your aid?"

"How so?"

"Heath mentioned that the two of you had been . . . involved. It occurs to me that your testimony to that effect could be influential."

"How do you figure that?"

"Mr. Parish, Heath is gay. It's in his best interest to establish that fact. The best way to do that is to have his lover testify."

"I'm not his lover," said David.

"But you were," said Ms. Menzies. "You're as close to a lover as he's presently got. Surely you must feel . . ."

"What?" asked David.

"Listen, I don't want to pressure you. Either you feel comfortable doing this or you don't."

"I don't think I would," said David.

"Why don't you think about it? Let me give you my number."

⁙ ⁙ ⁙ ⁙

David was reading Kate *Dear Mili*, which he had given her for her birthday, when the phone rang. "I'll be right back," he said, overturning the book across Kate's chest. "Don't look ahead."

"I won't," said Kate.

It was his mother, calling from River Hills, Wisconsin, to wish Kate a happy birthday. He summoned Kate to the phone.

"When is Ms. Mouse's birthday?" she asked as she entered the kitchen.

"In July," David said.

"Then am I older than her?"

"Older than she. No. Ms. Mouse is eight years old. Now Nana wants to wish you happy birthday. Don't forget to thank her for the pretty dress."

"What dress?"

"You remember the pretty dress she sent you. The one with bells on it. Nana made that for you. She sewed it."

"Thank you for the pretty dress with balls on it," Kate said in way of a greeting.

"Bells," David corrected.

Kate didn't hear. She was busy reporting. "I got a book and some toys and an ant farm, only the ants are dead. Daddy says they're sleeping, but they're not." She paused. "I have school every day." She paused again. "Do I have school on Christmas?" she asked her father.

"No," said David.

"No," said Kate. "I love you too. Good-bye." She handed the phone back to David.

"Can you talk?" his mother asked him.

"I was just putting her to bed," he said. "I'll call you back."

"Call before nine. I want to watch 'L.A. Law.' "

"Okay," said David.

He and Kate and Ms. Mouse and Mili returned to bed. Mili died after being reunited with her long-lost mother, a fate that seemed to please Kate.

"Did you have a nice birthday?" David asked, as he tucked her in.

"I still have my party at Mom's," said Kate.

"Yes," said David. "But did you like this party?"

"Yes," said Kate. She looked at the ant farm, which was beside her bed. "They still aren't moving."

"They're sleeping. They'll be moving tomorrow."

"Promise?"

"Well, I don't promise, but I think so."

"Ants are insects," said Kate.

"That's correct."

"Do ants have dreams?"

"I guess," said David.

"May I have another éclair?"

"No," said David. "It's time to sleep. Where do you want to kiss me tonight?" Kate had taken to depositing her good-night kiss in a different place each night.

She thought for a moment. "Your elbow," she decided.

David rolled up the sleeve of his shirt and crooked his arm above Kate's face. She kissed it. "Kiss Ms. Mouse," said Kate.

"I don't kiss cats," said David.

"I do," said Kate.

"No you don't," said David.

"Yes I do," said Kate. She kissed a reluctant Ms. Mouse on her tiny lips. "See," she said.

"That was very interesting," said David.

"I love Ms. Mouse," said Kate.

"I know," said David.

"Do I love Nana?"

"I think so," said David.

"I think so too," said Kate.

"Good." David kissed her. "Good night," he said. "Happy birthday."

In the kitchen he washed the dishes before calling his mother. They were not very close. His father had died when David was twelve years old by freezing in his car, which had stalled on the highway during a blizzard. Instead of bringing them closer together, this event served only to alienate David and his mother. They had two very separate griefs. When he was eighteen David learned that a woman—his father's mistress—had also died in the car, frozenly embraced by his father. Mrs. Parish had still never acknowledged this. David finished scouring the macaroni-and-cheese pan (Kate's choice) and dialed his mother's number.

She was calling about the holidays. "What are you planning?" she asked him.

"I hadn't really thought about it yet," David said.

"Well, I've just heard from Karen. She's arriving on the 23rd for a week. It would be swell if you could come then. What about Kate?"

"What about her?"

"Do you have her that week?"

"I'm not sure. I haven't talked it out with Loren yet."

"What are you doing for Thanksgiving?"

"We're having it together: Loren and I. And Loren's mother."

"That sounds lovely. How are things going with you two?"

"Fine."

"What does that mean?"

"It means things are fine. Back to normal."

"What's normal? Together or apart?"

"Apart," said David.

"That's a shame," said Mrs. Parish. "I was so hoping—"

"Come to think of it," said David, "I might have some trouble getting away this holiday season."

"Is work terribly busy?"

"No. A friend's going on trial, and I plan to testify on his behalf."

"Oh, dear," said Mrs. Parish. "A nasty custody battle?"

"No."

"What then?"

"It's a murder trial."

"Heavens! You're joshing. A friend of yours—a murderer!"

"He's not a murderer. That's the whole point—why I'm getting involved."

"Well, I suppose that's good of you, but even so, darling, one doesn't . . . I mean, nice people aren't accused of murder. At least not in Wisconsin. Perhaps you should reevaluate this friendship."

"It isn't really a friendship."

"I'm glad to hear that."

"It's more of a romance," said David.

"I thought you said it was a man friend."

"I did."

Mrs. Parish was silent for a moment. The whispery edges of another conversation could be heard at the corners of theirs.

"Well," Mrs. Parish finally managed. "You must do whatever . . . I can hardly presume to . . . are you all right?"

"Yes," said David.

"Is this romance . . . ongoing?"

"No," said David. "It's over."

"Does Loren know?"

"Yes."

She paused again. "You're careful, aren't you?"

"Of course," said David.

"One hears such awful things . . ."

"It's no big deal," said David. "I'm not even seeing him anymore."

"Then why this need?"

"What need?"

"The need to testify on his behalf. The need to tell me about it."

David thought for a moment. "Because it matters," he said. "Because it matters to me."

# CHAPTER
## 33

The candles had sputtered and gone out. The only sound was the traffic passing up the avenue. Solange and Anton lay, bloody and sweating, in the dark.

"It was good," said Solange.

"*Trés bon,*" said Anton.

"You're mine," said Solange.

"I am," said Anton. "I'm all yours."

"Every bit of you." She chewed his hair. "Your hair is mine."

"What I've got left."

She licked his ear. "Your ear is mine."

"Yes," he said.

"She's nothing."

"Who?"

"Amanda."

"Who's Amanda?"

Solange laughed. "Her heart is dead," she said.

"She never had a heart," said Anton.

"I want to go away," said Solange. "I want to be alive again, but not here. This city is dead to me, and I to it."

"Where shall we go?"

"I don't care. Paris, Mustique. Some sun would be lovely."

"As soon as the trial's over, we're gone, then. Forever."

"No," said Solange. "Now."

"But shouldn't we . . . the boy will go to jail, and Amanda will go free. I thought you wanted revenge."

"I have you." She held his cock. "That's my revenge."

"What about the boy?"

"I don't like boys," said Solange. "I like men."

।  ।  ।  ।  ।  ।  ।

"Why isn't Lillian having Thanksgiving with her family?" asked Judith. She stood in Loren's kitchen, breaking the pithy ends off of asparagus.

"Because she's starting to show, and her parents don't know she's pregnant. Besides, you know Lillian: She hates her family."

"She hasn't told them?"

"She didn't think it would go over too big with Harriet and Winston."

"I thought Harriet was dying for a grandchild."

"She is. I don't know. Lillian's gotten paranoid about this baby."

"That's a shame," said Judith. "It should be such a happy thing."

"She is happy," said Loren. "She's happy *and* paranoid."

"Do you have a steamer?" asked Judith. "I can't find it in here."

Loren wiped her floury hands above the pastry she was trying to roll large enough to fit the pie tin. "It's in the bathroom," she said. "Kate used it in her bath last night."

"I guess we don't need it yet anyway," said Judith. "I'll put these in some water. What time did you tell Lillian and David?"

"I told them to come at three and we'd eat at four. What's it now?"

"Two-thirty." Judith watched Loren roll the pastry. "If it's too thin, it will burn," she said.

Loren ignored this observation. "It's too bad Daddy isn't with us," she said.

"Well, it was his choice," said Judith. "He said he'd be happier at Aunt Peggy's."

"I find that hard to believe," said Loren.

"If he's going to sulk, there's nothing we can do," said Judith.

"Why are you acting like this?" asked Loren. "What's going on with you and Daddy? Why is he avoiding us?"

"You're the one who talked to him. What did he say?"

"He gave me some crazy story about your having a boyfriend. Something about some man at your apartment. It was really absurd."

"What's so absurd about that?" asked Judith.

"It even sounds absurd: a boyfriend. Sixty-year-old women don't usually have boyfriends. At least not as far as I know."

"What if he were a lover? Can a sixty-year-old woman have a lover?"

"Is this true? Are we talking about you?"

"Yes," said Judith. "We are."

Loren opened the oven and looked at the turkey. It just sat there, baking. She tried to picture it as a real turkey, with a head and everything, but she couldn't. It was just this naked thing baking.

"Of course you can have a lover," she said, addressing the turkey. "It's just that, well, you're my mother, and one doesn't think of one's mother . . . you know, in that way."

"In what way?"

Loren closed the oven. "You know what I mean," she said. "As being sexually active."

"It isn't just sex," said Judith. "It isn't even primarily sex."

"Than what is it?" asked Loren. "Are you in love?"

"A little," said Judith.

"Do you still love Daddy?"

"Of course," said Judith.

"So what are you going to do?"

"I don't know," said Judith. "I have a month left to figure that out."

ı ı ı ı ı ı ı ı

As dusk gathered, the party dispersed. The most senior (Judith) and junior (Kate) guests departed for a trip to the playground, leaving Loren, David, and Lillian to the washing up. David washed, Loren dried, and Lillian picked the turkey.

"I talked to my mother the other night," said David.

"How is she?" asked Loren.

"She's okay. She called to see what I was doing for Christmas. She wants Kate and me to go out there. I told her I'd talk to you."

"That might work out well," said Loren. "I was considering going away for Christmas."

"Without Kate?"

"With or without. So if you wanted to take her to River Hills, that would be fine. In fact, I think it would be nice: She sees your mother so infrequently."

"Lucky for her," said David. "Anyway, I might not go at all. It might conflict with Heath's trial."

"You want to watch Heath's trial?" asked Lillian.

"I'm going to be a witness."

"What kind of a witness? You weren't even there."

"I'm going to be a character witness," said David. "I'm attesting to Heath's homosexuality."

"Couldn't that get messy?" asked Loren.

"How do you mean?"

"I just mean, well, it's a very public thing, you know . . ."

"I know that."

"Poor Heath," said Lillian. "Have you talked to him?"

"No," said David.

"Why not?"

"Because I don't think he wants me to. I told him to call me if he needed anything, and he hasn't called."

"That doesn't mean you can't call him," said Lillian. "He's checking coats at the Wisteria. Loren and I went down there to see him. Only we didn't. They hide him in the basement."

They were silent a moment. The subject of Heath made them all a little uncomfortable. "You said before you were going away," Lillian said to Loren. "Where are you going?"

"I'd rather not say," said Loren.

"Oh, please," said Lillian. "Come off it. Where?"

"I was thinking of going to California."

"It's a big state," said Lillian. "Could you be a little more specific?"

"Lillian! Mind your own business."

"She's going to see Gregory," said David. "Right?"

"Yes," said Loren.

"You're not thinking of moving again, are you?"

"No. Jesus Christ, I'm just going to see Gregory for a couple of days. It's no big deal."

"It's what you make it," said Lillian, smiling cryptically at the turkey carcass.

"Speaking of which," said Loren, "what's the story with you and the guy?"

"What guy?" asked David.

"Didn't you hear about Lillian's romance?"

"No," said David. "Who?"

"The guy who owns the restaurant in Stone Ridge."

"Paul?"

"Claude."

"Oh, right. I thought there was something cooking between you two. Personally, I thought he was a little strange."

"What's going on?" asked Loren.

"Your basic nothing," said Lillian. "Or rather, *my* basic nothing."

"Have you seen him?"

"No. He invited me up there for today, but I said no."

"Why did you do that?"

"I don't know. I didn't want to, you know, go through that rejection again."

"What rejection?" asked David. "How come I don't know anything about this?"

He was ignored.

"Maybe this time would have been different," Loren said.

"I doubt it. I invited him here, but he wouldn't come. He said he never comes to New York anymore. I've given up on him. Plus, if I saw him now I'd have to tell him about the baby, and I'm just not into discussing that."

"You'd better get used it," said Loren, "since you're showing."

"I hate that word: showing. It sounds like you're an exhibitionist or something. Or that it's something to be kept secret."

"Are you sure you weren't you-know-what when you were up there? Maybe that's what freaked him out."

"He got freaked out?" said David. "I told you he was weird."

"He's not weird," said Lillian. "Maybe he is, a little, but I like him. I mean, I *liked* him. But I'm not going to pursue a relationship with a man who's scared of New York."

"I thought he used to live here," said Loren.

"He did. But he got freaked out over the crash and bolted."

"He sounds like a real loser," said David. "What doesn't freak him out?"

"Tranquility," said Lillian, pulling the last shreds of meat off the bones.

"God," said David. "Remember tranquility?"

Life seemed to stop for an instant while they stood there, silently, each engrossed in a different memory, but then they heard Kate and Judith laughing and racing down the hall, and life picked itself up again and rushed forward.

# CHAPTER
## 34

Something was wrong. Not only had Anton stopped returning her calls, but now his machine was turned off. Amanda decided to investigate and took a taxi uptown. She entered Trump Tower's darkened foyer and stood for a moment, wondering how to proceed.

Bernard looked up from a pad of doodles. "Good afternoon, Miss . . ."

"Paine," Amanda suggested. "It's so nice to see you."

"Likewise, I'm sure, Miss Paine."

"Did you have a nice turkey?"

"Very nice."

"I didn't know you were an artist, Bernard."

"I'm not, Miss Paine. It just helps pass the time. I'm doing a drawing of every resident."

"Speaking of residents, is Mr. Shawangunk in?"

"Mr. Shawangunk's left the country."

Amanda tried not to grimace. "Has he?" she managed to say. "When did he depart?"

"Oh, I'd say a week ago. At least a week. He didn't let you know?"

"Of course he did," said Amanda. "We're colleagues, as you'll recall. He'll be back this week, correct?"

"I don't think so, Miss Paine."

This is very bad, Amanda thought. She looked down to see her hand gripping the edge of the concierge's desk, her crimson nails making tiny serific indentations in the soft wood.

"I don't think he'll be back for some time," Bernard said.

"I expected him this week," Amanda said.

"All I know is what he told us, Miss Paine. He said he might . . ." Bernard paused, not sure if he should proceed. Miss Paine looked as though she might attack him.

"What?" she hissed. "What did he say?"

"He said he might not be back till the spring," Bernard muttered.

"You're mistaken! You misheard! The trial is next week."

"What trial, Miss Paine?"

"Heath Jackson's. Mrs. Shawangunk's murderer."

"Oh, that. Well, there's not much question about that, is there? I mean, they caught him with the gun."

This is true, Amanda told herself: They caught him with the gun. I was never seen entering or leaving the room. She tried to regain her composure by repeating, I was never seen entering or leaving the room, I was never—

"You don't look well, Miss Paine," Bernard said. She must have glared at him, because he added, "I mean you look great, really pretty and all, you just don't look . . . you look a little sick."

"I think I need some fresh air," said Amanda.

"That's one thing we don't got in New York." Bernard tried to laugh and then sighed in relief as Miss Paine disappeared through the tinted glass doors.

Amanda knew better than to fall apart on the street. Only common people fell apart on the street. She would do it in Bonwit's. She hastened around the corner and felt substantially better upon entering, reassured by the perfumed air and the serene, chimplike faces of the salesladies.

They were having a little fete in cruisewear with tea and canapés and models idling about in bathing suits with gooseflesh on their impossibly slender thighs. Amanda commandeered a cup of tea and disappeared into an empty dressing room. She sat for a moment, sipping tea, considering her reflection in the mirror. Why does it always happen like this? she wondered. Why are men so feeble? She had thought Anton was different, but he was not. He was a typical man—he loved neither properly nor enough. Perhaps Bernard is wrong, she thought. Perhaps Anton is coming back. Or perhaps it is all a story, and he has never really left. She tried for a moment to believe this, but she could not convince herself.

Where does it leave me? Without Anton's carefully formulated testimony linking Solange to Heath, the case would undoubtedly be weakened. And if Heath were cleared, surely they would begin looking for another suspect, and surely that suspect would be . . . perhaps I should kill Heath, Amanda thought. If I made it look like a suicide, his guilt would be assumed and the case closed. But no, she thought, I'm not promiscuously criminal. I kill for love and love alone . . .

Anton's gone, she reminded herself, swirling the dregs of her tea. Well, she thought, fuck him. God knows I've done everything myself so far; there's no reason I can't continue alone I'll put Heath Jackson behind bars. No one is going to make a chump out of me.

I I I I I I I

"Before I forget," said Tammi, "Anita told me to tell you Toinette Menzies called. You're supposed to call her back first thing in the morning."

"Colette Menzies," said Heath. "That's my lawyer."

"Maybe she has good news. Maybe they're calling the case off."

"I doubt it," said Heath.

"I think you need a new boyfriend," said Tammi. "A little romance would take your mind off all this trial shit." She was on her break and had come downstairs to try on fur coats, smoke, and talk to Heath. "How does this look?" she asked, modeling a full-length mink.

"I don't think it's you," said Heath.

"Of course it's not me," said Tammi. "None of these are. If they were me, I wouldn't be down here trying them on. I'd be upstairs eating fucking veal chops. Listen, I'm serious about this boyfriend thing. What about Howard?"

"Howard? Howard, the waiter?"

"No. Howard Hughes, the deceased billionaire. Of course

Howard the waiter. He thinks you're cute. He told me you reminded him of John Kennedy, Junior."

"You better take that off," said Heath. "You're getting ashes on it."

"Ashes are good for the pelt. They give it a certain woodsy aroma."

"Take it off," said Heath.

"So how about Howie? Do you like him?"

"No. I don't think he's my type."

"What is your type?"

"I don't know," said Heath.

"What don't you like about Howard?"

"He's too young and, I don't know . . . silly."

"So you want some old turd? Don't tell me you're still hung up on el yuppie."

"No," said Heath. "I just think he was more my type."

"So you're into cruelty?"

"David wasn't cruel."

"He ditched you for his wife."

"He didn't ditch me—it was a mutual decision."

"There's no such thing, bucko."

"Speak for yourself," said Heath.

"Anyone can speak for themselves," said Tammi. "I speak for the community of abandoned lovers. Anyway, if the yuppie was so great, why didn't you put up more of a fight?"

"I had other things on my mind," said Heath, "having just been arrested for murder."

"God, your life has been ultra shitty lately, hasn't it?" asked Tammi. She sat down beside Heath and patted his back. "I know you won't believe me, but I think you're going to get through this, and you'll be due for some major happiness."

"If I get through this without having to go to jail, I'd settle for more shit," said Heath.

⎪ ⎪ ⎪ ⎪ ⎪ ⎪ ⎪

"Margot," said Amanda, "what's going up next?"

Margot looked up from the pile of holiday cards she was sign-

ing. "You know very well," she said. "Gilberto Arnot. He was post-
poned from last summer, when we did Heath Jackson."

"Well, we may have to postpone him a bit longer. There's a
show I want up instead."

"I thought scheduling fell into my domain," said Margot.

"Don't be tiresome, Margot," said Amanda.

"Well, it's just that if I can't direct the gallery I don't see what
the point in being director is."

"Most girls in your position would be more than satisfied with
the title," said Amanda.

"I'm not like most girls," said Margot. "Who do you want to
put up?"

"Well, the details aren't finito yet, but I think it could be a
stunning—and lucrative—departure for the gallery. I've discovered
someone who does little doodly portraits of society types. They're
splendidly drawn, and I think they could be a big hit."

"They sound awful. I think we should stick with the Arnot. He
has some very fine new paintings. And he was so devoted to Solange."

"Solange is dead," said Amanda, "and fine paintings keep.
We'll open Bernard Zerener in January and do a big Arnot retro-
spective in the spring. How would that be?"

"Whatever you say," said Margot.

ı ı ı ı ı ı

"Sit down," said Colette Menzies. "I've good news and bad news.
Which do you want first?"

"Is the bad news badder than the good news is good?"

"I think they're just about equally bad and good."

"So they cancel each other out?"

"We'll see," she said. "They might."

"The bad news then."

Colette picked a copy of the *Post* off her desk and handed it
to Heath. "Page three," she said.

Heath opened the paper. On page three was a photograph of
a doorman standing beneath the Trump Tower awning. He read the
accompanying article.

## SHAWANGUNK LOVE NEST:
## DOORMAN HOLDS THE KEY

A Post Exclusive—Bernard Zerener, a doorman in the luxurious Trump Tower, has come forward as a surprise witness in the Solange Shawangunk murder case. As *Post* readers will remember, Shawangunk was shot point-black last July 13 at her SoHo gallery during the opening reception for a show of photographs by Heath Jackson. She died of complications two months later. Jackson, who was found with the gun moments after the shooting, has been charged with the murder. It has been the prosecution's assertion, long denied by the defendant, that he and Shawangunk were lovers.

Zerener told the *Post* in an exclusive interview yesterday that Jackson was a "frequent" visitor to the Shawangunk apartment on the 38th floor of Trump Tower. "I'd say he was there more than twenty times between January and June of this year," Zerener recalled. "I often saw him leaving or arriving at the apartment late at night, escorting Mrs. Shawangunk. They were real open about it—very physical and everything. I remember it because Mrs. Shawangunk was usually such a dignified woman. I especially remember an argument they had in the lobby on July 13, the day Mrs. Shawangunk was murdered. From what I overheard, it seemed as if she was trying to break the thing off and Mr. Jackson was resisting. He got a little rough with her and I had to interfere."

Asked why he had waited so long to come forward with this important testimony, Zerener said his conscience had troubled him. "I couldn't sleep anymore," he told the *Post.* "It's kind of an unwritten law for doormen not to get involved in the affairs of the residents, but a decent man can stay silent only for so long. The idea that this punk could go free prompted me to speak out. I heard him threaten Mrs. Shawangunk on the afternoon she was murdered. That's all the proof I need."

The Jackson trial begins next week. For exclusive photos of the love nest, and a DID HEATH DO IT? readers' survey, see page 46.

Heath replaced the paper on the desk. "Is this really as bad as it sounds?" he asked.

"I can't know," said Colette. "I haven't seen his actual testimony yet. And speaking of testimony, the prosecutor's alerted me that Anton Shawangunk has left town. We can subpoena him if we want, but I think it would be better to go after Amanda."

"They're both liars," said Heath.

"But Anton's better at it," said Colette. "Let's concentrate on Amanda."

"What's the good news?" asked Heath.

"The good news is that David Parish has agreed to testify on your behalf."

"He has? You talked to him?"

"Several times. And given this doorman garbage, his statement will be very helpful."

"What's he going to say?"

"He's going to say he had a love affair with you that began in December of 1987 and lasted through July of 1988. Which is exactly the same time the prosecution contends you were involved with Mrs. Shawangunk."

"Who will the jury believe?" asked Heath.

# CHAPTER
# 35

The prosecuting attorney was a short man named Ned Best who chain-ate Tic Tacs. His first witness was Amanda Paine. She was wearing a maroon schoolmarmish wool dress that made her look to Heath a little like Hester Prynn.

"Please raise your right hand," the clerk told her, once she had assumed the witness stand. "Do you swear that the testimony you are about to give this court and jury is the truth and the whole truth, so help you God?"

"I do."

"Please be seated. State your full name and spell your last name."

"My name is Amanda Paine. P-A-I-N-E."

Ned Best stood up. "Thank you, Ms. Paine. Could you begin your testimony by telling the jury something about your education and present occupation?"

"Certainly. I have a bachelor's degree in art history from Harvard University and an M.B.A. from Columbia University. I am presently the director emeritus of the Gallery Shawangunk. I was until recently director."

"How long have you been associated with the Gallery Shawangunk?"

"For five years. I began working there in 1983."

"And tell us, Ms. Paine, what kind of artwork does the gallery exhibit?"

Amanda laughed. "That's not an easy question. Let me see. Our stable is eclectic. I endeavor to show art that challenges the viewer by questioning the notion of aesthetics while at the same time making either veiled or pointed references to the historical spectrum in which it exists."

"Tell me, Ms. Paine, are you acquainted with Heath Jackson?"

"I am."

"In what manner?"

"Mr. Jackson is a photographer who recently had a show at the gallery."

"Was this show your idea?"

"It was not. The owner of the gallery, Solange Shawangunk, told me to mount a show of Heath's photographs."

"Would you have exhibited Mr. Jackson's photographs had it been your decision?"

"I would not have."

"Tell me, what is your opinion of Mr. Jackson's art?"

Colette stood up. "Objection. On the grounds of irrelevancy, Your Honor."

"Your Honor, the question is very relevant. I'm trying to determine the circumstances under which Mr. Jackson came to show at the Gallery Shawangunk."

"I'll allow it."

The question was repeated.

"I wouldn't really call it art. It's amateurish, visually illiterate, and derivative."

Although Heath had been instructed by Colette to remain expressionless, he couldn't help wincing at this pronouncement.

"Thank you," said Ned Best. "Now, getting back to the matter at hand. When was Mr. Jackson's show?"

"The show opened on July thirteenth, 1988, and closed on August twenty-seventh, 1988."

"Was there an opening reception for this show?"

"There was. On July thirteenth, from six p.m. to nine p.m."

"Could you tell us what transpired during those hours?"

"Well, I was at the gallery most of the day, working out the details of the show, with my assistant, Margot Geiger. The caterers came in around four and began setting up."

"When did Mr. Jackson arrive?"

"Mr. Jackson made his entrance about six-thirty. I greeted him and introduced him around."

"To whom did you introduce him?"

"Well, let me think. I remember introducing him to some media people. Then Heath and Solange went into the office together."

"How many doors does this office have?"

"It has one door. Well, it has a closet door as well."

"How many windows does it have?"

"It has two windows. One looks out onto the backyard and the other looks onto the gallery floor."

"Does the window that faces the gallery have a shade?"

"It does."

"Was the shade raised when Mr. Jackson and Mrs. Shawangunk entered the office."

"It was."

"Did it remain raised?"

"It was lowered."

"Miss Paine, tell us, what did you do while the defendant and Mrs. Shawangunk were in the office?"

"I was speaking with a journalist, Leonora Trumpet. We were talking about Mr. Jackson's photographs. I suggested she might like to see some of the photographs that weren't being shown, which were stored in the office closet, and Leonora agreed. We approached the office and I knocked on the door."

"How much time had elapsed since the defendant and Mrs. Shawangunk had entered the office?"

"I'd say about ten minutes. I'm not exactly sure."

"What happened after you knocked?"

"There was no answer. I knocked again, and I don't know, I just sensed something was wrong. I didn't hear any voices. So I opened the door."

"What did you see?"

"I saw Mr. Jackson standing, holding a gun. I saw Mrs. Shawangunk lying on the floor, bleeding. I think I screamed. And then I closed the door and yelled for someone to call the police."

"Did the police come?"

"Within a matter of minutes. They arrested Mr. Jackson and took Mrs. Shawangunk to the hospital."

"I have no further questions, Your Honor."

"Does the defense wish to cross-examine?"

Colette stood up. "I have a few questions, Your Honor. Ms. Paine, could you tell the jury how many of Mr. Jackson's derivative photographs were sold?"

"The show sold out. But the reason they sold—"

"We're interested in the facts, Ms. Paine, not your interpretation of them. Could you tell us about how much money Mr. Jackson's art has netted the gallery?"

"Well, I don't know the exact figures."

"Would you consider the show to be a financial success?"

"I suppose so."

"Would you consider Mr. Jackson to be a valuable asset to the gallery?"

"I suppose, yes, in strictly financial terms."

"Then would you suppose, Ms. Paine, that offering Mr. Jackson a show was an excellent business decision on Mrs. Shawangunk's part?"

"But when she offered him the show she had no idea what—"

"It's a yes-or-no question, Ms. Paine. Let me rephrase it for you. In your professional opinion, was Mrs. Shawangunk's decision to offer Mr. Jackson a show at the Gallery Shawangunk a smart one?"

"It could be seen that way in retrospect."

"Thank you. I just have one more question, Ms. Paine. Can you tell me why Harvard University has no record of ever awarding you a B.A. degree?"

"Did I imply they had?"

"I believe you did. Would you like me to have your sworn testimony read back to you?"

"No. What I meant to say was that I took several classes one summer at Harvard University. My degree itself is from another institution."

"What institution is that?"

"Slippery Rock State College."

"Thank you. Is there any other part of your testimony you'd like to reconsider?"

"There is not."

"Then I have no further questions."

"You may step down, Ms. Paine. Does the prosecution wish to call another witness?"

The prosecution called Bernard Zerener. While he was being sworn in, Heath looked around the courtroom. Everyone seemed to be staring back at him malevolently, except his father, who gave him a thumbs-up sign. His mother had her eyes scrunched shut, as if she were at a horror film.

"Mr. Zerener, could you tell the jury what you do for a living?"

"I'm a concierge at Trump Tower."

"How long have you been employed at Trump Tower?"

"Eighteen months."

"Do you know the Shawangunks?"

"I know Mr. Shawangunk. I knew the late Mrs. Shawangunk."

"Do you know the defendant?"

"I've never been formally introduced to Mr. Jackson, but I know him by sight."

"Where have you seen him?"

"In the lobby of Trump Tower."

"Could you tell us when you saw Mr. Jackson in the lobby of Trump Tower?"

"Several times between January and July of this year."

"And in what circumstances did you encounter Mr. Jackson?"

"He'd come through with Mrs. Shawangunk. They'd either be coming in or going out."

"Did they seem friendly?"

Colette half stood up. "Objection, Your Honor. Leading."

"Sustained."

"How did Mr. Jackson and Mrs. Shawangunk act toward each other?"

"Friendly. Very, very friendly."

"Did they touch each other?"

"Yes."

"Did you ever see them kiss each other?"

"Yes. Once, they were in the elevator, right before the door closed. They started kissing. French."

"Did you ever speak to Mr. Jackson in the lobby of the Trump Tower?"

"I did."

"Please describe those circumstances to the jury."

"It was on the afternoon of July thirteenth. I remember because the Shawangunks had been away, and they had just come back. Mr. Jackson was there waiting around for her. Mrs. Shawangunk came in alone, and he accosted her."

"What do you mean by 'accosted'?"

"He was grabbing at her. She was trying to get into the elevator, and he wouldn't let her."

"Did they speak to each other?"

"Yeah. I don't remember the whole thing. But I do remember Mrs. Shawangunk kept saying 'It's over,' and Mr. Jackson was saying stuff like 'Don't do this to me,' and 'I love you.' Loser stuff like that."

"What did you do?"

"At first I tried to ignore it. You know, mind my own business. But then Mr. Jackson, he starts to get rough with her, so I went over there and held him back while she gets on the elevator. And when she's gone, I let him go and tell him to get lost."

"Did he say anything to you, Mr. Zerener?"

"Well, he said something, but it wasn't really to me. It was more to Mrs. Shawangunk, even though she was gone."

"What did Mr. Jackson say?"

"He said, 'I'm going to kill you, baby.' "

Heath heard everyone gasp, and this time he did not have to turn his head to know that everyone was looking at him.

# CHAPTER
# 36

After David was sworn in, he looked around the courtroom. He almost didn't recognize Heath. He had never seen him in a suit before, and his hair, which was usually short but generally disheveled, had been furiously parted and slicked to his head. Heath looked to David like an older, more conservative brother of himself. Behind Heath, in the benches, David saw Loren and Lillian sitting beside each other. He had come downtown with Lillian, but he hadn't known Loren would be there. Heath, Lillian, Loren—their combined presence unnerved him. He felt a little as if his life, which he had heretofore worn loosely about him, had suddenly shrunk a size or two and was clinging uncomfortably to his skin. He shifted in his seat and returned his attention to Ms. Menzies.

"Mr. Parish, could you tell us how and when you met Mr. Jackson?"

"In December of 1987, my assistant took a four-week vacation. I hired Mr. Jackson through a temporary employment agency to replace her."

"So your original relationship was one of employer to employee?"

"Originally, yes."

"Did the nature of that relationship change?"

"It did."

"Could you tell us how it changed?"

"I could," said David. He paused and looked around. Heath was looking at him. Loren and Lillian were looking at him. Everyone was looking at him. "We fell in love." He had intended to proclaim this fact but it sounded rather more like an admission.

"Are you lovers at this time?" Colette asked.

David shook his head. "No."

"I don't mean to embarrass you, Mr. Parish, but for the jury's sake I'd like to clarify the nature of your relationship with Mr. Jackson. You said you were lovers. Did you have a sexual relationship with the defendant?"

"I did."

"Did you live with him?"

"Not exactly."

"What do you mean by 'not exactly'?"

"I mean, we spent a lot of time together but we didn't . . . we maintained separate residences."

"Did you ever spend the night with Mr. Jackson?"

"I did."

"How often?"

"Quite often, I'd say. Four or five nights a week from January to July of this year."

"Tell me, Mr. Parish, to the best of your knowledge, was Heath Jackson seeing a woman at the same time he was your lover?"

"To the best of my knowledge he was not."

"What do you base that answer on?"

"Well," said David, "Heath once told me he wasn't bisexual. He told me he had never slept with a woman and had no desire to do so. He never mentioned Solange Shawangunk. And moreover, I—well, my relationship with Heath may not have lasted very long, but while we were together, we had a . . . I believe we loved each other, and I think because of that I would have sensed if I were being betrayed in the manner you suggest."

Ned Best stood up. "Your Honor, I move to have that last answer stricken from the record. It hardly qualifies as objective testimony."

"The answer may stand. Mr. Parish, in the future please limit your testimony to what you know for a fact to be certain."

Nowadays, thought David, that's nothing.

"I have just one more question, Your Honor. Mr. Parish, is anyone paying you for your testimony here today?"

"No."

"I have no further questions. Your witness, counsel."

"Thank you, Ms. Menzies," said Ned Best. "Good morning, Mr. Parish."

"Good morning," said David.

"I'd like to begin by asking you to tell the jury what your marital status is."

"I'm divorced."

"So can we assume, then, that you were at one time married?"

"I was."

"Do you have any dependents?"

"I have one child."

"Is the mother of this child your ex-wife?"

"That's correct."

"Can we safely assume, then, Mr. Parish, and I here use Ms. Menzies' terminology, that you had a 'sexual relationship' with your wife?"

"I did."

"Can we assume, then, Mr. Parish, that you are bisexual?"

"You can assume whatever you want."

"I'd like a yes-or-no answer, Mr. Parish. Are you bisexual?"

"Your Honor, I object. I fail to see what relevancy Mr. Parish's sexual orientation has to this matter. I'd also argue this cross goes beyond the scope of my original examination of the witness."

"Your Honor, I disagree. Mr. Parish has testified as to Mr. Jackson's sexual orientation. I'd argue that his seeming confusion as to his own has bearing on that testimony."

"I think you've made your point, then, counsel. Please move on."

"Mr. Parish, during the time you had this 'sexual relationship' with Mr. Jackson, were you involved with anyone else?"

David didn't answer. He remembered that March night: Lillian's party, the cab ride through the dark park, Loren's hair in his mouth, the ringing telephone. "It depends what you mean by involved."

"I'll rephrase my question. Did you have sexual relations with a person other than Heath Jackson between January and July of this year?"

"I slept with my wife." David looked at Loren as he said this. She was looking down at her hands, studying them, turning them over in her lap.

"I assume you mean your ex-wife."

"I do." Loren looked up at him. Her face was expressionless.

"So concurrent with your *homo*sexual relationship with Mr. Jackson you were also involved in a *hetero*sexual relationship with your wife?"

"It was just one night."

"The duration of your sexual encounters does not interest me. Tell me, Mr. Parish, is it possible that Mr. Jackson had a similar heterosexual relationship?"

"Anything's possible."

"I suggest to you that anything is not possible, Mr. Parish. Fish do not fly. But some things are possible, and I ask you, most specifically, if it is possible that Heath Jackson had a relationship with Solange Shawangunk between January and July of 1988?"

"It is possible," David answered, trying to chose his words carefully, "But I don't believe he did. I believe, without a doubt in my heart or my mind, that Heath Jackson—"

"What you believe does not interest us, Mr. Parish. We're interested solely in what you know, which does not appear to be much."

ı ı ı ı ı ı ı

The nearer the end of the trial came, the less real it all seemed to Heath. One testimony clashed with another, and by the time he was called to the stand, on the afternoon of the trial's final day, the events of that long-ago July evening had taken on the patina of a dream.

But as Colette asked him question after question, details from that bizarre night swam slowly back into focus. He could see it all: the crowd in the gallery, his photographs lined up around the walls, the bare, tanned skin of the beautiful laughing women, the light sparkling in the glasses of champagne.

"Mr. Jackson," Colette finally said, "did you accompany Mrs. Solange Shawangunk into the gallery office at approximately six-fifty on the evening of July thirteenth, 1988?"

"I did."

"What was the gist of your conversation?"

"Mrs. Shawangunk tried to warn me about Amanda Paine. She told me Amanda was using me for her own purposes. That she had offered me the show to ridicule the gallery. I was very confused. I didn't really understand what Mrs. Shawangunk was trying to say."

"Did she have a chance to explain herself?"

"No. We were interrupted by Amanda Paine and Anton Shawangunk."

"Tell me exactly what happened, Mr. Jackson."

"Well, as I said, Mrs. Shawangunk and I were talking. There was a knock on the door, and then Ms. Paine and Mr. Shawangunk came in. Ms. Paine went over to the desk—she was wearing gloves—and took a gun from the top desk drawer. She pointed it at Solange and fired. Solange fell to the floor. Amanda threw the gun at me and then disappeared."

There was the briefest moment of silence before someone started shouting in the rear of the courtroom. It was Amanda Paine. "It's a lie!" she shouted. "He's lying! He's a sick little murdering liar!"

"I'm not lying," Heath said. "I'm telling the truth."

"I'm sorry, Your Honor," Amanda said. "I let my outrage get the better of me."

"See that it doesn't happen again. Let's continue."

"I have no further questions, Your Honor," Colette said.

"Mr. Best, do you wish to cross-examine this witness?"

"I do, Your Honor." Mr. Best stood up and looked at Heath for a moment. "Mr. Jackson, have you ever used the term 'schlitzed'?"

"Maybe," said Heath.

"If you're familiar with the term, would you define it for us?"

"If you're schlitzed, you're . . . um . . . you're a little wasted."

"And by wasted I assume you mean inebriated, Mr. Jackson?"

"Yes."

"I'd like to repeat my earlier question, Mr. Jackson, but I'll be more specific this time. Did you use this term in reference to your condition on the evening of July thirteenth, 1988, while sitting in a car hired from the Vanity Fair Car Leasing Corporation, driven by a certain Mr. Emil Taas?"

"I don't recall," said Heath.

"I'm not surprised," said Ned Best. "I'd be surprised if you could recall anything from that evening. You'd been drinking, hadn't you, Mr. Jackson?"

"I might have had a drink a two."

"Would it surprise you that Mr. Taas recalls hearing you say to your companion, 'I feel schlitzed'?"

"Not really."

"Did you also smoke some marijuana while in the car, Mr. Jackson?"

"I think I smoked a very small amount."

"I just have one more question. Mr. Jackson, given your self-described 'schlitzed' condition on the evening of July thirteenth, how can you expect this jury to believe your account of what transpired in the office of the Gallery Shawangunk?"

"I may have been a little . . . inebriated, but I know what I saw. I know a murder when I see one, even if I am a little . . . inebriated. I saw Amanda Paine shoot Solange Shawangunk. I'm certain of that."

"You're certain, Mr. Jackson? You're sure it wasn't a pink elephant you saw shooting Mrs. Shawangunk?"

"Objection!"

"Sustained. Mr. Best, if you have serious questions, ask them. Spare us your jokes."

"I'm sorry, Your Honor. I don't believe I have any more questions." Ned Best looked at the jury. "There isn't a question in my mind," he said, and sat down.

Heath resumed his seat. The closing statements and the judge's charge to the jury passed in a blur. He watched as twelve people walked by him, their eyes carefully averted, and disappeared through a door.

Colette turned to him. "Now comes the hard part," she said. "There's nothing worse than waiting."

# CHAPTER
## 37

Gregory was supposed to meet Loren at the L.A. airport, but he didn't. She was greeted by a fat blond woman holding a sign that read LOREN CONNOR PARISH. This woman explained that Gregory was "detained on location" and drove Loren to the ocean, where a production company was filming a picnic scene on the beach.

Loren took off her shoes and walked around the set. No one seemed to be doing anything, except for one woman who was dismembering a flock of roasted chickens with her bare hands.

"What are you doing?" Loren asked the woman, watching her tear hunks of meat off a chicken and toss them into a garbage bag.

"I'm the food stylist," the woman said. "I'm making these look eaten. We need one for each take."

The thought of all that perfectly good chicken going to waste infuriated Loren, but she refrained from commenting. "I'm looking for Gregory Mancini," she said. "Do you know if he's around?"

"He's probably in the trailer trying to get Patti straight."

"Who's Patti?"

"The fucking star. With the emphasis on fucking, if you know what I mean."

"Which trailer?"

"The one with a lot of hysterical crying coming from inside it," said the woman.

"What about in here?" asked Gregory. They were walking down Rodeo Drive looking for a shoe store. The fat blond woman had driven away with Loren's shoes and suitcase. Loren was wearing a pair of thongs borrowed from a P.A.

"It looks awfully expensive," she said. "I just need a pair for tonight. Don't you know any cheap shoe stores?"

"Not in L.A. I haven't done too much women's shoe shopping. Let's just go in here and get it over with. I don't want to miss our reservation. I'll pay. It's my fault, anyway, for not picking you up."

They rang the doorbell and were admitted to the shoe store, which looked more like a shoe museum. Inside glass cases, shoelike objects reclined on velvet pillows.

"This is absurd," said Loren.

"I told you I'd pay," said Gregory.

Something in the tone of his voice silenced her. She explained her dilemma to a saleswoman, who bade them sit, and disappeared into the stockroom, in search of some non-couture shoes.

The store was empty and freezing. "Are you all right?" Loren asked Gregory.

"I'm fine," said Gregory.

Loren reached out and touched his bare arm. "You're tan," she said. She leaned forward to kiss him, but he gave her a strange smile and stood up. He remained standing, examining the caged shoes, till the saleslady returned.

He was odd like that all evening: cordial and distant, as if Loren were a tiresome visiting relative rather than the woman he supposedly loved. At first Loren thought this uncharacteristic coldness was due to trouble at work: Things had been tense on the set. But her presence failed to thaw him. In fact, he seemed to get more tense as the evening progressed, and by the time they had returned to his rented house high in some canyon, she could stand it no longer.

"What's wrong?" she asked.

"Nothing," he said.

"Gregory, something's wrong. This is hardly right."

He shrugged.

"Tell me, what's wrong?"

They were standing on his terrace. There was a glimpse of dark lawn, moonlit pool, palm trees, and garden wall. Someone was watering his lawn, a dog barked. Under other circumstances it would have been beautiful, but to Loren it was all too quiet and so poignantly foreign she wanted to cry. She felt she was at the end of the world. In some abstract, nightmarish way she understood that Gregory had stopped loving her, but she could not believe that. It was impossible to believe. How could the warmth she felt in his presence not be reciprocated? It seemed to contradict some rule of physics, some basic ancient fact about the properties of objects. But the truth is that people fall out of love without the wonderful swooning symmetry that brings them together.

She touched him again, and this time he allowed it. "What's wrong?" she repeated.

"I think I'm angry at you," Gregory said.

"Angry? Why?"

"I think, I mean, I feel, I don't know, that you don't love me. That you never really did."

"That's not true," said Loren.

"But that's how I feel."

"Why?"

"Do you love David?"

"What do you mean?"

He looked at her. "You know what I mean: Do you love David?"

"No." Loren shook her head. "Not in the way I think you mean. I love you in that way."

He looked away. "I don't believe you do."

"But why? I just said I did. What more can I do?"

"Maybe I don't believe it," said Gregory, "because I don't really love you."

Loren was silent. She covered her mouth with her hand. A bird swooped low over the pool, ruffled its surface, winged itself away. "Why have you stopped loving me?"

"I'm sorry," said Gregory.

"But why?"

"When I heard you had left David this time, for a while I was so happy. I know that sounds mean, but, well, that's how I felt. I thought I had been right to let you go like I did, and I thought it would all work out . . ."

"And?" said Loren.

"It's all so shallow," said Gregory, "how you flip back and forth. It makes your love seem so arbitrary, so inconsequential. It made me sick to think about it."

Loren sat down. "And you had me fly all the way out here to tell me I make you sick?"

"No," said Gregory. "I mean, when I asked you to come, I wanted to see you. And then the more I thought, the more I realized how I felt. I couldn't tell you these things . . . I felt it was important I tell you this in person."

"I've had a very hard year," said Loren. "A lot has changed for me, but I . . . I mean, my God, I've finally figured things out, and I know what I want. I know who I love. You can't just leave me like this."

"You left me."

"But I had to do that. You understood. You said you did."

"I didn't really, though. In a way I understood, but I was very hurt by that."

"I'm sorry, Gregory. In retrospect I realize it was the wrong thing to do. But, I mean, I couldn't have known that then. I didn't mean to hurt you—"

"I know," said Gregory, "but you did."

"And I'm sorry." Loren stood up. She wanted to touch him, but she was afraid to. "I'll never hurt you again."

"I know you won't," said Gregory. "I'll never let you."

ı ı ı ı ı ı ı

David opened the door to the witness room. Heath was sitting at the table. He was alone.

"Hi," said David. "Colette told me you were in here. Is it okay if I come in?"

"Sure," said Heath.

David sat down. "I just wanted to see you—"

"Before they send me up the river?"

"No. I meant . . . well, I just wanted to see you."

"It was nice of you to come down."

"Lillian came too. She said to say hi."

Heath nodded. "I'm glad you came. I didn't get a chance to thank you the other day."

"I'm sorry I wasn't a better witness."

"You were fine. I really appreciate it. Thanks."

"You're welcome," said David. He sat down across the table from Heath. It was a beautiful old wood table. David touched it. He thought how a year ago he had met Heath. A year ago he had thought his life would change, and it might have—things might have happened very differently. There were a million ways things could have happened. But for some reason they had boiled down to this: this sitting on opposite sides of a table, waiting. David wanted, more than anything, to stop making such a muddle of things. To move through the world with assured, purposeful grace. To speak and act and love forthrightly. But he was a coward. He could not even reach out and touch Heath's hand, and there it was, lying just inches from his on the table.

"I thought your testimony went well," he said.

"Until that schlitzed business."

"That was just stupid, I thought. I'm sure the jury thought so, too. I was watching them."

"Well, we'll find out soon enough."

"When do you think they'll . . . you know, come back?"

"Colette says maybe tomorrow. But it could be anytime. She says the longer they're out, the better."

"It must be awful."

"It is. I don't really want to talk about it. Tell me something about you. How are things with Loren working out?"

"They didn't. I moved out a couple of months ago."

"Actually, I knew that. Lillian told me. What went wrong?"

"Nothing, really. It just wasn't right. It was a stupid thing to do because we both basically knew that. But the whole business with Kate confused us, I guess."

"How is Kate?"

"She's fine."

"I miss her. Tell her I said hi, okay?"

The door opened. It was Colette. "The jury's coming back," she said. "Can I see Heath alone for a minute?"

David looked at Heath, who had stood up when Colette came in. He looked awful.

"Sit down," Colette told him. "Would you leave us alone, David?"

"Sure," said David.

There were no seats left in the courtroom. David stood against the wall, beside a woman with long red hair and sunglasses. Heath and Colette came in and sat at their table. Heath looked a little better. The judge appeared. When everyone was assembled, the jury entered. It took them a while to weave through the crowd at the back of the room. The woman next to David was applying lipstick. A passing juror jostled her arm, causing her to draw a scarlet line across one cheek.

"*Merde,*" she said.

David could see only the back of Heath's head. He watched it as the jury seated themselves. There was a moment of silence, and then the court clerk stood up. "Madame Forelady, has the jury reached a verdict?"

The forelady stood up. She was an elderly woman. "We have," she said.

"In the matter of the State of New York versus Heath Edward Jackson, do you find the defendant guilty or not guilty?"

The forelady looked down at the slip of paper she clutched, as if she might get it wrong. "We find the defendant guilty," she said.

David watched Heath's head fall forward, ever so slowly. Beside him the red-haired woman began screaming, "Shame!" and pushing herself through the crowd.

"Shame! Shame!" she shouted, mounting the steps to the witness box.

"Silence!" yelled the judge, rapping for order. "What do you think you're doing? Who do you think you are?"

The woman waited a moment before answering. In her struggle to gain the stand her hair had become disheveled. She reached a hand up as if to smooth her coiffure but instead pulled it from her head, revealing her own dark, sleek hair.

Amanda Paine, who had been sitting in the front row, cradling a huge bouquet of red roses that she intended to give to the convicted murderer as a peace offering, stood up and promptly fainted.

The woman on the stand removed her sunglasses and turned to face the jury. "Shame on you," she told them. "How can he be guilty when I am alive?"

# CHAPTER
## 38

David was the first person to arrive at Lillian's New Year's Eve party. He lay his coat on her bed and followed her into the living room. "I thought you said you were never going to give another party," he said.

"Did I? When?"

"After your spring cocktail party. Remember?"

"Well, this isn't really a party. It's more of a get-together. I hardly invited anyone."

"Did you invite Loren?"

"Of course."

"Is she coming?"

"Later. She had a party at Charlotte Wallace's first. Do you want something to drink?

"What are you offering? What does one drink at a get-together?"

"I, myself, am drinking sparkling apple juice. But there's champagne and beer and seltzer. It's all in the refrigerator. I'm going to put some music on."

David went in the kitchen and helped himself to a glass of seltzer.

"Who do you want to hear?" Lillian called from the other room. "Chris Connor or Ella Fitzgerald?"

"It's your party," said David.

"Ella, then."

"Chris Connor was singing at Nell's a couple weeks ago. Not that I went."

"I thought Chris Connor was dead," said Lillian.

"Apparently not," said David. He sat down on Lillian's couch. Ella began singing "Things Are Looking Up." "Is that a sonogram on your refrigerator?"

"Yes," said Lillian. "Isn't it amazing?"

"It's great. Can't you tell the sex from a sonogram?"

"Not really. It's hard to tell penises from fingers."

"Have you decided on names yet?"

"Yes," said Lillian, "Marina, if it's a girl—Marina or Lesley."

"Marina Galton is very pretty. What about a boy?"

"I don't think it's going to be a boy."

"But what if it is?"

"Heath," said Lillian.

"What about him?"

"That's what I'll name my baby if he's a boy."

"It's a nice name."

"They're having a party for Heath at Cafe Wisteria tonight."

"I know," said David.

"Did he invite you?"

"Yes."

"Are you going?"

"No."

"Why not?"

"I get depressed when I see Heath. It just reminds me of all the mistakes I've made in the past year."

"But don't you think it would be nice to congratulate him on his victory?"

"I sent him a note." Actually David had sent flowers, but he was embarrassed to admit this.

"Actions speak louder than words," said Lillian.

"Yeah, but I'm a one-party-a-night kind of guy," said David. "Consider yourself lucky I came to yours."

"You always come to my parties," said Lillian. "That's why I love you. Anyway, this isn't really a party. Technically, it's a get-together."

Gilberto Arnot and Solange Shawangunk were sitting in the office of the Gallery Shawangunk, waiting for it to be late enough for them to make an appearance at Gilberto's opening. They drank champagne and smoked tiny cigars.

Solange exhaled fragrant blue smoke. "How often have we done this?"

"A thousand times, it seems," said Gilberto. "I'm getting too old for openings."

"Well, this year you almost didn't get one. That's why I'm opening it tonight, my dear—while it's still officially 1988. You should have seen what almost went up instead—doodles by a doorman. The thought of it still makes me quake. Luckily I reappeared in time to set things right."

"Yes," said Gilberto. "I heard about all that nasty murder business. How are you feeling? You're looking splendid."

"Thank you. There's nothing like a little death to rejuvenate one. I plan to rededicate myself to the gallery. It was obviously a mistake to entrust it to other people."

"Obviously. Although that Paine woman seemed to know what she was doing."

"Oh, she did. Until she became undone. It was all over Anton, you know."

"Was it? Fancy Anton—the old devil. I take it you've forgiven him?"

"Well, I don't know if 'forgiven' is the word I'd use. I'd say it's more like a conditional pardon. You see, I could easily incriminate him in my attempted murder, and I find the prospect of holding that over his head far too delicious to resist. It makes for a very doting husband."

The door opened, and Margot Geiger entered the office. "Excuse me," she said, "but there's quite a crowd, Mrs. Shawangunk. Everyone's asking for Mr. Arnot."

"Gilberto, have you meet Margot Geiger? Margot is the gallery assistant."

"It's a pleasure to meet you, Mr. Arnot."

"Likewise, I'm sure."

"So are you ready, Gilberto? Shall we make an appearance?"

"One supposes one must."

"The last time I did this, someone shot me," said Solange. "I do hope tonight passes less eventfully."

ı ı ı ı ı ı ı

The streets outside the China Bowl were thronged with revelers hurrying toward Times Square, but the restaurant itself was curiously deserted. Judith sat alone at the bar, nursing a Manhattan. She had ordered a Manhattan for the sound of it. Lately she had taken to saying "Manhattan" whenever the opportunity arose.

Through the slits in the Venetian blinds she saw Henry pause outside. He removed a pair of furry ear muffs, hid them in his coat pocket, and then entered the restaurant. He sat on the stool beside her. Judith leaned forward and kissed his cold cheek. "It's nice to see you," she said. "It's been a long time."

"Yes," said Henry.

The bartender, a tall Chinese man with a smile that revealed a combination of teeth that seemed to have been assembled from several different mouths, asked Henry if he would like a drink.

Henry pointed to Judith's. "I'll have one of that," he said.

"A Manhattan," said Judith.

"Yes," said Henry. "A Manhattan."

They were all three silent while the drink was concocted and delivered. Then Judith spoke. "I'm very excited," she said. "I've never spent New Year's in Times Square. Have you?"

"No," said Henry.

"How have you been?" asked Judith.

"I have been well," said Henry.

"Did you have a happy Christmas?" asked Judith.

"Very happy," said Henry.

"How is your family?"

"My family is fine. How is your family?"

"Pretty good. I spent Christmas with them in Pennsylvania. I've just come back."

"And your husband? Did he have a good travel in India?"

"Fairly good," said Judith. "He's glad to be home."

"And you? You are not also glad to be home?"

"At the moment I don't quite know where my home is," said Judith.

"Ah," said Henry. "That is a problem."

"Well, I'm planning to stay here in New York, at least until the summer. I've managed to sublet my apartment for another year."

"So it seems as if New York is your home."

"I think it may be," said Judith.

They sat for a moment looking at each other. "I would be very glad if New York were your home," said Henry. "If it would make you happy."

"It does make me happy," said Judith. "That's why I'm here."

. . . . . . .

Midnight loomed. Downtown herds of people migrated from one loft party to another. Outside the Cafe Wisteria, a line of people waited to be admitted to the Heath Jackson New Year's Eve Party. Inside pandemonium reigned. A dozen decorated Christmas trees hung upside down from the ceiling, like a surreal, inverted forest. From somewhere among them Shirley Bassey sang "Goldfinger."

Heath and Tammi were hanging out in the women's room, avoiding the mass of schlitzed well-wishers. Tammi had made an impromptu champagne bucket by filling a sink with cold water. She extracted the bottle they'd nipped from the bar and topped off Heath's nearly full flute.

"You don't seem to be having a very good time, bucko. Drink up."

Heath looked pensively at his effervescing beverage.

"What's wrong?" asked Tammi. "Doesn't being absolved of murder agree with you?"

"No," said Heath, "I'm happy about that."

"Then could you try to exhibit a little joy de viver?"

Heath smiled and sipped his champagne.

"Didn't I tell you you were due for some major happiness? Well, it's here. It's party time." She clinked her glass to his. "And listen," she continued, "now that you're independently wealthy as well as good-looking, talented, and famous, you're going to have to beat the boys off with a stick. Les girls, too, for that matter."

"I'm not independently wealthy," said Heath.

"Eighty thousand dollars in escrow sounds pretty I.W. to me."

"I owe it all to my grandmother. I've got to reimburse her for my legal expenses."

"Well, there's lots more where that came from. It's a known fact that once you start making money you can't stop. Of course, I don't know that from experience. It's something I've surmised."

"Actually, someone from Italian *Vogue* called me up the other day. They want me to take pictures at the Academy Awards. But I don't think I want to get involved with journalistic photography."

"Don't be such an elitist prick," said Tammi. "A photograph's a photograph, for Christ sake. You're going to the Oscars, bucko. And don't forget, I'm your official date. I'll have to start designing our gowns."

"I think it's time to make another swing through party hysteria," said Heath. "I want to see who's here."

"Looking for somebody in particular?"

"Isn't everyone?" said Heath.

ı ı ı ı ı ı ı

Kate had fallen asleep in the taxi, so Loren carried her up to Lillian's.

"Why don't you put her on my bed?" Lillian suggested. "We can close the door."

"Okay," said Loren. She lay Kate in a valley surrounded by coats.

Lillian turned off the light. "Let me get a blanket," she said.

"Don't bother," said Loren. "I can use my coat." She took her coat off and covered Kate with it. "I want to use your bathroom," she said. "I'll be right out."

"Hurry," said Lillian, "it's almost midnight."

When Loren came out of the bathroom David was sitting on the bed beside Kate. He had his coat on. "Hi," he said.

"Hi," said Loren. "Don't tell me you're leaving. It isn't even midnight."

"I've been here since eight. I'm ready to go home."

"Stay for a minute."

"How was your trip?" asked David. "How's Gregory?"

Loren sat down on the other side of the bed. Kate slept between them. "He dumped me," she said. It was funny how easy it was to say. It was a fact like the news or the weather. It's sunny, it's cold, the person who loved me doesn't, it's raining. The problem was saying it didn't mean you accepted it or understood it. It was like faking a knowledge of current events. You just hoped you weren't called on it.

"What do you mean, he dumped you? Is he seeing someone else?"

"I don't know. I don't think so. I think he just got fed up with me. Kind of retroactively fed up."

"Are you okay?"

Loren nodded. "Yeah," she said. "I don't know what's going to happen. But I realized . . ."

"What?"

"I don't know. That it wouldn't be the worst thing in the world for me to be by myself for a while."

"I thought you really loved Gregory."

"I do. I think I do. But maybe I don't. I mean, who knows at this point? Sometimes I think the older I get, the less I know about love."

"I know," said David. "It just gets more and more complicated. It was very simple in the beginning."

"The beginning is always simple."

They were quiet a moment and then David said, "I can still remember this feeling I used to have when I lay in bed with you. It was as if I had found my place in the world. Like when I lay down with you all the bad things in my life lay down and were still. And it's gone. I don't know what to do about it. Sometimes I think my heart is broken—I mean irreparably. Like I'll never fall in love like that again."

"I don't think your heart is broken," Loren said. "I think you have a very sweet, intact heart. It's just disengaged. And not very brave."

There was a tiny celebratory roar from the living room. They sat and listened to it.

"Happy New Year," Loren said. She leaned across Kate and kissed David. "Why don't you stay a while? Take off your coat."

"No," said David. "I'm going home. Should I take Kate now?"

"Don't wake her up," said Loren. "Plus, all her stuff is downtown."

"I'll pick her up tomorrow, then."

Loren stood up. "Listen, are you sure you won't stay? We could all go out for breakfast or something?"

"No," said David. "I'm just going to sit here with Kate for a minute."

"Will you say good night before you leave?"

"Sure," said David. "Listen, I'm sorry about Gregory."

"Thanks," said Loren. She came around the bed and touched David's shoulder. "Will you do me a favor?" she asked.

"What?"

"Will you promise me you won't go home and mope?"

"I wasn't planning on it," said David.

"Yes you were. I can always tell when you're descending toward mopedom."

"That's a hard thing to promise," said David. He paused. "What did you mean before about my heart not being brave?"

Loren moved her hand from David's shoulder to his chest. She felt his heart beating. "Maybe I was wrong about that," she said. She left him alone with Kate.

David couldn't resist waking his daughter. He kissed her and then blew on her cheek. Kate opened her eyes. "Daddy," she said.

He took her warm hand. "Hi," he said.

"Where am I?" she asked.

"You're at Lillian's. This is Lillian's bed."

"It's big," said Kate. "Where's Mommy?"

"She's in the other room. Lillian's having a New Year's Eve party."

"I went to a New Year's Eve party at Kate Wallace's. I didn't get kidnapped, though."

"That's good," said David. "I didn't like it when you were kidnapped."

"Why not?"

"Because I missed you. Because I love you so much."

"Were you ever kidnapped?"

"No," said David.

"I'd miss you if you were kidnapped."

"Well, you don't have to worry about that. Neither one of us will ever be kidnapped. We'll always be together."

"Except when I'm at Mom's," said Kate.

"Yes," said David. "Except for then."

ı ı ı ı ı ı

Lillian was right: Her party was a get-together. It hovered at that awkward stage between everyone sitting down and everyone standing up. She and Loren surveyed it from a corner of the living room.

"Isn't Adrienne coming?" Loren asked.

"No. She's gone on a lesbian cruise to the Greek Islands."

"I didn't know Adrienne was a lesbian."

"She's not. It was just a freebie, and you know Adrienne. She'd take a cruise to Hell if it were free."

"Who's that woman with Julian?"

"Her name is Eva. She's South American."

"Whatever happened to Betsy? I thought she and Julian were getting married?"

"She choked. It's the Galton sibling curse: We'll never get married."

"Never is a long time," said Loren. "Any word from the French chef?"

"Nada."

"Good riddance," said Loren. "We can be single together again. It will be fun." She raised her glass.

Lillian was unconvinced. Sometimes I think the only reason I've gotten this far in my life is because people keep telling me the next part will be fun, she thought. But she raised her glass anyway and touched it to Loren's.

ı ı ı ı ı ı

David left Lillian's and took a cab home. Life is strange, he thought. The streets of our hearts are poorly lit and dangerous. All the traffic lights are amber. All the signs say DON'T WALK.

The cab emerged from the park and found its way to David's building. He sat for a second, looking up at its ugly facade. He could picture his apartment, how it would look in the dark before he turned on the lights: the silhouettes of the furniture, the gleam of Ms. Mouse's eyes. He could picture himself moving about the small rooms, drinking a glass of seltzer, brushing his teeth, undressing, setting the alarm, getting into bed. The cold sheets and silence.

"Didn't you want 124?" asked the cab driver.

"I've changed my mind," said David. "I want to go someplace else."

"Where?" The cabdriver turned around.

"I want to go to the Cafe Wisteria. It's downtown, on Church Street."

The driver grunted and swung back into the traffic. He turned left and headed south. The beautiful city flew by outside. The taxi stopped at a red light and was instantly surrounded by pedestrians and honking cars. David sat back and looked out the window. He thought he saw Judith on the sidewalk, but when he looked more closely he realized it couldn't possibly be her: This woman was passionately kissing an Asian man, something that Judith would never do.

The light turned green.

ı ı ı ı ı ı ı

Lillian was trying to clean up enough so that she could go to bed and not dream about soiled glasses and rinds of cheese when the phone rang. Somebody must have left something here, she thought.

"Hello," she said.

"Lillian?"

"Yes," she said.

"Happy New Year," the voice said.

"Who is this?" Lillian asked.

"It's Claude. Remember me?"

"Vaguely. How are you?"

"Cold," said Claude.

"Where are you?"

"Down on the street. I'm on your corner."

"What are you doing there? I thought you never came to New York."

"I never did. Not once, in all of 1988. But it's not 1988 anymore. Can I come up and talk to you?"

"I'm kind of in the middle of something," said Lillian. Like a pregnancy, she thought.

"Oh," said Claude. "Just for a minute? I'd really like to see you."

"What about tomorrow?"

"Well, I guess tomorrow would be okay. Are you mad at me?"

"Not mad, really," said Lillian. "More like frustrated."

"Will you listen for just a minute? So I can explain?"

"Sure," said Lillian. "For a minute."

"I made a resolution last year—actually I made two. One was to stay out of New York City and the other was to refrain from having sex."

"Are you planning to join a religious order?" asked Lillian.

"No. They were important resolutions for me. My life was very fucked up in New York. I told you that. And I, well, I decided to do something completely different. To regain control. So I moved upstate and started Chez Claude and lived by myself and everything was okay till I met you. You probably think I'm totally messed up, but I'm not. I mean, comparatively speaking, I'm not."

"Why didn't you tell me any of this last summer?"

"Because I knew if I told you about the resolutions I'd break them. It had to be a secret. But it's over and it's 1989, and I want to come see you. It's the first thing I want to do this year."

"You may not want to," said Lillian. "There's something you should know about me."

"What?"

"I'm seven months pregnant."

"Wow," said Claude. "Talk about resolutions. What's going on?"

"Not much," said Lillian. "That was the problem."

"I mean, are you involved? Who's the father?"

"I don't know. Actually, I think I do, but technically I don't. I went to a sperm bank last May."

"Wow," said Claude. "And I was going to suggest we go skating tomorrow. I brought my skates and everything."

"I'm not exactly in skating shape," said Lillian. Not that I'd be caught dead skating if I were, she thought.

"Listen, my money's running out. Can I come up? Just for a second?"

Lillian paused, but not for long. "Yes," she said.

ı ı ı ı ı ı ı

Heath kept thinking he saw David's face in the crowd, but he was consistently mistaken. Finally he gave up on him, and once given up, it seemed ridiculous: the idea of David dancing with him in the Cafe Hysteria.

At midnight he was asked to make a speech, but he refused. He had done his testifying for the year. He decided he would be having a much better time at the party if the party weren't for him. The fact that everyone expected him to be euphoric only made him feel worse.

He danced with Tammi and Gerard, who had come down from City Center postperformance, in a tight little triumvirate. As the evening wore on, the music seemed to get louder and louder. It was nice to just dance. To forget things and dance. Heath closed his eyes.

He felt a hand on his arm. He opened his eyes. David was standing there. Tammi and Gerard had disappeared. It seemed to have gotten darker. David was shouting something Heath couldn't hear.

Heath shrugged. "I can't hear you!" he shouted.

David smiled. He leaned up so that his lips almost touched Heath's ear. "Later," he said.

ı ı ı ı ı ı ı

Kate awoke during the taxi ride home. She looked at her mother.

"Hi, pookie," whispered Loren. "Happy New Year."

"Is it late?" asked Kate. She sat up and looked out the window.

"It's very late. It's tomorrow already."

"It's past my bedtime," said Kate.

"It's way, way past your bedtime," said Loren. "It's past *my* bedtime."

"I like New Year's," said Kate.

"I know," said Loren. "It's nice to start all over again."

"You only start when you're born," said Kate.

"Well, you can pretend to start again," said Loren.

"But it's not a real start," said Kate.

"I need a hug," said Loren. "It's cold."

Kate hugged her mother and then resnuggled herself on Loren's lap. Loren stroked her hair. "When we get home, will you carry me up?" Kate asked.

"Maybe," said Loren. "If you're asleep."

Kate closed her eyes. She felt the pattern of streetlights cross her eyelids. She felt her mother stroking her hair. The taxi stopped. Loren leaned forward and paid the driver. Kate shut her eyes tighter. She felt herself being lifted. The cold of the street was followed by the sudden fragrant warmth of the vestibule. Kate heard the clanking doors of the elevator pulled open. She felt her mother's arms around her. She felt herself going up.

Abacus now offers an exciting range of quality titles by both established and new authors. All of the books in this series are available from:

Sphere Books,
Cash Sales Department,
P.O. Box 11,
Falmouth,
Cornwall TR10 9EN.

Alternatively you may fax your order to the above address. Fax No. 0326 76423.

Payments can be made as follows: Cheque, postal order (payable to Macdonald & Co (Publishers) Ltd) or by credit cards, Visa/Access. Do not send cash or currency. UK customers: please send a cheque or postal order (no currency) and allow 80p for postage and packing for the first book plus 20p for each additional book up to a maximum charge of £2.00.

B.F.P.O. customers please allow 80p for the first book plus 20p for each additional book.

Overseas customers including Ireland, please allow £1.50 for postage and packing for the first book, £1.00 for the second book, and 30p for each additional book.

NAME (Block Letters) ...........................................................

ADDRESS ..........................................................................

..........................................................................................

☐ I enclose my remittance for  _____

☐ I wish to pay by Access/Visa Card

Number ☐☐☐☐☐☐☐☐☐☐☐☐☐☐☐☐

Card Expiry Date ☐☐☐☐